# fake

"Hey listen, I meant it on the phone the other day," he said. "I'm really sorry I hit you with that thing. Like I said, I thought I had to in order to make it look good."

Keith waved his hand dismissively. "Big deal. I've been hurt a lot worse than that. It's nothing compared to what we're facing now. Nothing."

"What do you mean? What's the big deal?" asked Danny.

Keith raised his head and gave Danny a piercing stare with his slightly crossed pale blue eyes. He lowered his voice to a whisper. "The big deal is that one of those guys died. We're wanted for murder!"

"What?"

"I swear to God." Keith looked down at the ground. "It's a pretty weird feeling knowing we took a human life. Life is hella weird."

"*We?*" yelled Danny. "*We* took a human life?"

"Well, you drove the getaway car," said Keith. "Your ass is on the line too. Just stay away from the Blakelys. And don't call your family in California, either."

# fake

# K. K. Beck

**SCHOLASTIC**

Scholastic Children's Books,
Commonwealth House, 1-19 New Oxford Street,
London, WC1A 1NU, UK
a division of Scholastic Ltd
London ~ New York ~ Toronto ~ Sydney ~ Auckland
Mexico City ~ New Delhi ~ Hong Kong

First published in the UK by Scholastic Ltd, 2002
This edition published by Scholastic Ltd, 2003

ISBN 0 439 98207 3

Printed and bound in Great Britain by Cox and Wyman Ltd, Reading, Berkshire

10 9 8 7 6 5 4 3 2 1

For Emma

When the men entered the ground floor bedroom of the ranch-style home in a quiet Southern California suburb, Danny Murdock was asleep. He was usually asleep at one in the afternoon on a Saturday.

Danny had had a relatively quiet night the evening before. He and his best friend Scott Mitchell had sat in Scott's room playing video games, and calling everyone they knew to see if there were any parties happening. While they heard rumours of festive gatherings in homes where parents had gone away for the weekend, they were unable to nail down any specifics.

Later, after Scott's parents went out to a movie, the boys had taken some of Mr Mitchell's weed from the Delft pottery canister hidden in the bedroom closet behind a stack of sweaters, replacing the amount they took with some dried oregano from the spice cabinet, and smoked it. After ordering a pizza and eating it, the boys fell asleep while watching TV, but Danny was able to awaken shortly before dawn, make his way five blocks home, and crawl into the house through his bedroom window, the latch of which he had jimmied to facilitate surreptitious entry.

Danny had awoken briefly a few minutes before the men arrived in his room. Then, he had had only one thought and it was a pleasant one. This was the first day of spring break. No school for two weeks. He snuggled back under the covers and drifted back to sleep.

Suddenly, he was being shaken roughly, and someone was yelling. "Get up, Danny. We're going!"

He opened his eyes and stared in horror. A blond, muscular, thick-necked man with a pockmarked face was grabbing him by the shoulders, and yanking him out of bed.

A noise came out of Danny's mouth, a cross between a shout and a scream, that broke in the middle like his voice sometimes did. Although he realized he had produced this noise himself, it still scared him. He now saw that there was another guy behind the first one. This one had the same bull-like physique, but his hair was black. Danny knew he didn't have a chance against two of them.

"What do you want?" he yelled, twisting away from the first man who still held on to his shoulders.

"We're taking you on a trip," said the second man in a smoother, more menacing voice. "You'll find it's better if you co-operate."

Danny, now fully awake, sat on the edge of the bed in his plaid boxer shorts feeling small and weak and completely overwhelmed. He blinked in terror.

The first man looked around at Danny's room with its litter of dirty socks, empty glasses, and sloppy piles of books and papers. "This room is a fucking pigsty!" he said.

Wanda couldn't hear him through the glass, but Danny clearly mouthed "I hate you, Mom!" through the back window as the big white Bronco pulled out of the driveway. His face was pink and twisted with rage. Suddenly, she saw his infant features superimposed on the face he had now. She remembered him in his crib about a year or sixteen months old, clutching and shaking the rail with his

2

chubby little hands. His face had been that same shade of pink, and it had had that same accusing look.

He was, as far as she could tell, dry-eyed now, but back then he had shed copious, bright tears that coated his lashes and rolled down his fat cheeks and aroused her deep pity. He had been a fussy baby and he was still fussy, but he hadn't hated her until now.

Wanda was large, soft, blonde and tremulous, with a nervous prettiness. She wore her hair in a centre-parted ballerina's chignon, which gave her a dramatic air. She stood on the porch next to her husband, Carl. As soon as the car turned into the street and drove out of sight, she planned to collapse against his shoulder and burst into tears of her own.

But she couldn't, because her twelve-year-old daughter, Amy, and Amy's friend from next door, Rachel, trotted up the driveway. The girls were carrying a large box full of CDs and magazines.

Wanda was irritated. This wasn't how she had planned it. She had told Amy to stay over at Rachel's until she called her. She didn't want Amy traumatized, and neither did she want Rachel's parents to hear all about Danny's departure in lurid terms. She glared at Amy. "What are you doing back here?" she demanded.

"We're just going to my room to listen to some music," said Amy, giving Wanda a challenging level gaze and systematically flicking the rubber bands on her braces with the tip of her tongue, a little tic she knew really bugged her mom.

"My dad has a migraine," explained Rachel, in more eager-to-please tones. "And we only have one set of earphones that works at my house."

"OK," said Wanda, as the girls went inside. Now that she'd been forced to maintain her composure in front of them, she didn't feel like sobbing any more. This was slightly disappointing. Instead she said, "I hope we did the right thing. I feel bad."

"We did the right thing," said Carl, a dark, neat man with a pointed nose and a small moustache. "Believe me, he'll thank us some day." He put his arm around his wife and led her back into the house.

They went into the family room and she collapsed heavily on the sofa across from the TV. The shopping channel was on, advertising a cuckoo clock, but the sound was off. She stared blankly at the screen as the little bird popped in and out and silently opened its beak. Carl went to the sliding window that led to the patio and gazed out at the small fenced yard.

"Maybe we overreacted," said Wanda. "I mean he's always been kind of emotional. Adolescence is such a difficult time."

Carl didn't turn around. "We've been through all of this," he said in a tone that sounded patient, but managed to imply that his patience wouldn't last much longer. "He's been diagnosed by experts. He has oppositional defiant disorder. It's a fact and we have to deal with it. Ignoring it is like not doing anything about your kid's dyslexia or crooked teeth."

"I hope we did the right thing," Wanda repeated. The cuckoos were still at it on the TV.

"Of course we did," snapped Carl, turning to face her. "We agreed. Heck, he has a substance abuse problem too. We can't let that go! We can't have Amy raised in a dysfunctional environment and become co-dependent!"

"I know, I know," said Wanda wearily, reaching for the remote and turning off the TV. She let the remote drop on the sofa beside her, then put her hand over her eyes. She hoped Carl wouldn't get all wound up and start telling her how everything that was wrong with Danny was her fault.

4

Carl came over to his wife, touching her shoulder. "I know this has been hard on you, honey. Remember, we did what any caring, loving family would do."

She let her hand fall from her eyes to her lap and smiled up at him wanly, hoping he'd admire her bravery, and respect her maternal dignity.

He returned her sad smile, then headed towards the kitchen with a thoughtful air.

In the kitchen, Carl measured out coffee and poured water into the coffee maker with a look of grim satisfaction. The little shit was gone! Out of the picture for two whole weeks!

As he walked over to the cupboard to get cups, Carl executed a little victory dance, then made a fist and yanked his forearm downwards in a gesture of triumph, simultaneously hissing the word "Yes!" God, he felt great!

Down the hall, in Amy's bedroom, the girls cranked up their music and leaned back against Amy's ruffly pink bed. "What's up with your brother?" asked Rachel. "Who were those guys he was with? He looked really mad."

Amy shrugged. "My dad caught him smoking dope and they're sending him to this rehab thing. They like live out in the desert and eat gerbils they catch or something. I heard them talking about it this morning."

"Gross," said Rachel. After a moment she narrowed her eyes and stared fiercely at Amy. "Why didn't you tell me? You're supposed to be my best friend."

Amy shrugged. "I think I was kind of embarrassed because my parents are weird," she said.

A few weeks before, Danny had been looking for stamps in his stepfather's desk when he found the brochure. On the front was a photograph of a guy who appeared to be about thirty. He was wearing a leather jacket, and he had a real fuck-you expression – chin raised, eyes smouldering, lips curled into a sneer. Next to him was a scowling, slouching, slutty-looking girl, arms crossed across her chest. She had an eighties-style spiky hairdo and a pierced nose. Underneath it read *Fed Up? There's Help for your Out-of-Control Teen.*

Inside, it said: *When conventional counselling isn't enough, decisive action is required. We offer a programme that addresses such behavioural issues as substance abuse, poor academic performance, low self-esteem, resistance to authority, sexual acting out, a lack of forward planning, poorly developed anger-management skills, hysteria, self-mutilation, and moodiness.*

*Even if your teen isn't impacted by these issues yet, the wilderness experience enhances his or her ability to resist harmful peer pressure to engage in negative behaviour. And, we get fast results!*

*The two-week wilderness survival experience works because it teaches teenagers that co-operation with the adults in charge is essential to their survival. We take your troubled, angry, unco-operative boy or girl and put him or her through a gruelling course that gives him or her the belief in him or herself, and others, that is necessary if he or she is to truly succeed in today's competitive world.*

Horrified, Danny had read a description of the course intended to break the will and spirit of any adolescent. From what he could tell, it involved being dumped out in a barren part of Utah with some other troubled teens, under the control of scary militia types. There was a picture of one of them yelling at a bunch of frightened-looking kids in a bleak landscape. He had a military haircut and wrap-around sunglasses and wore desert camouflage-gear. All the scene needed was a collection of circling vultures overhead.

The worst part was that you had to go into the desert with nothing more than a compass, a canteen of water, a box of matches and some pieces of string or something. You had to find your own food!

He had grabbed the brochure and run into the kitchen where his mother was loading the dishwasher. He flapped it in her face. "Have you seen this?" he demanded.

"Oh," she said, as if it were no big deal. "Yeah. Carl showed it to me. He thought it might be an interesting challenge for you."

"You can't be serious? Just because my room's messy and stuff? That is seriously sick. Carl is mentally ill!"

"Well honey, things have been very stressful around here. You don't pay attention to anything we say. And your grades are terrible. This programme is supposed to get you focused."

"Mom, they don't give you food! Don't you get it? I'm hungry all the time. I drink a gallon of milk a day, and you want me to be living off lizards and bugs?"

She had the grace to squirm. "Oh, it can't be that bad," she said.

"I absolutely refuse to have anything to do with this," he said, flinging the brochure down on the counter, where he was pleased to see that it got wet. "It's way worse than making me stay in Boy Scouts way after everyone else quit. This is serious. I could die."

"Don't be so dramatic, honey," she said with a nervous little laugh. "They can't let people die. They'd get sued."

Danny remembered this conversation as the white Bronco sped down the freeway. OK, maybe he wouldn't die but he would definitely suffer. What a way to spend spring break! Scott and his family were going to Hawaii, and he was going to be brutalized out in the desert by these thugs.

Danny had been contemptuous of his mother and her

husband for some time, especially since they had dragged him to that unpleasant counsellor, a nerdy guy in his twenties who said things like "Yo, wuzzup?" and tried to high five him while suggesting he participate in more school activities.

Danny had already come to the conclusion that his parents were majorly stupid. Now, however, he despised them and he was beginning to think they were actually evil. How could his mother let this happen to him? She'd promised him, after he'd found the brochure, that they wouldn't force him to go.

And now, here he was, sitting by himself in the back seat, feeling about ten years old, and staring at the two seal-like heads, one blond, one black, and the shaven necks of the men in the front seat. "Where are we going?" he asked. He felt completely betrayed.

"You'll find out after it's over," said the blond pock-marked one, the driver. "Clients aren't told until afterwards. It's a security thing."

The car turned off the freeway and slowed down. Why were they leaving the freeway if they were going to Utah? Maybe this wasn't the same deal as the brochure. Maybe it was worse. Maybe it was one of those fundamentalist Christian boarding schools he'd heard about where they kept kids until they were twenty and brainwashed them into a zombie-like state.

The car slowed down as they approached a stoplight. They were in a kind of rundown part of LA that Danny didn't recognize. Maybe they were going to take him to an airport and fly him to some compound with barbed wire in Texas, or some other state where you could legally beat kids.

He'd heard horror stories about this gulag where people were declared insane and locked up. It had happened to

8

someone's cousin at school just because she'd dyed her hair green.

They were stopped at the light now, on a tired-looking street corner opposite a liquor store. Danny took a deep breath. He had no choice, really. He was going to go for it. He checked out an escape route between two buildings and over a dumpster. He was small but he was pretty fast. Silently, he unlatched the seat belt. He just might make it. He yanked on the door handle.

"Forget it," said the driver without turning around. "The childproof locks are on. Put your seat belt back on."

"Yeah," said the black-haired man sarcastically. "You're precious cargo." He appeared to be going over some paperwork. "This next guy is coming back on the thirty-day guarantee," he said to his partner. "I remember him. Keith. A real hard case. We better cuff him."

Great! He was going to be shut up with criminals. God, now he actually hoped they *were* going to that place in Utah described in the brochure, the place that scared him to death ten minutes ago. At least on that wilderness thing he couldn't be attacked in the showers by hardcore guys like this desperado, Keith. They'd all be out together in the open air. And there were girls. Girls would make it better. They couldn't make it too brutal if there were girls there, having periods and stuff.

The Bronco turned left, and Danny looked out the window at the scruffy neighbourhood of small stucco houses in dirty pastels surrounded by weedy yards, mangy palms and cracked sidewalks. They pulled up in front of one of the houses. Danny wondered whether both of the men would leave the car. If they did, maybe he could get away somehow, defeating the child locks by pulling the fuses out or something, and just take off. But where would he go? The surrounding neighbourhood didn't look too hospitable.

Danny, who only a few minutes ago had felt enough adrenaline surging through him to leap out of the car and run like hell, scale fences and zip into alleys, now felt completely helpless. In fact, he actually felt a little faint.

In the end, only the driver left the car. Danny laid his head back and closed his eyes and thought about how he had ended up in this situation. He wasn't a bad kid. He'd never been a bad kid. In fact, he'd been a perfect little kid, getting As and never getting in trouble. Maybe if he hadn't been such a good *little* kid, his parents wouldn't have been so shocked that now he cut class once in a while, and forgot to call home and say where he was, and got Cs and Ds like normal people.

Danny knew that the troubled-teen shock treatment was Carl's idea. Last year, the year he'd gotten one inch taller than Carl, was also the year Danny had realized his step-father was a dork; an irritating, snappish little man, issuing orders and nagging all the time. Carl wasn't even that smart, and he never shut up about his stupid, boring job selling packaging. There were plenty of times Danny had just wanted to say "Aw, shut up," and backhand the little jerk, but mostly he just ignored his stepfather when he started ranting about Danny washing the car or launched into a solemn dinner table monologue about shrink-wrapping and blister packs.

Being ignored really bugged Carl. He'd yell, "Look at me when I talk to you. It's like talking to a wall!" and Danny would shrug and mumble, "Whatever," and let his eyes go kind of out of focus, which Carl hated.

But right now it was his mother with whom he was most angry. She should have stopped Carl from doing this to him. When Carl yelled at Mom because Danny wouldn't do what he said, Mom always started crying and got hysterical, and mostly felt sorry for herself, then caved in and let Carl do whatever he wanted.

Lately, Danny had thought once or twice about finding his real father, but he'd always rejected the idea on the grounds that no adult was very satisfactory. They were a thickheaded bunch of dull worrywarts who had little insight into the nuances of real life, and lacked the ability to live for the moment.

His musings were interrupted by loud yelling, and he looked through the window at the sad little pink house where they were parked. The blond Nazi was dragging a tall, dark-haired kid in a pair of jeans and a wife-beater undershirt towards the car. His wrists were pinned together behind his back, and his face was twisted with fury. He was screaming, "Fuck you! Thanks a lot, bitch!" at a hard-looking, skinny woman in a bathrobe who stood on the porch sucking hard on a cigarette and glaring. "Fuck you too, Keith," she said calmly.

The car door was opened, and the kid was hurled in next to him. Danny could see that his wrists were bound with plastic handcuffs. Keith fell back against the seat, while the blond man fastened his seat belt. "Get the fucking cuffs off me!" the boy shouted. The door was slammed. The driver silently resumed his position in the front seat and merged into traffic. Keith turned around and stared out the back window at the little pink house until it disappeared from view.

He flopped his head back and stared upwards, then produced a hollow laugh. "I can't believe this," he began now. "This is so totally stupid. I can't believe the bitch called you guys again!"

"Her insurance covered the second visit, in case the first one didn't take," said the driver pleasantly. "Apparently, you need a little refresher course, Keith."

"Oh, man!" wailed Keith loudly. "This sucks!" Danny

11

checked him out. He had longish, dark hair, down past his earlobes, a straight nose, heavy eyebrows, a square jaw line. It looked like he'd been shaving for quite a while. In fact, he needed a shave right now. On his upper arm was a tattoo of a grinning skull with a knife stuck through it.

The car proceeded back to the freeway, and merged on to it. After a while, Danny cleared his throat. "So where are we going?" he asked Keith.

Keith turned and looked at him for the first time. "Who are you?" he demanded. Danny noted that his pale blue eyes were slightly crossed.

"Um, Danny, uh, Daniel Murdock."

"Yeah?" Keith turned away, no longer interested.

"Seriously. You've been there before. Where exactly are we going?" persisted Danny.

"To hell," replied Keith, with another phony-sounding laugh.

The two men in the front seat laughed too.

Flora and her best friend, Claire, were in Flora's messy bedroom in Seattle, sitting side by side on the floor using Claire's bed as a backrest. They were both flipping through magazines, Claire extremely carefully because she'd just painted her nails baby blue.

"So things are better with your stepdad, huh?"

"Yeah. He's kind of backed off on some stuff," said Flora. She pointed at a picture of a little dress in black and white zigzags in her magazine. "Isn't that cute?"

Claire nodded. "Very retro, kind of early sixties. I like it. But if you wore that to school no one would get it. Really. It's too interesting."

The girls sighed. They were best friends partly because they both shared the conviction that they were just a little too sophisticated for Madison High School, where an odious bunch of superficial preppie kids with no sense of taste or style had somehow managed to socially terrorize everyone there, and con the faculty into thinking they were wholesome young people and natural leaders.

"So what's Richard backing off on?" said Claire.

"Oh, borrowing the car and stuff. We really are getting along better."

"At least you don't have any more steps beside him," said Claire. "You know. Like what happened to Nora Sinclair."

Flora clicked her tongue in sympathy. Poor Nora Sinclair. Her mom had married Lewis Aitkens's dad, and now every other weekend, Lewis Aitkens, a very obnoxious preppie guy who was on the football team and had a lot of loud friends who all thought they were too cool for Nora and her friends, lived at her house, and they even had to share a bathroom.

"Thank God Richard never had kids," said Flora.

One flight below, in the den, Richard Blakely sighed. He was watching TV with his wife, Flora's mother, Louise, and there was a preview for a new movie with a blonde actress with a soft, kind of blobby face. The actress who looked like Wanda. Louise could never see this actress's face without referring to Wanda. Richard wished this woman's career would end.

Sure enough, Louise piped up, "Hey, there's that actress who looks like your old girlfriend."

He was sorry his mother had ever let Louise see all those photos. He felt strongly that husbands and wives didn't need to discuss the past, especially the sexual past. But soon after he had met Louise and took her to meet his family, Richard's mother had dragged out that box of old pictures, and sure enough, there was a stupid shot of him with his arm around Wanda at his brother's wedding, seventeen years ago.

"And that's Richard's girlfriend at the time, Wanda," his mother had said.

Louise had grabbed the photo, peered at it, and said, "She's so pretty!"

"She was very highly strung," Richard's mother had said primly.

"She reminds me of someone. Some movie star," Louise had said.

Now she turned to Richard next to her on the sofa, and

14

said, "Judging by her picture, she was sure pretty."

Richard knew what he was supposed to say now. "Not nearly as pretty as you." He kissed her. He hoped this would end the conversation about Wanda. Richard hated thinking about the past.

"I never asked you why you broke up with her," said Louise thoughtfully.

"She got pregnant," said Richard impatiently. "Accidentally on purpose. I told you she was nuts."

Richard felt her body stiffen next to him on the sofa. "You never told me that," she said.

They were driving east on an old two-lane blacktop road. For some time now, there had been absolutely nothing outside the window except greyish vegetation and outcroppings of prickly pear, illuminated by a harsh, flat light. For some reason, this empty landscape was fenced in with barbed wire. What was the point of that? Nobody would want to trespass here. Maybe the whole place was radioactive or something.

Danny had always hated the desert, preferring green, lush surroundings. The desert looked like Mars to him. Mom knew that and she still let Carl send him out here for two weeks without food or shelter. Just a few years before she had smeared factor 24 sun block all over him when he went out to play in the back yard.

Looking through the windshield, Danny saw that the air shimmered in the heat, creating fleeting mirages of water up ahead. They sped past a battered metal sign with peeling red and white paint that said in big letters: "Gas. Two Miles". and underneath, "Last Chance". This reminded him of that bastard Carl. "This is your last chance," he'd said over and over again. Danny hadn't really understood what Carl was talking about. Last chance before what? Now he knew.

Keith had been silent for most of the time, usually with his head flopped back and his pale eyes just staring up at the roof of the car. Danny had kind of hoped he could bond with him, partly to find out about what awaited them, but also on the theory that if the whole thing turned into some Lord of the Flies scenario, with kids terrorizing each other and fighting over food, Keith would be a good ally to have. Conversely, Danny felt he would be a very bad enemy.

Suddenly Keith's head snapped into an upright position. "I gotta take a leak," he shouted belligerently.

The blond driver sighed. "OK," he said. A huge truck came barrelling past them, hit the horn, and passed with a whoosh that sent the car shuddering. "I'll find somewhere to stop."

After about thirty seconds, Keith said, "I mean it! You want me to piss all over the fucking upholstery?"

"All right, hold on," said the driver. He pulled off the highway into a white stucco gas station with a red-tiled roof. This presumably was the last-chance place referred to on the metal sign. But it had been a lie. The gas station was completely abandoned, with rusting pumps, vegetation growing through the concrete and warped plywood over the windows.

As the blond driver opened his door, a blast of heat rushed into the air-conditioned interior of the car. A second blast joined it when he opened Keith's door. As he unbuckled the seat belt and pulled the boy out of the car, he said to his partner, "You keep an eye on the other one."

"Are you taking these off, or are you going to hold my dick for me?" Keith snarled. The driver removed the plastic cuffs. "How about some shade?" Keith added, as he massaged his wrists. The two of them went around the corner of the building to the shady side of the old garage.

16

The man in the front seat picked up a cellphone and punched some buttons. "Hi Steve. We got both of them and we're proceeding to the terminal point," he said, checking his watch. "We should be there right on schedule." He paused, and said, "Naw, no problems," in a bored tone of voice, then replaced the phone in its cradle.

Just then, they heard someone yell. It was a kind of surprised, scared yell in a deep voice.

The man dropped the cellphone and clambered out of the car. "Stay there!" he told Danny as he ran to the garage.

Well, duh. Where the hell did he think Danny would go? Out into the desert? The buzzards would be gnawing on his bones within twenty-four hours.

As soon as the man disappeared around the corner of the building, Danny climbed into the front and over the gear-shift into the passenger seat. He grabbed the phone. He was going to call Mom and tell her he was being tortured, and that he had to go home. Or maybe he'd say he was sick and he had a weird pain that he thought might be his appendix about to burst. They'd have to come get him then.

Before he had a chance to punch in his home phone number, he heard panting and running feet. He looked up and saw Keith running towards the car, his hair flapping around. He was carrying a crowbar.

Keith yanked open the door and flung the crowbar into the back seat before diving behind the wheel. "Keys! All right!" he shouted with a big grin.

While Danny watched, fascinated, Keith started the car, then struggled with the gear-shift. "Fuck! It's a stick!" he said. Finally he managed to get the car, bucking and stuttering, to move forward to a position where it could turn back on to the road.

He peered down at the pedals, apparently trying to find

17

the clutch, as he steered haphazardly. He succeeded in getting it going forward at a pretty fast rate, but Danny could hear from the way the engine was protesting that Keith would have to get out of first gear pretty soon.

Keith seemed to realize this too and jammed at the pedals. He seized the gear-shift lever and yanked it around. The engine quit and the car came to a violent stop. Danny was flung forward into the windshield. It felt as if someone had taken a hammer to his temple, and he heard a ringing in his head.

Keith pounded the steering wheel with his fist and yelled in a plaintive tone, like a howling coyote, "Fuck! I can't drive a stick!"

"I can!" said Danny through his throbbing pain.

Keith couldn't ditch him now. He had something Keith needed.

Richard thought husbands and wives should probably shut up about the past. This applied even to Louise's first husband, who by virtue of having died was now out of the fleshly running. He was more of a genial, ghostly figure like Tom Hanks in a soft focus montage of domestic scenes, but Richard still didn't want to think about him.

Neither did Richard like thinking about his own past. The past was over and finished with. Richard didn't like to dwell on it, even the happy parts. He certainly didn't want to think about Wanda.

But ever since he'd let down his guard, and blabbed about Wanda's pregnancy, Louise had asked him a whole bunch of questions. It all brought the whole ghastly time with Wanda back. He remembered it only too well. Wanda giving him a goofy look and taking him to a cupboard to show him her home pregnancy test, as if she were very proud of herself, and smiling at him as if he'd be so happy.

Instead he'd shouted at her. "You said you were on the pill!"

"It was making me fat," she had replied, blinking stupidly.

"What! And you'd rather be pregnant? That is so dumb!" He realized he sounded insensitive. He tried not to yell. "I'm sorry, Wanda," he said. Her family was Polish. That meant they were probably Catholics. That might make it hard for her to go through with the abortion. He'd try and be as supportive as possible, pay for everything, go with her to the doctor.

And when it was all over he would dump her fast. He'd already been trying to figure out a way to get out of the relationship. The thought of her yelling and screaming, which she did with alarming frequency, was the only thing that had stopped him so far.

"I didn't think you'd mind," she had said. "I thought it would bring us closer together."

While Richard had stood there in shock, she'd continued in calm tones. "If it's a boy I want to name it after my dad. Daniel. And if it's a girl I can't decide between Sarah and Amy."

"Wanda," he'd said, grabbing her by the shoulders, "I don't think you understand. I don't want this baby. I don't know if I want any baby, ever. And if I did, I wouldn't want a baby now. And if I ever did want a baby, I wouldn't want one with you."

She appeared not to have heard him. "When I found out about the baby," here she had touched her stomach, which gave Richard the creeps, "I thought maybe it meant we should be together." She assumed the pose of some Madonna from an Annunciation painting – hands crossed over her breast, eyelids lowered. Her long blonde hair, parted in the centre, added to the effect.

When he didn't respond tenderly, when he in fact told her that she had behaved badly and what she had done was the female equivalent of rape, her serene features re-arranged themselves into a contorted mask of fury, and she started screaming at him. Her pale face turned bright pink, and she began drumming his chest with her fists.

In the end she agreed to the abortion, but she didn't want him to go with her. In fact, she said, he was a cruel, horrible psycho, who needed years of therapy, and she never wanted to see him again. Apparently, her own therapist agreed.

This was a huge relief.

Later, though, he wondered if maybe he shouldn't have insisted on going with her, just to make sure she went through with it. He'd sweated out the following months, wondering if she'd pop up again with the kid, and try and get back together or something, but she never did and he had finally relaxed.

Louise had made a big deal out of all this. "So it's possible she had the child?" she'd said. "You could have a son or daughter?"

"Well, it's possible," he'd conceded, "but it's not very likely. Don't you think she would have come around asking for child support?"

But Louise had persisted. She was, Richard felt, a little fanatical on the subject of children, always smiling at babies in the grocery store even if they weren't particularly attractive – probably because after Flora was born they'd told her she couldn't have any more. "How old would it be?"

"I don't know." He frowned and counted. "Fifteen or sixteen, I guess."

"The fact she had names picked out—" began Louise.

Finally, he'd had enough. "Look," he said, "if you don't mind, I want to drop this. It's very painful, all right?"

"All right," she said, but she gave him a funny look. It

was a look that indicated she thought that he'd screwed up somehow. This was clearly unfair. How could he have been expected to know Wanda had quit taking the pill?

After Danny had pulled the car out on to the road and headed back to the main freeway, the road unreeled in front of him, and he shifted into fourth gear. He had the heady sensation of being in a movie. One of those road type movies where people just took off and no one bothered them, and they had fabulous adventures and when they got bored they just hit the road again. To enhance the feeling, he turned on the radio. Now it sounded like the movie he was in had a road-music-type soundtrack.

He felt a wonderful, soaring sensation, that began right behind his breastbone and suffused his whole being. No one knew where he was. And, for the first time in his life, he was absolutely free and unsupervised. Those two sadistic thugs, who were dragging him off to torture him with his parents' consent, plus his evil parents themselves, were out of his life.

He glanced over at Keith. "Um, what the hell happened back there?" he said, trying to sound casual.

Danny laughed. "Those fools! As soon as I get around the corner, I grab the guy by the throat and push his head real hard against the wall. He kind of groans, so I slam him harder and he just goes kind of all limp and falls down."

Danny replied with a noncommittal, "Wow."

"Then I look around and there's this like, metal thing laying there." He gestured into the back seat. "So I do this fake yell thing so the other guy will come out and try to save his buddy. And I kind of flatten myself against the wall and as soon as he comes around the corner I just give it to him real hard upside the head."

"Seriously?"

"Yeah. And then, just so the guy wouldn't follow me, I jumped up and down on his knees, thinking maybe I could break his legs or something. I didn't hear anything snap, though." Keith sounded a little disappointed.

"You could get in real trouble," said Danny.

"We sure could," said Keith.

After a few miles it occurred to Danny that the men back there, hateful as they were, might need some help. What if they were knocked out and lying in a pool of blood and needed medical attention? The gas station had been completely abandoned. It might be weeks before anyone found them. Maybe Danny and Keith could leave an anonymous tip to someone to go find the men. Then, if they got in trouble later they could say they'd tried to help.

He eyed the cellphone. "There's a phone. Maybe we should—" he began.

Keith followed his gaze and finished his sentence, "Get rid of it. Good idea." He rolled down the passenger window and tossed the phone out into a roadside ditch. "That's how they busted those guys who killed Michael Jordan's dad. Those idiots used the guy's cellphone."

"We've got to get as far away as possible," he went on. "We can't go back to LA because they'll look for us there. I don't know. Maybe Mexico."

Danny wasn't sure where he wanted to go. His first impulse had been to go home to Arleta, but that was before he got that soaring feeling. Home didn't make sense, anyway. Mom and Carl would send him right back to Camp Starvation.

God, he hated them. It would serve them right if he just disappeared. Carl wouldn't care, but Mom would. She would blame and berate Carl for ever, in that kind of whiny way she had now that she was on meds and she'd stopped screaming at people. This thought cheered him up a little.

As Danny barrelled down the two-lane blacktop he had thrilling thoughts of pulling up to his parents' house in a Lamborghini many years later, rich and successful with a beautiful and sophisticated wife. Perhaps the wife would have a French accent and be named Dominique.

Or maybe he'd be famous, and they'd see him on TV one day, accepting a Grammy award or an Oscar or something. And you'd better believe he wouldn't mention Mom or Carl in his thank you speech.

"I don't know about Mexico," said Danny doubtfully. "I think if you're a minor you need a note from your parents to get across the border. And you need a driver's licence or something. I only have my learner's and, anyway, it's at home. Plus, I'm flunking Spanish."

"OK, Canada then," said Keith. "They speak English. We just go north."

"We'll need a lot of gas," said Danny. It suddenly occurred to him that to buy gas they would need money. They would need money for other things, too. Like food. In fact, Danny was getting hungry. He could handle about three burgers and a chocolate shake right now. "Do you have any money?" he asked Keith.

"No problem," said Keith. "We can get some."

## 3

"A lot of it is a matter of territoriality and traffic patterns," Louise had explained to Richard, when he first complained about living in what he called a child-centred household. "If we change those patterns it will all be much easier."

Louise had thought the house would be big enough for all of them, but she hadn't had a realistic idea of how much space Richard needed. It wasn't as if he were a child who could play in his room. Now it all seemed rather a tight fit. Still, as Flora would be off to college in a year and a half, moving into something bigger just for a short while seemed silly too.

Louise had been adamant about not wanting to disrupt Flora's life more than necessary. It was hard enough for poor Flora to have to share her mother with someone else after all those years, without the added burden of moving, and maybe even changing schools.

The solution Louise had hit upon was to upgrade their basement. It consisted of a laundry room and a rather grim, unused rec room with green marbled linoleum, ugly fifties fake wood-panelling, and a neglected workbench, all poorly installed by the home handyman who had owned the house previously.

This would be replaced by a sort of mother-in-law apartment for Flora – a large bedroom and a teen lounge where she could have a TV and a stereo and entertain her friends. The small windows would be enlarged and the outside door replaced with one with glass panels to make it all lighter. The laundry room would be transformed into a bathroom – not prohibitively expensive, as most of the plumbing was there. A smaller, quieter washer and dryer would be installed upstairs in the dressing room of the new master suite, made from combining Louise and Richard's bedroom with Flora's.

Louise was very excited that Dave Fraticelli, their contractor, would be coming soon. After the work was done, everything would be much better. She wouldn't have to mediate so much between Richard and Flora, dashing back and forth placating them both in turn.

And no longer would she be watching Richard's jaw for signs of tension when Flora and her friends descended on them – their young, loud, slightly hysterical voices ricocheting through the house, their relentless music throbbing along in a droning continuo.

When she had first sidled up to her daughter apologetically and said, "Darling, can't you entertain your friends in your own room?" Flora's face had taken on that accusing, hurt look.

"Fine, I guess you and Richard want the living room. There are only two of you and there are eight of us. But if you want us all cramped into my room – God, Mom, you used to say you really liked it that I brought friends home." Pause. Narrowing of eyes. Final thrust. "But I guess you've changed."

Why were teenagers so huffy about people changing? She remembered people writing earnestly in high school yearbooks, "Don't change over the summer". Maybe the poor things were reeling so much from the changes within that they couldn't bear to have anyone else behave unpredictably.

"But darling, our lives *have* changed," she'd explained, trying to keep her tone sweet and reasonable in the hope that Flora would ease up. "I'm married now, and I think I'm entitled to some space, too."

Before Richard, Louise had greeted Flora's friends warmly, flashed welcoming smiles, pointed out snack availability, and withdrawn to her bedroom to read or watch TV. It had worked well when there had just been Louise and her daughter.

Richard, however, was appalled at the idea the two of them should creep away and allow a gaggle of sixteen-year-old girls to take over the living room. Louise had thought of her daughter's set of friends as nice, wholesome young girls, self-confident in a way she had never been. She was so happy that Flora's friends were good students who weren't obsessed with boys, who played in the school orchestra and whose body parts remained unpierced and untattooed, that she hadn't minded their girlish whoops and the way they strode over to the refrigerator and helped themselves to food.

But the first time Richard walked in to see them all lounging around the living room applying polish to each other's nails, cutting pictures out of magazines, eating bowls of ice cream, laughing shrilly and cranking up the stereo, she saw them through his eyes. All that busy, giddy, nubile young womanhood sprawling around seemed to produce a slightly disturbing aura of claustrophobia tinged with hysteria.

Suddenly, Flora and her schoolgirl friends resembled bored young women behind harem walls, restless odalisques splayed over the sofas, ignored by the sultan and left to amuse each other with pointless grooming and malicious gossip.

Louise never remembered entertaining her friends in

26

the living room. She never remembered having eight of them over at once, either. She wasn't sure she'd even had eight friends in high school. She had dim memories of herself at Flora's age spending quiet hours in the gloom of her bedroom with her best friend, Caroline – another bookish, plain girl. The two of them would sit on the floor torturing themselves by leafing through the pages of *Seventeen* magazine, *Glamour* and *Mademoiselle*, and studying photographs of pretty, perky girls with bangs and pink lipstick and coquettish, confident smiles. Sometimes, she and Caroline took personality tests to determine what kind of perfume should become their signature fragrance, or read their horoscopes. And while they sat quietly in her room, her parents and little brother had sat quietly in the living room watching *Happy Days*.

Anyway, after Dave Fraticelli and his crew were finished, Flora would have her own space where she and her friends could loll to their hearts' content. The upstairs living room would be reclaimed. Louise would pop down occasionally, smile at the girls, and be pleasant, re-establishing her friendly relationship with her daughter's peers. She suspected from the surly looks that some of the girls were giving her lately, that Flora had been complaining about her mother's traitorous changing. Changing, specifically, into a bitch and throwing her own flesh and blood out of the living room.

Dave Fraticelli had been so reassuring. He was a small, fastidious man, a perfectionist with a measuring tape on his belt, making notes on a clipboard and squinting thoughtfully at the area to be redone. He asked lots of questions and suggested that Louise and Richard think of ways to use the space after Flora left – a sewing room, a guestroom, and perhaps a wine cellar.

These options startled Louise, conjuring up as they did an unfamiliar, pleasant, but slightly threatening post-child

27

life of civilized leisure. Post-child life could have been a lot more threatening she realized, with a sense of having been saved at the last minute. If Richard hadn't come into her life, and Flora had left her all alone, she might have gone slightly crazy. She had never lived alone. It seemed selfish and pointless somehow, looking after no one but yourself.

After about twenty minutes on the road, Danny was pleased that Keith started talking and acting friendly. Keith's silence had unnerved him and made him seem more like a weirdo and less like a normal kid.

"Man," Keith said, "I really lost it back there with those guys, but I wasn't going to be shipped back to that fucking desert. No way."

"How bad was it there?"

"Bad, believe me," said Keith with a sidelong glance. "If you didn't do what they said, or if you didn't do it fast enough, they knocked you down and kicked you. They made the other kids beat you up. And there wasn't any food. You were like weak and dizzy the whole time. It's fucking child abuse."

"You're kidding! I can't believe my parents would send me there."

"Believe it," said Keith. "They think you're cute and stuff when you're little, but when you get bigger, they turn on you. They wish they never had you. My mom tells me that all the time."

Danny's mother had never said that to him, but maybe she thought it. "I can't go back home," he said. "They'd just send me back."

"That's right. And it might even be worse. You might end up in juvie because of what I did to those guys back there. They might say you were an accessory, even if I tell them it was all my idea."

This had never occurred to Danny.

"Hell," Keith went on, "I heard about this guy, he drove a getaway car for some other guy holding up a liquor store, and they sent him to the gas chamber because the guy inside the store killed the clerk. This guy that got the gas chamber never even saw the guy that got killed."

"Really?" Danny swerved to avoid a flattened possum. He knew it was already dead, but the idea of squishing it some more kind of grossed him out.

"Yeah," continued Keith, stretching out and putting his clasped hands behind his neck. "God, they might even want to try us as adults. Then we could go to like a state penitentiary. Vacaville, or San Quentin or whatever." He sounded terribly blasé about all this. "Did you say your name was Danny?"

"That's right."

"So the thing is, Danny, we have to get the fuck out of Dodge," said Keith.

"What *exactly* did you do to those guys anyway?" asked Danny.

"Just what I had to do," said Keith with a resolute clench of his jaw. "You didn't want to go to the desert, did you?"

"Well no, but it sounds better than jail." Maybe he would have to be a fugitive his whole life. Everyone else would be off at college then they'd get married and have kids and normal lives, and he'd be on the run, friendless, down and out. He saw himself as an older guy, maybe twenty or so, unshaven, poorly nourished, furtively washing dishes in the dark shadows of a restaurant kitchen.

"Hey, it'll be OK," said Keith. He actually chuckled, which calmed Danny down a little. "I bet I just knocked them out. They think they're really hardcore guys. They're not going to complain. It would make them seem like wusses."

"Maybe so." Danny wanted to believe this.

29

"I think we should wait a while and see if there's anything about it on *America's Most Wanted* or whatever," said Keith.

"We can check on the Internet," said Danny eagerly. "We can go to a library and search for our names and see if we're in some news report or something."

"Yeah, OK," said Keith, sounding uninterested. "It's Saturday, right? What we could use right now is a mall. Someplace with a lot of cars. And some kids."

Carl put down the phone. Thank God Wanda was driving Amy to soccer practice. He'd have some time to figure out how to tell her that her son had vanished. He rehearsed a couple of approaches.

Option One. He could downplay the whole thing, and act as if the boy's disappearance was no big deal. "I'm sure they'll find him. How far can he get, anyway? The kid can't even get downtown on a bus by himself. He'll probably call us collect any minute now."

He didn't think Wanda would buy this.

Option Two. He could dwell on the incompetence and carelessness of Youth Intervention Therapies, Incorporated. "I can't believe they can't keep track of a bunch of goofball kids! How hard can it be?"

This indignant attitude was closest to Carl's real feelings. He felt strongly that Wanda, however, would be more interested in knowing where the hell her child was than in consumer issues.

Option Three. He could blame Danny himself, and by implication, Wanda's overindulgence through the years. "The kid's a criminal. He stole a car! My God, if you'd only let me send him to that place when this first came up. Now he's a thief on the run! I knew the kid was sliding downhill fast!"

On the whole, he thought this time-tested approach was

probably his best bet. Putting Wanda on the defensive was always a good way to go.

Then it occurred to him that he had a lot of time. Danny wasn't due back home for two weeks, and the kids were supposed to be incommunicado the whole time. Option Four. Say nothing and hope Danny turned up sometime in the next two weeks, preferably not in jail.

The offices of Youth Intervention Therapies, Incorporated, were located in Century City on the twenty-third floor of a building constructed during the era of brutal concrete plazas and Darth Vaderesque black glass. As it was after hours, there were no surly clients or stressed-out parents around.

The empty lobby resembled a dentist's, doctor's or psychiatrist's waiting room with bland décor, pastel carpeting, a large, shiny-leafed philodendron, a gurgling fish tank and a lithograph of soaring seagulls against a turquoise- and rose-coloured sunset. Back issues of *Parenting Magazine*, *Psychology Today*, and *Readers' Digest* were stacked neatly on the coffee tables.

Beyond the lobby was a small interview room with comfortable chairs, more plants and lithographs of leaping dolphins. Here, members of the company's Diagnostic Intake Team interviewed adolescents to determine which of an array of disorders described in the American Psychiatric Association's diagnostic manual and covered by major health insurance plans, was most applicable.

Beyond this room lay the office of the director, Dr Eugene Philbreck, and his wife and partner, Charmaine Philbreck. This was an informal, rather cosy room with a beat-up old filing cabinet, stacks of boxes full of brochures, a coffee machine and a little fridge, some family photos of the Philbrecks' grown daughters and a pair of cheap metal desks.

The Philbrecks were here today with their two client escorts, Brad and Brian. Blond Brad had a large gauze bandage wrapped around his head, and some scrapes on his scrofulous skin, and dark-haired Brian sported a large bruise that was just becoming apparent around one eye. A butterfly bandage covered the fresh stitches in his left eyebrow.

Usually, Dr Philbreck had the breezy, take-charge manner of a successful salesman. Now, however, he looked worried. After putting down the receiver he continued to stare at the phone.

Charmaine, blonde and carefully groomed, put a well-manicured hand on his, the light playing with her large diamond and emerald cocktail ring. "You did real good, Gene," she said in her cigarette-cured baritone.

"He didn't say anything about suing, and I think he got the hint when I said we wouldn't necessarily press charges on the car theft." Dr Philbreck was a short, well-built man in his late fifties with a thick neck, and steel-grey crew cut. He glanced over at Brad and Brian with thinly disguised contempt. "I suppose if he really gets nasty we could bring in the assault thing, which I didn't think we should mention just yet. Heck, if we have to, we can say both kids beat on you. How would you know? You were out cold."

"I don't think we want to bring up any of that unless we really have to," said Charmaine. "We're selling client control. The customers don't want to think the little bastards can beat the shit out of our counsellors and escorts."

Dr Philbreck sighed. "Yeah, you're right. But let's take out the Polaroid and get a few shots of the damage just in case." He gazed over at Brad and Steve. "Maybe wait till that shiner gets a little more spectacular."

"OK, hon. One down, one to go," said Charmaine in an encouraging tone of voice. She waved her hand at the phone.

"All right," said her husband in a resigned way. "I'll call the other one now. What's the kid's name? Keith?"

"Piece of cake," said Brad. "His mom will be delighted to hear he's missing."

# 4

Shortly after reaching the interstate and turning north, Keith yelled, "All right! Turn in here." The mall, surrounded by farmland, was situated at the junction of two freeways. It consisted of a huge pile of silvery buildings in the middle of a sea of cars, with some warehouse-scale businesses – a big furniture store, a Home Depot, and a Toys 'R Us – off by themselves at the edges of the parking lot.

Danny got on the exit ramp, and shifted down. "Think we can get something to eat?" he asked hopefully, scanning the perimeter for fast food outlets. "I heard somewhere that they have to throw away burgers if they don't sell them by a certain time."

Keith laughed. "We can get whatever we want," he said, flipping down the visor to check himself out in the mirror. He ran a hand through his hair. "Park over at the side of that Home Depot and wait for me."

After Keith hopped out of the car, Danny investigated the bump on his head in the rear-view mirror. It was starting to bruise up and it still hurt. Then, he fiddled around unsuccessfully with the radio to see if there were any decent radio stations out here in the sticks. Fifteen minutes later, Keith emerged from Home Depot and got back in the car. "OK, let's find a nice quiet spot some-where," he said. "Like behind that movie theatre." Danny drove over to a far corner of the mall where a multiplex theatre sat. The cars were sparser here.

Keith pulled up his undershirt and produced a screwdriver from the waistband of his jeans, then directed Danny to a parking slot behind the theatre, next to a beat-up old Nissan sitting alongside a dumpster and a rear exit door.

"Probably belongs to somebody who works here," said Keith. "They won't be back any time soon." He jumped out of the car and proceeded to unscrew the front plate from the Nissan. A minute later he was unscrewing the rear plate.

Danny was extremely nervous throughout the operation. They could get in really big trouble for this.

At the same time, he was excited. This was actually pretty cool. And Keith seemed to know what he was doing. He was wielding that screwdriver really fast, just like a guy in a movie who only has a few seconds to disarm a bomb or something. Suddenly, Danny felt very lucky. There probably wasn't any better or more competent companion than Keith here, for the kind of cinematic road trip on which Danny was now embarked.

A few minutes later, with the licence plates switched, they drove to another parking place up by the main cluster of buildings. "Now we need some girls," announced Keith. "Kind of skanky-looking."

Danny was surprised at Keith's priorities. Of course, in a road movie there would be a couple of girls. Presumably, though, they would be attractive. Right now, however, Danny was more interested in about four cheeseburgers, fries, and a quart of milk.

Unclear about what precisely Keith was up to, and not wanting to appear dumb by asking, Danny simply said, "Whatever," then fell silent and followed him down the main concourse and into a Gap store.

Was Keith going to shoplift more stuff from stores? Keith hardly looked like a preppy Gap shopper in that undershirt and sporting that scary skull and knife tattoo. Danny felt sure that the clerks would be keeping a beady eye on him. Maybe he wanted a better shirt than that gangsterish wife beater, but was it worth the risk?

The screwdriver, that was different. They had needed it to get the job done and it was small and everything, but the merchandise here at the Gap all had those plastic alarm things you needed a special tool to remove, and they probably had cameras too. Keith began sliding hangers and looking at shirts. Danny decided to steer clear of him. If Keith got himself busted, Danny didn't want to look like he had any part in it.

From the opposite side of the store, Danny feigned interest in a pile of T-shirts and watched Keith as he carried some khakis up to a clerk. He seemed to be asking for another size. The clerk started searching through the stacks shelved against the wall, while Keith stood next to him, checking out the room. What was he doing? Danny was getting hungrier and hungrier.

After the clerk failed to find the right size, Keith began to follow two girls around, as he pawed half-heartedly here and there through the merchandise. At one point, he smiled at the girls. From where he was positioned, Danny couldn't see if they smiled back.

They sure were ugly. One was fat with frizzy hair, and a mouth full of heavy metal orthodontia. The other one was skinny, had a mean face and looked about twelve. God! Did Keith want to hook up with them? Danny's opinion of Keith's ability to handle the world in a suave and competent manner took a sudden plunge.

After hassling around for at least twenty minutes, the last five or so of which Keith spent scrutinizing socks in a display near the register while the fat girl bought a sweater with a credit card, Keith finally left. He indicated to Danny with an unsmiling jerk of his head that he should follow. Danny was relieved to see that Keith made it through the electronic sensor without tripping it.

Outside, Keith was waiting for him. "We gotta follow those girls."

Danny gave a man-of-the-world smirk and held up his hands, palms out in an include-me-out gesture. "Hey, no offence but they're not my types," he said.

"No kidding!" said Keith, rolling his eyes. "But they look seriously stupid and they've got a credit card."

"We can't steal a credit card," said Danny.

"Right. Did you forget we just stole a fuckin' car?"

Danny mulled this over. That didn't seem so bad because it belonged to those creeps who were kidnapping him.

Keith pulled at his sleeve and dragged him along. "Chill, OK? We don't have to steal nothin'."

The boys caught up with the two girls in the Food Circus. Danny stared at some nearby enchiladas while Keith said to the fat girl, "I really like the sweater you got at the Gap. It's really cool."

Half an hour later, they were sitting at a white metal table littered with styrofoam cups, paper plates, and dirty napkins. The fat girl, whose name turned out to be Amanda, asked, "Are you sure I won't get in trouble?"

"Absolutely," said Keith with complete confidence. "You just tell your parents that some creepy guys were standing behind you at the cash machine and they probably memorized your PIN number, then followed you and jacked the card out of your purse later. You could say they were Mexicans or Cambodians or something. Not black. That sounds bogus."

Danny felt so much better. He'd eaten three tacos, two

cheeseburgers and an ice cream sundae. Amanda had paid for everything with her credit card. She said her mom felt it was safer for her than walking around with a lot of cash.

"The reason it's all cool with everyone," continued Keith, "is that when you call the credit card company and report the card is stolen within 48 hours, it's like illegal for them to charge you for anything. So nobody actually loses any money."

"Except the credit card company," pointed out the mean-looking skinny one, whose name was Lydia, and who seemed smarter than Amanda. Because she was more sceptical, and clearly the dominant half of this best-friend pairing, Danny thought maybe he and Keith were doomed to failure. On the other hand, it was Amanda who actually had possession of the card.

"Exactly!" Keith sounded like a teacher speaking to a pupil who has grasped an important principle. "And the credit card company is *not a real person*. They're like some huge corporate bureaucracy thing. So like I say, it's all good."

Amanda was chewing on her moist bottom lip. She seemed to be thinking it over, but she looked uncertain. Her plump hand lay on the table, and Danny placed his hand on it and squeezed. "Hey, you know what? I'm sorry I even brought it up. I guess it's out of line. If you're not cool with it, well maybe we can figure something else out. Just telling you about our problems has been really helpful."

He sighed deeply and withdrew his hand. Amanda watched it go. "I just hope we can make it to my aunt's farm somehow," he went on, gazing into the middle distance. "My brother and I will be safe then." He gave Danny a protective look, full of compassion and concern. "How's that bump on your head, guy?"

Danny winced and remained silent.

"I can't believe your parents did all those things to you," said Lydia. "They should be in jail."

Keith lowered his voice to a conspiratorial whisper. "Like I said, the FBI needs them as, like, witnesses. They can do whatever they like and they'll never be arrested."

"Are you sure they can't get you back from your aunt?"

"No way. She has legal custody in Ohio. They can't get us back. And our parents have to keep using their new, fake identity or the mafia will find them, like I explained. All we have to do is get to her farm and everything will be OK."

Danny felt that he hadn't contributed enough to the conversation. He cleared his throat and said, "Our aunt has always been there for us. Life on the farm will help us, like, heal. She's a really good person."

The girls nodded solemnly.

To Danny's astonishment, Keith's eyes glazed over with tears. "Yeah, that's for sure," he said, his voice choking a little.

As soon as Amanda handed over the card, Keith got up and tugged at Danny's sleeve. "We'll never forget you girls," he said in a trembling voice. "You saved our lives."

Amanda scribbled on a paper napkin smeared with taco sauce. "Wait! Here's my address," she said gazing up at Keith with huge, round eyes. "Let me know if you make it. Otherwise, I'll always wonder my whole life."

Keith favoured her with a big, bear-like embrace, while Lydia and Danny eyed each other skittishly. "Wow! You're really a good person, Amanda," Keith said. "I'll be in touch. Definitely."

They didn't use the cash machine in the mall. Keith said there might be surveillance cameras there. Instead, they went to a big gas station at the next freeway exit and filled the tank, paying for the gas with the credit card at the pump, which didn't require a signature. Then they went inside and used the cash machine inside the mini mart.

The cash advance limit on the card was two hundred. Keith picked up the handful of twenties and rolled them up and stuffed into his front pocket. After they were under way again, he pulled out this fat roll, and, looking like an old-time mob boss, peeled off three twenties.

"Here you go, Danny," he said. "Some walking-around money."

Danny thought he deserved at least half because he was the only one who could drive a stick, but he didn't say anything. It seemed best not to. Instead, he just concentrated on the road ahead. All they had to do was keep going and before long they'd be in Oregon, which Danny imagined to be all green, with exotic Nordic forests and cool mists. God, he loved driving. He sighed happily, thrilled by the knowledge that he was free, unstoppable, and in control of his life at last.

## 5

"Do I have to go?" Flora, in the kitchen with her mother, kept her voice low, presumably because Richard was sitting nearby in the living room.

"Oh honey, is it that big of a deal?" Louise was tossing a salad of mixed greens to take to her in-laws. Marcia always wanted them to bring something.

Louise resented this. She certainly never asked guests to bring their own food. Her revenge was to make it as simple as possible – just the standard gourmet mix from the supermarket with some salt and expensive olive oil. Five minutes preparation time max. She would present it in a kind of reverse-snobbish way, as if anything more complex would have been vulgar. "I didn't want to bring anything that would clash with what you're having," she would say. "Simple fresh greens and this nice Tuscan olive oil I found at Trader Joe's should go with just about anything, don't you think?"

"No one will care if I'm there or not except you," said Flora decisively.

Louise thought she might be right, but she said, "Aunt Marcia is expecting you. You can't ditch out at the last minute. She already planned dinner and all that. It would be rude." The last thing Louise wanted was to give Marcia the opportunity for one of her sly little digs at Flora.

"God!" said Flora, her voice heavy with the disgust that seemed to have become her normal manner of speaking lately. "What's up with this Aunt Marcia stuff?"

"Well, you know," said Louise vaguely, sampling an oil-coated leaf. "She's sort of an aunt by marriage."

"*Your* marriage," said Flora. "If you hadn't married Richard, we wouldn't even know them. You would *never* choose Marcia as your friend, admit it."

"Probably not, but so what?" said Louise. "You can't pick family. You just have to hang in there for everyone's sake."

"Why?" asked Flora.

"Listen," said Louise irritably, "maybe you could put those dishes in the sink in the dishwasher while you're giving me a hard time. That way, something will get accomplished."

Flora sighed. "I'm sorry, Mom." She began to slam dishes noisily. "I just don't see why it's so important for me to be there."

"Because it means a lot to me, OK? Richard and Gordon are close, and they run a business together and see each other every day. I think we should all get along as well as we can, even if it is kind of superficial."

"I can't believe you think superficial is good."

Louise snapped cling wrap and sealed the salad bowl. "I find Marcia kind of trying, OK? But I want to do the right thing, and I want everyone to be happy, and I want you to help me."

"OK, OK," said Flora, sullen but vanquished. Then, managing to get in the last word, as was her habit, she added, "Jeez, Mom, that guilt thing you do really works."

Good! thought Louise. While she wasn't proud of it, she knew that most of the time that guilt thing was all she really had going for her.

\* \* \*

It was after they had driven across the Oregon border, and seen the first green and white freeway sign that showed the mileage to Seattle, that Danny first had the idea of going to find his real dad. Why not? Maybe he was an OK guy. After all, anything had to be better than Mom and Carl. And one of the only things Danny knew about his real dad was that he probably lived in Seattle.

It was the fake aunt in Ohio that had first given him the idea. He wished he had some real relatives like that where he could go, and then he thought about his real dad. The whole time Keith was fooling those stupid girls with that lame story about protected child-abuser witnesses testifying against the mafia, Danny had had a vivid picture of the pretend aunt.

He saw her as kind of a smiley, healthy-looking woman with freckles and big teeth and wavy brown hair out in the barn with a pitchfork throwing hay around or whatever, and making pies, like someone in one of those commercials that talked about products that had real farm freshness.

She had a pleasant, low voice, and a nice laugh, and she didn't make a huge big deal about everything and nag and nag and nag, because she was too busy taking care of cows and whipping up fabulous scratch meals. Big, glazed stuffed turkeys and sizzling steaks. Piles of butter-drenched corn on the cob. Mashed potatoes and gravy. Bacon and eggs. All that high cholesterol stuff that they told you not to eat at school, and that Mom kept saying made her fat.

He turned to Keith. "I'm getting kind of tired of driving. Wanna eat? Let's find a truck stop." Danny had never eaten at a truck stop, but he liked the idea of rough, masculine surroundings and copious amounts of the old-fashioned food that he had been daydreaming about.

About twenty minutes later, they found one, and parked the Bronco next to an awesome collection of giant rigs. Danny had always wanted Carl to stop at one of these places on family outings, but of course, Carl never did, explaining that they weren't "family oriented".

A lot of the truckers were fat, so maybe Mom was right about high-cholesterol food, but these guys had a pleasant swagger and a no bullshit manner, and some of them wore cowboy boots which was kind of cool. There was an agreeable smell of diesel in the air and inside the atmosphere was blue with cigarette smoke.

It was in a back booth over a chicken-fried steak with country gravy that Danny told Keith his idea, "So I figure why not check the guy out? I mean, I never even met him."

"What do you know about him?" asked Keith.

"Only his name. Richard Jerome Blakely. I found it on the birth certificate. And I was born in Seattle, so that must be where he is."

"What makes you think he's still there?"

"Mom told me his family ran a furniture business there. Like one of those been-in-business-fifty-years type of things. My mom said his family was rich. He probably still works there."

Keith looked thoughtful and dug into his bowl of chilli topped with masses of chopped onion. "How come you never met him?" said Keith.

Danny frowned. "I guess he didn't really plan on me," he said. "My mom wasn't real clear on that. Anyway, he's never seen me."

Keith laughed. "He's not gonna want to see you. Are you crazy?"

"Well maybe he's curious," said Danny, trying not to sound hurt. "Wouldn't you be curious?"

"Maybe. Is your mom hooked up with someone else?"

Danny explained about Carl, who had married his mother when Danny was two and a half and she was working as a secretary at this place in Seattle where Carl went to sell packaging — a rush order of special reinforced cartons with styrofoam insulation inserts — and how they had moved to Arleta, California, soon after and had his little sister Amy.

"Your stepfather is retarded. He could be getting baby bucks from this rich guy that knocked up your mom," said Keith matter-of-factly.

Danny bristled a little at this description of his conception. Mom had told him in a deep whisper with dramatically-rolled eyes that she and his real father were very much in love but that they were too young and their romance was too stormy to work out.

Keith seemed to notice Danny's irked reaction. "No offence," he said with a reassuring, friendly smile.

"Mom said she and Carl decided it was better if I thought of Carl as my dad. They figured it was better if this other guy wasn't in the picture at all." As he explained this, Danny thought for the first time that this was probably because Carl was afraid that he'd look bad next to the rich, suave, debonair Richard Blakely.

"Still, even if he doesn't want to see you, you could get something out of him I bet," said Keith thoughtfully. "You could screw him good. He's your dad and he hasn't done a fucking thing for you all these years. There's laws, man."

"Maybe he tried to find me and couldn't," said Danny, who had imagined this scenario many times. "I mean my mom has a different name now. Perhaps Richard Blakely was lonely and wanted a son to hang with and take fishing and to Disney World or whatever. He could be looking for me right now."

"Don't count on it," said Keith.

"Well, I just thought I'd check it out," said Danny. "It can't hurt."

"Hell no," agreed Keith. "I'll help you find him if you want. I'm good at that kind of stuff."

After dinner, Gordon asked Richard out to the garage, ostensibly to examine the progress he had made installing his new pegboard-and-hook tool storage system. Richard knew this was just a pretext, as the project had been initiated by Marcia and held no interest for Gordon. He had already explained that he was only doing it because otherwise Marcia would lie next to him in bed at night obsessing about it, sighing loudly, and waiting for him to ask her what was the matter so she could start in about how much the mess in the garage upset her, and how what they needed *immediately* was a pegboard system with outlines for all the tools, just like her dad had in his basement.

The brothers knew each other too well to bother with the pegboard cover story once they got into the garage. "What's up?" asked Richard. They leaned side by side against the workbench sipping the wine they had brought with them from the dinner table.

"Listen," said Gordon. "We gotta get this owners' draw thing squared away. Have you had a chance to think about it?"

"Kind of. But I have to tell you, Louise doesn't like it. I mean, you guys are already taking a lot more than we are. After all, this remodel is setting me back a lot, and I didn't ask for any more out of the business."

"Yeah, I know, but we got three kids, and they're not getting any cheaper. I added up Jessica's gymnastic expenses, and I figure it's setting us back about twenty-five thousand a year in coaching, travel, all that. And it's going to get worse now that Coach Bela is on board."

"Well maybe you can't afford it, then," said Richard, in his usual sensible big brother way. He had always thought that his fourteen-year-old niece's gymnastic career was a big waste of time, and resented having been expected to show up at an occasional meet. The sight of grinning little munchkins flipping around struck him as grotesque.

"Marcia says she'll never get over it if she doesn't go as far as her dream takes her," said Gordon, gnawing on a cuticle.

"That's ridiculous. It sounds like a commercial. I don't get it. When we were kids, we just went outside and played."

"I know. But there could be big scholarship money down the road. If she doesn't grow too much. They can't get too big or they bump their heads on the bars or something."

"Yeah, you explained that before," said Richard. "Well, if you took that twenty-five thou' a year and put it in some kind of an investment for her education, between now and the time she's ready to go to college you could probably have enough to send her to Harvard. And then she could hit six feet and two hundred pounds and it wouldn't matter."

"Yeah, yeah. But it's not just about that. Listen Ricky, when you're a parent you feel like you have to do whatever you can for your kids. You can't stifle them. They have to be able to feel they can go as far as they want to."

"But they can't! No one can. That's bullshit. I mean how many major-league ball player and astronaut and President-of-the-United-States slots are there, for Christ's sake?"

"Yeah, OK, I see your point, but it's different when it's your kid."

"I wouldn't know," said Richard coldly. Louise was always telling him he couldn't understand because he didn't have kids of his own, and now his brother was starting. Did it occur to any of these people that maybe having children actually impaired your judgment?

"Hey, I'm sorry," said Gordon. "Maybe Marcia's got me all worked up about this. I don't know."

Richard immediately thawed. Blaming wives was one of the brothers' secrets to getting along. "I understand. But listen, Gordie, if you guys take more, then maybe we should too. Just to be fair. And maybe that will put too much strain on the business. You know, Mom and Dad never lived like we do. Remember those cheap camping vacations?"

"Marcia wouldn't put up with that for a minute," Gordon replied.

Louise, sitting on the sofa drinking coffee with Marcia, was becoming aware that the two men had been gone longer than the time strictly required for inspection and admiration of the pegboard-and-hook storage system.

After dinner, the two younger children had gone to the rec room to watch a video. Louise was pleased to see that Flora was making an effort to be nice and had dutifully trooped off with Jessica, who was two years younger, to teach her how to French-braid her hair.

"Of course, when you only have one child it's a lot different," Marcia was saying. "Things are getting so complicated around here that I've developed a new system. I use a different colour magic marker on the calendar for each kid. That way I can check anyone's schedule really quickly. Jessica's pink, Troy's blue, and Samantha's yellow. The yellow's a little hard to read, but all she has right now is Brownies and Gymboree."

"I read somewhere that kids are getting stressed from all these activities," said Louise blandly. "This article said children should have to figure out how to fill some time themselves."

"That's true," said Marcia with a thoughtful expression. "I think that enhances creativity."

"Exactly. I remember when Flora was small she spent a lot of time by herself reading and playing imaginative games and drawing." Marcia's hyperactive children seemed to have no inner life. How could they? And poor Jessica was missing so much school with all her gymnastics activities that she would probably grow up ignorant.

"I guess only children do learn to amuse themselves," said Marcia. "Especially when they have just one parent who has to work. But I think it's also important to make sure kids are well rounded. You know. Music, sports, team things so they learn to co-operate and function well in groups. And then, once in a while, you discover that a child really has special ability. Like Jessica."

Louise smiled pleasantly, but refrained from showing any interest in Jessica's achievements.

"Her new coach says she has incredible potential," Marcia continued. "Did I tell you about him?" She had. He was from some former Eastern bloc country, and was taking Jessica away for the summer to his gymnastics camp in Florida. "Of course, he's very expensive."

Louise felt herself tightening. Here it was. The pitch. She knew Marcia and Gordon wanted to take a bigger draw from Blakely Home Furnishings. While Louise had started out not paying much attention to the family business, lately, she had decided that Richard was being taken advantage of. His brother Gordon was a nice enough guy, if nowhere nearly as intelligent as Richard. But Marcia's plans for her family bordered on the grandiose.

"Yes, I'm sure it is expensive," she replied tartly. "Flora is expensive, even though she's in public school. That remodel is mostly for her sake, for instance, and college is coming up. That's why I'm glad I have my job."

There! That ought to settle her hash. Marcia hadn't had a job since Jessica was born.

"I know how you feel about your career, Louise." This was a low blow. Louise had worked ever since her first husband had died simply and solely because she had to. "And of course with just one child, who's so much older, you can probably go to work without worrying."

"Oh, you never stop worrying." Marcia always acted as if she were the only caring mother in the world.

Marcia sighed. "I know. I'm so worried about Jessica. She has a chance at a really great gymnastics career. If I thought we'd made that dream impossible because we weren't in a position to give her the tools she needed – the coaching, the right meets, the visibility."

Where were the men? Louise began to panic. She was terrified that Marcia would lean right across the coffee table and ask for Louise to say Marcia and Gordon should take more money out of the business. She knew Richard thought that wasn't wise. How dare this woman make their lives difficult!

Louise had never realized how fraught a family business could be. As a young widow with a child, she had worried a lot about money and jobs. She had always assumed it must be delightful to step into a going concern, and know you always had a secure job and income. But she was beginning to realize that blood and money were a tricky combination. Thankfully, Richard and Gordon soon returned, and there was no further discussion of money.

On the way home in the car, Richard tried to contain himself. While he always felt that he could tell his brother just what he thought, he didn't like to criticize him behind his back. Finally, he could stand it no longer. "Can you believe it! They're spending twenty-five thousand bucks a year on Jessica's gymnastics!" he said. "It's nuts. For what? So she and a bunch of other flat-chested little girls can jump around like performers in a flea circus!"

From the back seat Flora eagerly announced, "She told me she really wants to have periods, but that with all that exercise it won't happen until she's twenty. Some weird hormonal thing."

Richard sometimes wished he wasn't surrounded by women. He really didn't want to know about his niece's menses.

Louise turned to Richard. "You should have a talk with Gordon. They're ruining that girl's life! She might not be able to have children!"

"It's not Gordon's fault," said Richard defensively. "Stop picking on my brother."

## 6

Danny was disappointed. He had assumed that when the Bronco went over the side of the cliff, it would roll over about five times with some satisfying crunching-metal sound effects, then burst into flames before bouncing into the river below.

Instead, it had made it halfway down, then wedged itself between a boulder and a tree that grew at a strange angle out of the side of the cliff.

The two boys looked down over the guard-rail that ran around the deserted Scenic Vista Lookout Point in a mountainous national park. The early light of dawn cast a peaceful, rosy glow over the white car.

"Damn!" said Keith.

"That is so lame," said Danny. "Look at that!" They had worked hard at getting the car in just the right position in a spot beyond the guard-rail that provided a steep angle, over a stretch of river that looked reasonably deep.

It hadn't been easy hooking the front tyres over the edge, either. Danny had been at the wheel, with Keith standing at the cliff's edge motioning him forward inch by inch. In the end, Danny had stopped about a foot before Keith's last urging wave, and it had worked out just right.

When they gave the Bronco its final push, it eased slowly over the side in an irritating, ponderous way. There was nothing left but to hope that its momentum would increase as it proceeded down the side of the cliff. Unfortunately, however, it never picked up much speed, slid downward in an upright position rather than rolled, and settled quietly into its undignified spot about thirty feet below them.

"Oh well, it'll take them a while to get it out of there," said Keith with a philosophical shrug. "That'll give us time to move on."

They walked back to their new vehicle, a green Toyota now bearing the plates they'd taken from the car at the mall back in California, and tossed in the sleeping bags meant for their desert sojourn and the small amount of luggage they'd transferred from the Bronco. Keith had thrown the crowbar away into some bushes by the side of the road a few miles back. Danny had been horrified to see blood on it, and that it had left a smear of blood on the upholstery too.

They'd found the Toyota in the parking lot at a nearby trailhead. Keith explained that leaving the car open and completely empty was one way people tried to avoid having stuff stolen from their cars when they were hiking.

Of course, if it was the car itself you were after, this made it much easier. All you had to do was open the door, get in, fiddle around under the dashboard, hot-wire it, and peel out of there. And with any luck, the hikers wouldn't be back for days.

"Is it worse to steal two cars than one car?" Danny had asked. Keith seemed to have a working knowledge of the criminal justice system.

"Hell, we aren't really stealing them. We're joyriding. It's totally different."

"Oh. OK." Keith had made sure the new vehicle was an automatic, and he was now driving. Danny found this slightly irksome, as if he had been demoted somehow.

"So tell me again about your mom and stepdad," Keith said. "What kind of a job does he have?"

Danny regaled him with Carl's obsessive need to discuss packaging options, and, because Danny seemed so interested, told him all about his house in California, his half sister, his mom and her part-time job at a company that sold bottled water. "God, he's so fucking boring!"

"Yeah, well maybe your real dad will be more cool," said Keith.

"If I can find him."

"We probably can. He's probably right in the phone book. But if he isn't, we know he has a furniture store in Seattle, right? We just call a bunch of furniture stores in the yellow pages, call 'em and ask for someone named Blakely."

"I guess so."

"But it could be dangerous. What if they're looking for you? Your parents, or whatever. Maybe the cops. The first place they'll look is your dad's."

"Yeah. So?"

"We could be wanted. There could be warrants out for us," said Keith. "We have to plan this really carefully." He paused. "The thing is," Keith went on, "you don't want to go knock on the guy's door and be cuffed in the back of a squad car ten minutes later, right?"

"That wouldn't happen, would it?"

Keith's voice grew solemn. "Listen Danny, I didn't tell you before, because I didn't want you to freak out, but now I feel like we're real friends, so I'll give it to you straight."

Danny felt his stomach lurch.

"The thing of it is," continued Keith, "those two guys were hurt bad." His face took on a serious cast that made him look suddenly like an adult. He lowered his voice. "I think it's pretty likely at least one of them won't make it. I mean I saw, like, brain tissue and a big chunk of like, skull bone open. Maybe the guy's just brain damaged. But we could be talking homicide here. For both of us. That's how the law works, you know."

Danny felt himself start to tremble.

Keith reached out and squeezed Danny's hand and kept holding it for a long time, which Danny found weird but reassuring at the same time. "I know you're scared. I'm scared too." Keith didn't look or sound scared. "But in a way, I got you into this, and you're a good guy. I'll do what I can to help you hook up with your dad. Maybe you'll be safe there."

"I see. I understand. I'm sure you're doing the best you can." Carl kept his voice neutral and low, whispering directly into the receiver. He worried that Wanda, in the next room, would hear him.

"I appreciate your understanding," said Dr Philbreck smoothly. "Naturally, I know you're concerned. But let's face it, with the kind of oppositionally defiant kids we deal with, anything can happen. Believe me, these kids are time bombs waiting to go off. I just wanted to check and see if you've taken any independent action."

"Independent action? Like what?"

"Oh, you know," said Dr Philbreck vaguely, "called the police or anything."

"Well, no," said Carl. "I thought you'd do that. I mean you lost him."

"Well, he lost himself, didn't he?" Dr Philbreck's voice took on a snippy edge. "And he stole our car. Not that we're planning to press charges at this time," he added in a reassuring tone.

Carl grunted. "Might do him some good if you did."

"Our primary concern is the emotional health of Sammy."

"Danny," corrected Carl.

"Yes, of course. Anyway, no need for you to get involved in any official way. Let me assure you, we're working the problem. As I say, I'm sure the boys will turn up. If, by any chance yours turns up at home, my professional advice is that the best thing to do is ship him right back to Wilderness Survival School. We'll deal with him there.

"It's therapeutically contraindicated to let these kids get away with this kind of stuff. They must learn that adults are in charge. And I think, considering the, um, unusual circumstances that we could see our way to giving you a discount on our usual rate."

"I appreciate that. But depending on when he surfaces, he might miss some more school that way," said Carl. "His mother wanted to make sure he didn't miss too much."

"Well, it's up to you, of course, but I think that a clear course correction is more important for your boy right now than anything else. He can always make up his schoolwork at summer school. Um, how is your wife taking all this, by the way?"

"To be honest," said Carl, "I haven't told her. I was afraid she'd get upset that her kid disappeared."

"A valid concern," conceded Dr Philbreck.

"As far as she knows, he's out in the desert doing his thing there with your people."

"Really?" Dr Philbreck paused. "I think you're handling this wisely," he went on, sounding genuinely pleased. "I encourage you to continue with this course of action. No point getting her all riled up. I'll just make a note of that. If I get any updates, I'll only talk to you."

"Good. It's better not to call the house. Let me give you my work number and my pager number."

Wanda came into the room just as Carl was saying, "Thank you, Dr Philbreck. I appreciate your keeping me updated." He spotted his wife, gave her a nervous grin, said a hasty goodbye and hung up.

"Who was that?" she asked. "Was it Wilderness Survival School?" She clutched her husband's arm. "Is he OK?"

"He's fine," said Carl. "Apparently he's responding very well. This will be the making of him. The doc says he's having the time of his life."

Monday morning the boys woke up in damp sleeping bags. It had rained in the night and Danny had slept very little. They were tucked inside some shrubbery in a large park in Seattle, and had found a little burrow that, by the evidence of old potato chip packages, cigarette butts, and empty beer cans, had served as a hiding place for others before them. Keith had surveyed the debris and pronounced the spot safe. "It's not like anyone else is living here. There's just stuff left over from kids partying."

Danny had looked around warily, and unrolled the sleeping bag on the damp ground, terrified of discovering old condoms or syringes there. "Why can't we sleep in the car?" he'd asked.

"Too risky," said Keith. "It's stolen. They'd haul us in then find out about – you know." He looked away. "The other thing."

Besides the rain, there had been ominous nocturnal rustlings in the bushes. "Probably rats," Keith had said, before curling into a ball and falling asleep.

Cold, wet and miserable, Danny spent most of the night coming up with a plan. Something for the next couple of weeks until school started again. Carl always told him he had to plan ahead, and now, damn it, he was going to. Danny did not want to spend another night here.

The main part of the plan was to stay here in Seattle and live with his dad. The two of them could live in some cool apartment with a view of the city, like in *Frasier*, and a great stereo, two bachelors living in the lap of luxury, with a couple of nice cars, going out to restaurants and renting videos and stuff and he could start in a new school where no one knew him, and things would be completely different, and he would have cooler friends than Scott Mitchell, who had been his best friend since fifth grade. And maybe he would have a really nice girlfriend.

By dawn, Danny had added some details. The girlfriend would be really pretty but, miraculously, sweet and friendly, not snobby, and she would realize how interesting he really was.

And, as soon as he hooked up with Richard Blakely, he was going to come totally clean. Well, not totally. But he was going to tell his dad what had happened back in California with those two goons and Keith and the crowbar. He would explain that he had no choice but to run because Keith drove off with him as a virtual prisoner in the car. This part was actually true. He could hardly have been expected to jump out of a moving car. No need to mention he'd been behind the wheel.

He could even say Keith had tied him up and put him in the trunk, if there'd been a trunk in the Bronco — maybe the trunk thing happened in the Toyota — for possible use as a hostage at some point. And that he'd escaped from Keith at a truck stop and gotten a ride with a friendly trucker who drove him to Seattle.

This story, he decided, wouldn't be snitching, because Keith had said he was going to keep running. They'd never catch Keith.

Danny would also make it clear to his real dad that Mom and Carl had been shipping him off to a desert concentration camp for no good reason. Carl, he would explain, was some kind of religious fanatic, and wanted to brainwash Danny into complete obedience. He'd seen a guy like that on Jerry Springer, who tried to run his home like some cult and beat his kids because he believed God wanted men to totally control their families. Mom, he would explain, was completely dominated by wacky Carl and was too afraid to stick up for her son. That part was certainly true.

After hearing his tale of madness and treachery on the part of Mom and Carl, and abuse by hardened criminal Keith, Richard Blakely was bound to be sympathetic. Danny imagined his real father as a smooth, classy, competent type with silver hair at the temples, saying, "My God, you've been through hell!" and getting him an elegant lawyer who would make the phone calls to California that would clear everything up right away. And the cool part of the plan was that tomorrow, it could begin. Danny and Keith had already found Richard Blakely's home address right in the phone book.

## 7

Louise was pleased when the doorbell chimed precisely at eight. Good. Dave's employees were on time. She opened the door and saw the demolition crew standing on the porch – a pair of rough-looking young men. The tall one had a menacing expression and didn't look clean. The short one wore a black T-shirt, with "Sexual Deviant" written across it in cracked white rubber letters, and smiled too broadly. The two of them reminded Louise of hollow-chested young men being led off in handcuffs to a squad car shouting, "I didn't do nothin'" on a TV programme that showed documentary footage of the police in action.

Despite her revulsion, Louise forced herself to smile at the unattractive young men. Anyway, she told herself, the skilled workers – electricians and carpenters who would soon be on the job – would be more like the reassuring Dave Fraticelli.

The two fellows seemed eager to begin smashing things. Clutching a crowbar and a sledgehammer each, they had thudded down the stairs and gone at their task with an unseemly relish. The first blow from the basement scared the hell out of Louise. The floor shuddered under her feet, and brought to mind an alarming description of poltergeist phenomena she had once read.

The subsequent sounds from the basement continued

to make her uneasy – splintering wood, nails being pulled from beams with abrupt squeaks, sheets of panelling falling to the floor with ringing slaps. As they smashed and crunched, the men shouted at each other with harsh, excitable, male voices.

Louise found those young men's voices threatening. She told herself it was because she had lived for many man-less years alone with Flora. Since meeting Richard and falling in love, she realized that over those years she had developed some of the reflexes of a nervous old maid.

She was about to go upstairs and check on Flora to see if she was well enough to go to school when the doorbell rang again.

When she opened it, a third young man was standing there. He was as unprepossessing as the other two demolishers, with a greasy backpack hanging from one arm, and what appeared to be a rolled-up sleeping bag under the other. His pale blue eyes were slightly crossed. When he smiled, however, he looked suddenly quite charming and less alarming.

"Is this the Blakely residence?" he asked.

"Yes, it is."

"I'm Daniel."

"Come on in. There's the door to the basement right there. Go on down." The sleeping bag puzzled her. Had the kindly Dave Fraticelli gone down to some homeless encampment under the freeway to recruit his workers? Despite the nice smile, the kid did look as if he had been deprived of a shower for a while. Louise had unpleasant fantasies of all three of these guys asking to use the shower while they were here, and she wondered what she should say if they actually did ask.

Behind her, she heard Flora's heavy tread on the stairs. "Mo-om?"

61

Flora was wearing her usual sleep attire — a pair of wrinkled men's boxer shorts worn low on the hips, and a shrunken ribbed tank top. Between the two garments was a wide swathe of pale young stomach. If she wouldn't wear pyjamas or a nightgown, couldn't she at least wear the nice, cosy bathrobe Louise had bought her for Christmas, for God's sake?

When she was sleepy, Flora always looked appealingly like she had when she was five or six. She rubbed her eyes with the heel of her hand. "Why didn't you wake me up?" she asked, sniffing.

Louise glanced at the boy in the doorway. He was staring up at Flora, and seemed to be directing his gaze up one of the wide legs of the hideous boxer shorts.

"I thought you should stay in bed because of your cold," Louise said impatiently. She was eager to get the young man to work and away from her half-naked daughter.

"But I have a chemistry test first period." Flora blinked, scratched her stomach, and then seemed to become aware of the boy's presence. Louise gave him a stern look, meant to get him moving, but he was still staring up at Flora.

"The door to the basement is right there," she snapped.

He ignored her and kept staring at Flora. "I didn't think there would be other kids here," he said. "I guess she must be my sister."

"What!" said Flora. Who was this geek, and what was he talking about? Mom was staring at the boy with this surprised but sad expression, like she was about to start crying.

"Daniel!" she said. "My God. Are you Richard's son?"

"Richard has a *kid*?" said Flora.

"Yes, yes, he does have a child. I thought he might." Mom kept staring at the boy.

Flora was angry. "He never told me and neither did you!"

The boy gave her a kind of pitying look, like she was clueless. "I'm Richard's son," he said. "Daniel." Then he smiled at Mom, who smiled back, tilting her head slightly to one side. She clutched at his sleeve and pulled him through the doorway. "We'll call your dad right away, Daniel," she said eagerly. "Come in! Please come in! He's at work. I know he'll be so excited. I'm Louise, his wife, and this is my daughter, Flora."

"But I'm Richard's stepkid," said Flora. "So we're not related."

Mom ignored her. "I knew this would happen some day, Daniel," she said. "I just felt it."

He laughed. "Wow! Really?"

Flora watched him look around the hall, taking in the sailing ship pictures on the walls, the antique chest, the curving, white-painted banister leading upstairs.

Now Mom was grabbing the hall phone and frantically punching the numbers. "We'll call your dad right away," she said. "He's at work. He'll be so excited."

"OK," the boy said. "Then I better call home and tell them I'm here. It's really important."

"You can use my phone," said Flora. "We have a kid line." She went down to the bottom of the stairs, bent over and picked up the portable where she'd left it last night, and handed it to him. The boy slid the backpack from his shoulders and let it settle on the Oriental carpet. "Thanks." He was about three inches taller than she was, and Flora thought he had a seriously bad haircut.

"Oh, I'm on hold," Mom said, all excited. "Daniel, he didn't know. He wasn't sure you even existed. But I just felt that you were out there."

"He didn't know I existed?" said the boy in what Flora thought was a pretty casual way. But maybe he was blown away because suddenly he looked kind of agitated and said, "Wow. Listen, I'm gonna call my mom now. Can I go out on the porch, and make it like, private?"

On the porch, Keith punched in the number of the telephone booth in the park that they'd staked out. He closed the front door.

"Hello?"

"Danny," he whispered. "It's me. Keith. I found your dad all right."

For the fifth time, Louise heard the recording with Marcia's overly-genteel voice explaining sorrowfully, "We are helping other customers now. But your call is important to us. Please stay on the line and we'll help you as soon as possible. Thank you for your patience." Sprightly Vivaldi followed.

Louise watched Flora withdraw reluctantly back upstairs. Flora looked shocked and hurt, feeling no doubt that they hadn't been truthful with her. Louise would have to explain very delicately that Richard hadn't even known about Daniel, hadn't suspected, really. But, Louise thought with some satisfaction, she herself had guessed. Guessed that Wanda had gone through with the pregnancy and guessed also that the child would arrive someday looking for its father.

This wasn't how she had imagined the reunion, however. If only Richard had been home! Father and son could have rushed into an embrace, relieved, despite not knowing about each other all these years, that the unnatural separation between parent and child was over at last.

When Keith called, Danny had been sitting on the wet

64

grass, waiting for the payphone to ring for an hour. While he waited, he had been nervous and also resentful, regretting not having gone with Keith to reconnoitre the Blakely residence. It wasn't fair that Keith got to go see his dad's home first.

But Keith had been adamant about going there alone. He seemed to think they had a good chance of getting arrested and doing hard time as adults. "Even if the guy I wasted is alive, they'll bring him into court in a wheel-chair, paralysed and drooling and stuff. The jury will for sure want us to rot in prison. But listen, man, you're a friend, so I want to help you out before I bounce outta here."

"What happened?" asked Danny now, gripping the receiver.

"Hey, it's really bad, man," Keith's voice was urgent and hurried. "Be very, very glad I checked it out for you first, or you'd be in jail for sure. The FBI had already been there, and told them you and a companion are wanted in California for a very major felony.

"I gave them the story, like we talked about. I was a homeless kid looking for you."

"Had they heard of me?" asked Danny.

"Yeah. But they told me they hadn't ever seen you and if they ever did, they'd turn you in. Danny, I'm telling you, you better get out of town fast. I'm sure as hell going to. They tried to stop me to find out what I knew about you, but I just took off running, jumped a couple of fences, then worked my way over to the freeway. I'm hitchhiking north, man. If we can remain at large until we're adults, then get like really good lawyers or something, we might be OK. I don't know. But for sure, we're hot now."

"What's my dad like?"

Keith sighed. "I only talked to the wife or girlfriend,

whatever. What a cold bitch! She said they didn't want trouble. She said if I did find you to tell you to leave them alone."

"Really?"

"That's right. And if I were you that's just what I'd do. That woman is mean."

"But maybe my dad would feel differently," said Danny.

"I doubt it. The old bitch said 'You tell him my husband is sorry he ever fucked that skanky trailer trash ho, Wanda.' Exact words, man!"

"Wow," said Danny. He felt suddenly dizzy, as if someone had pushed a two by four into his gut. He couldn't believe anyone would talk about his mom like that!

"Anyway," continued Keith, "even if he isn't as mean as his wife, so what? She calls the shots. I can tell."

"But if you'd talked to my actual dad—" began Danny. Keith had screwed it all up! He hadn't even found his dad.

Keith sighed elaborately. "OK, I didn't want to tell you, I didn't want you to feel bad, but the deal is, he was there too. He didn't say much. Just nodded at whatever she said. A short, fat guy with a bald head. Really whipped by that bitch, I gotta tell you. I don't think you get it, Danny. You better flee and fast. Gotta run. Love you man. Peace and good luck, brother."

Keith hung up, and Danny stood there in the phone booth, listening to the dial tone for a minute, then stepped outside the booth and vomited into some damp shrubbery.

Richard's glassed-in office at the back of Blakely Home Furnishings was a big, airy space, with a large desk dotted with papers and an abstract painting in autumnal colours above a black credenza. A pair of burnt-orange leather guest chairs with asymmetrical flaring backs flanked a black, trapezoidal marble coffee table.

The items in the office had been chosen by one of the store's designers, and Richard felt out of place here. A slightly rumpled man, Richard's hair was often in need of a trim, and he wore khakis and sweaters and plaid shirts. More than once, he had been described as looking like a professor. He suspected that the decorator would have preferred he wear Italian silk suits to match the office.

He especially hated his glass walls. They made him feel like a zoo exhibit, scrutinized all day by the employees who occupied the collection of desks in the bullpen on the other side of the glass. Since his back had begun acting up a little, he had taken to pacing around his enclosure, making the zoo analogy even more apt.

Sometimes he would look up and catch one of them staring at him with an inscrutable expression. He could only assume they were looking for signs of frivolity or sloth. There was no way he could ever relax with a book or anything. They wanted him to look like he was working really hard, even though the brothers had a terrific sales manager, and had delegated most of the operations to other equally efficient staff members.

Of course, the employees knew that and resented him and his brother for it. Despite the fact that Gordon wanted to pull more money out of the business and, goaded on by Marcia, whined about their income, Richard knew that he and his brother had lucked into a pretty good thing – an up-and-running business with a three-generation reputation, and a prosperous, growing market with new people in need of new furniture moving in all the time. Dad had also had the foresight to move from his own father's downtown storefront to a more spacious suburban location with lots of parking, back in the sixties when land was still cheap. The mortgage had been paid off long ago. The only fly in the ointment was the new, second location in a suburb to the east, which seemed to be taking a while to get off the ground.

Richard was in pacing mode, carrying a print-out of budget figures as a prop to avoid employee scorn, and musing over his good fortune – a secure middle age and maybe early retirement – when the phone rang. It was Louise. She said simply, "I have wonderful news. You have a son, Daniel. He's here now."

Richard's initial response to stress was always centred in the pit of his stomach. Now, he felt as if he were standing in an elevator that had plummeted twenty floors, and as if his knees might buckle at any moment. "What!" he shouted.

Despite his reaction, he had sufficient presence of mind to turn away from the glass, lest the spectators notice his reaction, before sinking into his chair.

If it hadn't been for the fact that the kid's name was Daniel, Richard would have immediately said there must be some mistake. He had no children. But Wanda had said if it were a boy she would name him Daniel. This had to be her child. There certainly wasn't anyone else he'd impregnated. Not that he knew about anyway.

"Yes, it is wonderful, isn't it?" Louise now said, presumably for the kid's benefit. "Here he is. You can talk to him yourself."

"Wait!" said Richard. What the hell was he going to say to this person? "Gosh, Daniel, what a surprise, your mother promised to abort you?"

A slightly shaky teenaged voice came on the line. "Wow. Hi," it said.

"Daniel?" said Richard stupidly. "I didn't know. Your mother—"

"Wanda. Wanda Murdock. I know. She never told you about me."

"No, she didn't. She should have."

"I know. Um, that's why I decided to, you know, find you myself. I found your name on my birth certificate. I hope that's OK."

"Yeah, sure. Of course." Richard was completely at a loss. What did one say to a stranger who was also your son?

"Um, I was, like, afraid you wouldn't believe that I was your kid. Or that you wouldn't want to meet me." The voice sounded more mature now.

"Of course I want to meet you," said Richard. And then, feeling cornered, he said in as affable a voice as he could muster, "Stay right there, Daniel. I'm on my way home to meet you now."

He put down the phone, and walked, zombie-like to his brother's office. God! Why had Louise seemed so pleased and excited? Perhaps she relished her own supporting role in the drama. Somehow, he found himself blaming her for this development. It was as if by carrying on about a phantom child she had actually produced one by some spooky Faustian method of conception.

Gordon had the same sliding glass door arrangement, but his office was situated behind a storage area, so he was spared the scrutiny of the employees. Richard found him there drinking coffee with his feet on the desk and flipping half-heartedly through a copy of *Furniture Retailing* magazine. "It says here that the Gen-Xers are finally getting around to buying some decent furniture," he said.

"Never mind all that," said Richard collapsing in the guest chair. "Remember my old girlfriend Wanda?"

Gordon put down the magazine. "Kind of. Blonde with big tits, right? Mom hated her. What about her?"

"Yeah, well, it seems she had my kid about sixteen years ago, and now the boy's found me."

"Jesus!" Gordon flung aside the magazine, yanked his feet off the desk and leaned forward. "Are you sure?"

"I just spoke to him on the phone. He's over at the house, waiting to meet me."

"Weird," said Gordon. "I can't imagine. How do you feel about it?"

"I don't know. It's very strange. I mean I never even knew this person existed."

"Gosh, I guess that means he's my nephew." The brothers fell silent and stared at each other for a while, companionably overwhelmed.

"This could be real expensive," mused Gordon after a while. "That Wanda could come back to you for a bunch of back child support. And the kid'll want you to put him through college. It doesn't seem fair for you to have responsibility dumped on you when you didn't even know. You might get stuck with orthodonture too. That can really get into big bucks, believe me. We just made the down payment on Troy's mouth."

"If I just have to write a cheque, I can handle that," said Richard. "It's the emotional part that creeps me out. What do I say to the guy? Am I supposed to love him or something? I don't get it."

"Well, yeah, I guess so. You probably will love him, eventually, once you get to know him." Gordon sounded unsure on this point. "I mean, I sure love my kids." He glanced over at the framed pictures on the shelf behind him, including the grinning, tubular little Jessica in her leotard, flexed out with her arms raised in triumph after a landing.

"I saw them born, the whole nine yards. You know, the bonding thing. It was supposed to be like love at first sight. But to tell you the truth, at first they looked kind of like pink slugs. I had to fake it. Maybe it'll take you a while."

70

Richard didn't know if he could ever love Danny. But he did know if he couldn't, he would have to fake it. If he didn't appear to care about this boy, everyone, especially Louise, would think he was the coldest bastard in history.

## 8

After he was sure he'd finished vomiting, Danny made his way to a park restroom and rinsed out his mouth at the water fountain there. Then he carefully hid his backpack and sleeping bag behind a huge clump of ferns and started walking along a woodsy path with his hands in his pockets and his head down. There were a few morning joggers who ran past him panting, and some dog walkers who eyed him warily, but mostly he was alone, frantically trying to keep panic at bay.

He was so scared, that he couldn't do anything but just keep plodding along while he tried to figure out what the hell he should do. At one point, he stopped walking for a while, and sat on a bench, watching a squirrel. But he got too nervous, his heart pounding in his chest, and went back to his pacing.

The trail took him past ferns and evergreen shrubs he didn't recognize, and through groves shaded by tall conifers. It was hard to believe that he was inside a city. Parks in Southern California didn't look like this. The strange, dream-like surroundings made it all seem even more unreal. Danny kept saying, "This is not happening!" over and over to himself.

He had only been gone from home for three days, and already it seemed as if his old life belonged to someone else. That Danny Murdock was another kid, a normal kid with normal parents.

But Mom and Carl weren't really normal, he reflected bitterly. They'd turned out to be psychos, paying a bunch of sadists to take him away and torture him! Keith had told him just how bad it was. He'd had no choice but to take his chances on the road! It was totally his parents' fault he was in such deep shit.

For a brief moment, he'd had high hopes for his real dad but he'd turned out to be a jerk, too. And that wife sounded like a real piece of work. Danny had already had to put up with one horrible stepparent, and this woman sounded just as bad as Carl.

What were you supposed to do when you ran out of decent parents? But even nice parents would be of little use to him now. He was a wanted criminal.

The path curved widely, and Danny found himself emerging from a shadowy grove into an open grassy area where he was astonished to see a little old-fashioned white house. It looked like something out of some old black and white sitcom from the fifties. The house sat inside a chain link fence, surrounded by a perfect green lawn. There were some geraniums in pots by the door.

What was it doing here all by itself? Maybe it belonged to a caretaker or something. Danny found himself wanting to go inside. Wouldn't it be great if he could just walk in, and find a nice mom like the one on the farm that he and Keith made up for those girls?

"Hi, Mom, I'm home," he would say, and then go collapse on his bed and listen to music on a killer stereo while the mom made him a fabulous snack — maybe a sandwich with three or four kinds of meat and cheese, and tomatoes and lettuce and lots of mustard, and brought it to him on a tray.

The little house had a mirage-like quality. He found himself heading up the path to see if it was real. When he reached the front porch, he saw that there was a clear plastic box screwed to the front door. Inside was a stack of brochures that said *Learn Lawn Bowling. We'll Teach You How. The Seattle Lawn Bowling Club, founded in 1922, welcomes beginners who want to learn this pleasant and relaxing sport.*

There was a picture of a group of chunky old people of both sexes, wearing white outfits and standing around a green lawn staring at large spheres.

*Lawn bowling is thought to have originated over 5,000 years ago, and was brought to America by the English in the 17th century.*

Suddenly, the door opened, and a lady stood there. Danny was never sure how old adults were, but this one was older than his mom – more of a grandmotherly type. She had grey hair in neat waves, and a pleasant, kind of snubby face. She was wearing an apron over navy blue polyester slacks and a plaid blouse. "Hello," she said.

Feeling panicky at being caught standing on the porch for no reason, which might seem suspicious, he held up the brochure and said as sincerely as possible, "Um, I'm here about the lawn bowling classes."

The old lady smiled sweetly. "Lovely. Do come in, and we'll sign you up," she said. "So nice to see some younger people interested. I was just tidying up a little. Would you like some left-over cake? We had a tournament yesterday, and we always have a few refreshments afterwards."

"That would be great!" said Danny enthusiastically.

The woman gave him a thoughtful look and said, "There's some milk, too. A lot of lawn bowlers like milk in their tea. So many of them are from Britain or Commonwealth countries, you know." She bustled through a large room that resembled a living room, with coffee tables and stuffed furniture, to a small kitchen – Danny following eagerly. On the walls were pictures of more old people in white outfits standing in rows. The lady gestured to Danny to sit down at a small formica kitchen table and opened a noisy avocado-green fridge. "I'll get you a piece of cake, then you can fill out the paperwork. How did you hear about us?"

"I don't know," said Danny stupidly. He had to get a grip and do better than this. There was a piece of cake and some milk at stake here. He had to sound legitimate. "I mean I've always been kind of interested in it. After all, it does go back five thousand years. It must be pretty fun if people kept playing it so long."

"Well that's an interesting point of view," the woman said, smiling. She carried over a glass of milk and a paper plate with some cake on it and put it in front of him, then sat down opposite him. "Oh my, that's a bad bump on your head! How did you get it?"

"Oh. This?" said Danny, touching his forehead. "I'm not sure exactly." This, he realized, was a dumb answer. He had to start thinking faster. This old lady would think he was retarded. He also noticed, when he touched the bump, that it still hurt.

She looked at him sharply. "You're not sure what happened?" She peered intensely into his eyes while he self-consciously chewed some kind of lemon cake. Danny noticed she had green eyes with little brown sparkles in them. It occurred to him that old people's eyes didn't get wrinkly or anything, so the actual eye part stayed normal looking.

The lady clicked her tongue. "Well, your pupils are both the same size but you could still have a concussion. A blow to the head can be very serious. Have you been to the doctor?"

"I can't remember," said Danny in a quavery voice. He stared past her, through a window hung with fluffy white curtains, out at the perfect lawn. A dreamy expression came over his features. "In fact, I don't think I can remember anything!" he said, turning back to renew eye contact, then widening his eyes in a look of surprise.

She stood up, scraping back her chair. "We'd better call your parents," she said, clearly alarmed. "What's your name, dear?"

"I don't know!" said Danny, dropping his fork, placing one hand on either side of his face and assuming a horrified expression. "I don't know who I am! I can't even remember my own name!"

Danny stared at her trying to look overwhelmed, all the while gauging her reaction. She looked very worried about him, but he sensed something else in her alert green eyes. She seemed to think having an amnesiac wander into her little house had made this her lucky day. He could tell she thought that he was an interesting project.

"We'll have to take you right to a doctor," said the old lady decisively. "And then we need to find out who you are. Your parents must be so worried about you! What's the last thing you remember?"

"Waking up. Here in the park. With my head hurting."

"Do you think you live in the neighbourhood?"

"I don't know." Danny scrunched up his eyes to indicate mental effort. "I don't know anything. But I think I remember being thrown out of a car! Yes, I'm almost sure of it. I was with some dangerous person and he threw me out of the car, and I was relieved because I was getting away from him, but then I landed on the road and passed out. And crawled to the park and passed out again."

He congratulated himself on setting up this victim scenario. It provided a little more drama for this lady to enjoy, and it also fitted in nicely with the idea that Keith had taken him against his will, which might come in handy later.

"My God!" said the woman. "What's in your pockets? Is there a wallet?"

Danny knew his pockets were empty, but now he made a show of frantic checking.

"Nothing," he said.

"I'm taking you to the emergency room to make sure you're not badly hurt, and then we'll call the police. Your parents have probably called them already."

"I have a feeling I'm not from around here," said Danny. Not the police. He didn't want her to call the police.

"They might put you on television and ask any member of the public with information to come forward," she said with a certain relish. "Or maybe you've been missing for some time. They send around pictures of children and teenagers every week on the back of ads for carpet cleaning and venetian blinds and things. 'Have You Seen Me?' it says. Maybe you're on one of those."

If the FBI had been over to Richard Blakely's house, then the local police might also be looking for him. Danny imagined a scene like in a really old movie, in which a couple of serious-looking FBI agents in overcoats and hats handed over blown-up versions of his yearbook picture to some uniformed policeman, saying, "We have reason to believe he may be in the area. He and a companion brutally beat two men to death in California."

"Can I finish my cake first?" he asked. "I'm kind of hungry."

"Oh my goodness! I wonder how long it's been since you've eaten."

"I don't know," said Danny. "It feels like a long time."

She smiled at him tenderly. "Of course, boys your age

are always hungry. You can never get enough to eat."

"That's right," Danny responded with feeling. "That is, I'm not sure how old I am, but that sounds familiar somehow."

"You finish your cake, and then we'll get you a proper breakfast on the way to the emergency room, how does that sound?" The lady had removed her apron and was now pulling on a cardigan and picking up her purse and car keys. She had two bright pink spots in her cheeks and looked eager to get started.

"Great," said Danny. "Wow! Thanks so much!"

He'd have to ditch. He couldn't risk the police and being arrested. But he'd wait until after he finished breakfast. Maybe he'd just say he was going to the men's room, and leave the restaurant. It seemed kind of mean to do that to the old lady, but she'd probably just figure he had another blackout or something, and had wandered away in some kind of a daze.

"My name is Olive," she said as they got into an ancient but well-kept Buick. "Olive Chapman. What's yours?"

"Um," began Danny, "I don't know." Was this a trick? He had almost told her his name. He'd have to be very alert.

"Oh, of course," she said, looking genuinely sad. "Oh dear, I'm so sorry."

"It's all right," he said, staring out the window with a haunted expression. "Maybe there's a reason I've forgotten. Maybe the truth about my life was too terrible." This was certainly true. Danny was beginning to wish he really did have amnesia. He would love to be able to forget about Mom and Carl and start fresh. A crashed hard drive would also wipe out Keith and those men who had bled to death in the desert, and Richard Blakely and his stepmom-from-hell wife, too.

"Listen," said Olive in a bossy voice Danny found kind of soothing. "I know you must feel scared and upset, and I suppose it's normal to expect the worst. But you'll feel better after a bite to eat. I believe I've read somewhere that most amnesia is temporary. I'm sure there are a lovely mother and father worried just sick about you — most parents are perfectly nice and mean well no matter how foolishly they sometimes act — and you'll be home with them soon."

"I just don't know," said Danny. "It's so frustrating."

Olive drove into the parking lot of a nearby Denny's. As they entered the restaurant, Danny seized a newspaper machine and yelled, "Seattle Post-Intelligencer. So we're in Seattle!" That was a nice touch, he thought.

Olive had a cup of coffee and smiled approvingly while he ate three eggs, bacon, sausage, ham, hash browns, muffins, milk and orange juice. Unlike Mom, she just watched him eat and didn't ask him a lot of stupid questions while his mouth was full.

As he ate, it occurred to him this might be his last good meal for a long time. As soon as he finished he'd have to get up, excuse himself to go to the bathroom, dive behind a glass case full of pies, and head for the front door.

And then what?

Maybe he should go along with Olive to the emergency room. Maybe they'd put him in the hospital for observation. At least he'd have a bed to sleep in and he could lie there and watch TV and they'd bring him trays of food. He'd have time to think about his next move.

But would they call the cops?

Well, what if they did? Even if they figured out who he was, and asked him about those men Keith had murdered or maimed, all he had to say was he didn't remember. They couldn't trip him up on any little details either, like Carl

79

always tried to do, because there wouldn't be details. God, it was so simple.

Louise had decided to go to work late because she wanted to stay with the boy until Richard arrived. Daniel had been polite but quiet, taking in his new surroundings, eating a bowl of granola with banana slices in silence, and hungrily. Flora had gone off to school, acting blasé about the whole drama, scolding her mother for not having woken her earlier, and apparently more interested in a note for the attendance office than in Daniel. From the basement, the disturbing sounds of demolition continued.

As Louise had fluttered around the kitchen, Daniel, who seemed tired, had drifted into the study, parked himself in front of the television, and watched MTV. Louise had stuck her head in once to see a screen full of writhing young women in hot pants and tank tops fronted by a mumbling, glowering, chubby rapper. Daniel had a curiously dispassionate look on his face. Louise marvelled at his calm. He must be using those intense images to distract himself from the powerful emotions bound to be brought to the surface by the prospect of finally meeting his long-lost father.

As it turned out, when Richard did arrive, Louise was downstairs with the workmen, discussing the various options for the temporary plugging up of the old dryer outlet hose, so she missed the actual reunion. When she came upstairs the two of them were already standing in the front hall about two feet apart, smiling awkwardly at each other and looking as if they might start giggling nervously.

Louise had felt completely at a loss. Should she fling herself at them, and get some kind of three-way hug going? She had no experience at this sort of thing. The closest she had come was observing such reunions on cheesy afternoon talk shows – a guilty, solitary pleasure in which she indulged when home from work in bed with a bad cold.

On these programmes, the hostess would announce in businesslike tones to some tearful middle-aged woman who had given up a baby for adoption many years ago, that the long-lost child was in the wings ready to come out and meet its mother on national television. Parent and child would run to each other, and alternate moments of clutching at arm's-length and staring deeply into each other's eyes, with episodes of sobbing, heaving, full-body embraces, all to the approving purring murmurs and hearty applause of the studio audience.

Nothing like that seemed to be happening with Richard and Daniel. Maybe it was the absence of a studio audience. After an awkward interlude, Louise excused herself to go to work, explaining that she could hardly wait to come back and learn all about Daniel.

Louise worked in the community relations department of a large engineering firm, overseeing the company's charitable giving programme. She and another woman, Jill, managed the department by themselves and had very little idea what the company actually did. The first thing she had done when she arrived at work was tell Jill all about the morning's extraordinary events.

"Oh, my God!" Jill had said in her teenaged way, even though she was in her late thirties. "This could be really messy. There is going to be major emotional baggage being unloaded. Just make sure it doesn't all get dumped on you, Louise. You'll be doing all the emotional heavy lifting."

Louise was irritated. "We'll all do our best. All problems can be solved if people are willing to work at them." What did Jill know, anyway? What could anyone whose cubicle was decorated only with pictures of its occupant's cats, and who hadn't spoken to her own mother for a year and a half, know about happy, well-adjusted, non-dysfunctional family life?

## 9

The emergency room wasn't like on TV. There were no people biting their lips and holding on to bleeding shotgun wounds, or firemen dragging in burn victims, or doctors screaming at each other about what to do while they snapped on latex gloves. Instead, it turned out to be a normal-looking waiting room with magazines on coffee tables, and one old man watching *Oprah* on TV with the volume blasting. Oprah was talking about angels.

A woman of about twenty-five sat behind a receptionist's desk at a computer terminal and said brightly, "Hi! What can we do for you today?"

"This young man had a blow to his head and he has amnesia!" Olive told her.

"Oh my! That's too bad! We better take a look at you. Have you been here before?" she said, smiling, her fingertips poised over the keyboard.

"I don't know," said Danny.

"Well, what's your name?"

"I don't remember." Danny tried not to smile. This was so cool! If you didn't have any answers to questions, no one could do a damn thing about it!

The clerk frowned and turned to Olive.

"Are you a relative?"

"If I knew who he was, I would certainly have supplied

his name," she said. "I don't think you understand. He can't remember anything. I found him wandering around the park."

The clerk gave Olive a slightly huffy look. "Well, I need his social security number," she said.

"I don't think you understand," repeated Olive. "He can't remember anything. That's why we came here."

"But I can't process this. We're not set up to deal with this. Does he have insurance?"

"I don't know!" said Danny, raising his voice. He turned to Olive. "Maybe we should just forget about it."

The clerk looked as if she hoped that they would.

"He needs to be examined by a doctor," said Olive.

The clerk chewed her lip. "How old is he? Is he eighteen yet?"

"I don't think so," said Danny.

She turned back to him with a smirk of triumph. "Then we can't treat you without the consent of a parent or guardian."

"You have to treat him," snapped Olive. "It's an emergency. This is an emergency room, isn't it?"

"Just a minute," said the clerk snippily. She disappeared out of a door and returned with an older woman with blonde, puffy hair and glasses around her neck. She looked at Danny.

"How are you feeling?" she asked.

"OK, I guess."

"We may ask you to go to Harborview Hospital if it's not life-threatening."

Olive sighed elaborately. "He's had a head injury. It might be life-threatening. He might go into convulsions or something. I can give you my name and social security number. I'll take responsibility. But you can't deny him treatment. It's against the Hippocratic oath! Are you a doctor? I'd like to speak to a doctor."

The blonde woman clicked her tongue and shrugged and led Danny off to an examination room. Here, a nurse took his blood pressure and temperature. From outside, he heard Olive talking to someone else. "He thinks he may have been thrown out of a car," she was explaining.

"In that case, seeing as there might have been a crime committed, we have to call the police," a male voice answered.

"Good," said Olive. "The sooner the better. His parents must be frantic!"

"You don't think he could be faking it?" asked the male voice.

Danny started shaking. The nurse noticed it. "Are you OK?" She removed his thermometer, and looked at him suspiciously.

"I guess so," he answered, "except I don't even know who I am." He started looking around for an exit. Maybe he'd have to do what he'd planned to do at the restaurant. Ask to use the bathroom, then escape. He simply couldn't face the police.

But a second later, a man came in, and introduced himself as a doctor in the voice he'd heard talking to Olive. Danny realized he was stuck here for a while. Well, he'd have to stick to his amnesia story, but not offer too many details. All he knew about amnesia was seeing some woman on *Inside Edition* who said she forgot who she was for seven years but still remembered every plot of *Gilligan's Island*.

The doctor looked at the bump on his head, and asked him to follow a fingertip with his eyes, then hit his knees with a triangular rubber hammer. Danny followed all the doctor's instructions and decided not to fake any actual physical symptoms. That might backfire.

He lay on the examining table and the doctor asked if he had any other injuries, then asked him to strip down to his shorts and looked at his arms and legs.

"You seem all right to me. Except for the memory loss, of course," said the doctor. "Amnesia is very rare, but almost always temporary. Memory usually returns within seventy-two hours. Meanwhile, sometime soon I want you to get a CAT scan, and maybe an X-ray." He was scribbling on a piece of paper. "You really need to see a neurologist. And maybe a psychiatrist. Some amnesia is brought on by emotional trauma."

Danny didn't like the sound of that. Would they put him in an insane asylum, with wackos beating their heads on the wall all around him? If it came to that, he'd have to pretend he'd got his memory back fast.

The doctor went with him back to the lobby, where Danny was horrified to see Olive talking to two police officers – a woman with wide hips and a cheerful face and an older guy with silvery hair. The man was talking into a crackling walkie-talkie. The woman said to Olive, "Is this the boy?"

"Yes," said Olive.

The doctor explained to Olive and the police about the CAT scan and the X-ray. The bossy administrator piped up and said, "But we can't go ahead with any tests until we have someone who can sign a consent form."

The female officer nodded. "We need to get someone to take legal custody," she said. She peered at him with kindly interest. "I hear you got a bump on your head."

"I think I fell out of a car. Or was pushed. I'm not sure. I don't remember anything after that."

"There's a bump on his head but no abrasions and contusions anywhere else," said the doctor. "I wouldn't say it's consistent with falling out of a moving vehicle."

86

"Maybe I was hit on the head and imagined the car part," said Danny, shrugging. Why did he say he'd been thrown out of a car? From now one, no more details. "I just don't know."

The policewoman nodded. "And you don't know who you are?"

"No. It's pretty scary."

"I bet," said the policewoman. Danny wasn't sure that she believed him.

Olive seemed to, though. "I told them how you just knocked on the door of the clubhouse." She turned to the police officers. "The lawn bowling clubhouse at the park," she explained. "He was very hungry."

The policeman on the walkie-talkie clicked it off and said, "Sergeant says we're supposed to clear it with the doc to get him out of here, then turn him over to DSHS."

"What's that?" asked Danny nervously.

"Department of Social and Health Services," said the woman. "They're responsible for juveniles. How old are you?"

"I don't know," said Danny.

"Well you don't look eighteen yet. The social workers there will find a placement for you. And they'll decide what to do next. Find your parents or whatever. We'll file a report. Check you against any missing kids."

"A placement?"

"A temporary foster home, probably."

"A foster home?" said Danny. "I've heard they're pretty bad." He stepped closer to Olive.

"The social workers down at DSHS will tell you all about it. We'll take you down to their intake office. It's down by juvenile hall."

"Can't I take him down there?" said Olive. "I feel somehow responsible."

The two police officers conferred and the silver-haired one called in to his sergeant on the walkie-talkie again. "He says DSHS says we can turn him over to anyone we think is OK." He turned to Olive. "We'll just need your name and address and phone number for the incident report."

When Louise came home from work, she found her husband and his son sitting silently, side by side, in front of the TV in the study. Daniel and Richard were watching a baseball game. This struck her as pathetic. Richard didn't even like baseball, but there he sat like a zombie, reaching now and then into a bowl of tortilla chips.

Flora, whom she had hoped to be the source of information on how things were going, was holed up in her room chatting on the phone. She waggled her fingers at her mother in a distracted way while she kept on talking about somebody's hair problems. "It's too poofy. She needs to unpump it. It looks like a marshmallow."

Louise withdrew to her own bedroom, only to be cornered by Richard demanding in a whisper they all go out to dinner together. She hated whispering behind closed doors. This was a feature of life she had come to associate with all the painful turmoil of the recent past, as she had tried to get Richard and Flora to be kind to each other.

"I think just the two of you should go out to dinner," Louise urged under her breath. She knew what would happen if they all went. She and Flora would be left to try and carry the conversational ball, and Richard would avoid developing any intimacy with his son. "You can get to know each other a little more. And for heaven's sake, find out how long he's staying. I can't believe you didn't find that out."

"I'm working up to all that. Apparently, he just took off without telling them. Wanda drove him to it. And there's a sadistic jerk named Carl in the picture."

"Poor kid!"

"He doesn't look like her," Richard said, suddenly thoughtful. Louise felt a stab of jealousy. How dare he even remember what Wanda had looked like?

"Listen, darling," Richard said, "Flora should come too. They're about the same age. It'll be a lot easier for everyone."

A moment later, Louise was back in Flora's bedroom, trying to sound bright and casual. Flora was off the phone now and doing homework. "I'm glad your cold is so much better, because we're all going out to dinner. Richard thought Ray's would be nice."

"Oh, no thanks," said Flora. "I've got to write a paper for Language Arts and I'm expecting a really important phone call."

Once again, Louise lowered her voice to an urgent whisper. "Oh, sweetheart, I wish you'd come. It would mean a lot to Richard. He's kind of nervous about Daniel. He thought it would make it all easier if you came."

"Since when do you guys go out to dinner with me tagging along, anyway?" said Flora with a proud little laugh. "Now that his kid is here, all of a sudden we're the perfect family of four instead of the couple and the third wheel." She reached for *Roget's Thesaurus* and started leafing through the pages.

"Oh, please! We just thought if you were there it would make it all easier. To be honest, I don't think they quite know what to say to each other. It's a weird situation."

Flora flung *Roget's* aside. "Look, I feel sorry for them too, but they will have to just deal with it. It's not our problem."

Louise's face took on a stubborn, clenched-jaw look.

"OK. I'm not asking you to come along for Daniel's sake, even though he's obviously going through a major life event. And I'm not asking you to do it for Richard, even though he seems blown away by it all. I'm asking you to do it for me. I just want everyone to be happy."

Flora sighed. "OK, OK. I'm doing it for you. But Mom, don't get sucked in and think if things go wrong it's your fault. Richard will have to deal with Daniel."

Aware that everyone had disappeared upstairs and that doors were opening and closing up there, Keith sat on the sofa of the TV room with his feet on the coffee table, drank his Coke, and reviewed his situation while he watched some pouting women caress their breasts and stomachs and thighs as they sauntered to a pumping beat through a Disneyland ghetto landscape.

One thing was for sure – the Blakelys definitely had a nice house. That Danny kid had told him about the family business, and said they were rich, but a furniture store, hell that could have been some loser selling ghetto water-beds and futons in some strip mall. This house, however, made it pretty clear that the Blakelys were seriously rich.

There was a big, quiet living room that looked as if it was never used, with paintings on the walls and soft sofas. Off the formal dining room, through glass-paned doors, was a pretty garden with clumps of flowering shrubs and a white-painted latticework fence all around it. The kitchen had counters made of polished stone, warm, terracotta floors, new-looking stainless steel appliances, and a break-fast nook with a skylight and another view of the garden.

And then there was this little room where he was right now, with bookshelves and a TV that was shut up in a cabinet when not in use, like it was too tacky to be seen or something, and a great sound system. Keith had noticed more speakers in the living room and the kitchen, too. It was all definitely classy, even considering they must get a huge discount on all the furniture.

Keith had been in houses like this before, but he'd usually been in a hurry to get out in case the owners returned. It was kind of nice to be able to relax and enjoy all the nice stuff. There was a nice, fresh, lemony smell to the place.

Danny's dad hadn't been what he expected at all. He thought the guy might have been really pissed off that he had to deal with his kid. Instead, Richard had tried to be nice in a kind of guilty way, and made a big deal of saying how bad he felt about being out of touch. Keith had just watched and smiled and nodded and mumbled his appreciation.

Maybe Richard was sincere, but maybe he was one of those guys who liked to believe they always do the right thing, even when they're just a typical, selfish asshole. There was no way to know yet.

Keith felt that Louise however, was definitely good news. She had a soft, sweet face, that crumpled up with emotion in a way Keith knew well, and she would be very easy to deal with. The girl, though, was a spoiled little bitch. Keith was also irritated by the fact that she had a nice, tight little body and she knew it.

He rose and went over to the desk in the corner, noted the presence of an IBM laptop and began systematically inspecting the contents of drawers. Paperwork mostly, old cheques and things, and a few photographs that he flipped through without interest. There were also a couple of passports – something Danny found intriguing, as he had never seen one before. They were probably worth bucks if you knew where to get rid of them.

In the third drawer he found a little leather bag. Inside,

there was a handful of gold coins. Boy, that Blakely was just begging to get ripped off. There was bound to be plenty more good stuff in this house. The wife probably had some jewellery that was worth something. Keith had the pleasant thought that with these workmen on the premises, if something got jacked, they would get blamed. For now, though, he'd limit himself to taking inventory and just chill.

Keith liked the restful hush of the place. He felt good here – warm and comfortable, and happy in the knowledge that everything was nice and clean. These people were used to a pleasant life. He deserved a pleasant life too.

## 10

Olive had a difficult time finding the Department of Social and Health Services office. It was in a seedy part of town, and getting into the office required pushing an intercom button and yelling your business into it, then being buzzed in.

The lobby was full of people sitting on a pair of dirty couches and a collection of orange plastic chairs. There was a large woman in white leggings and a big sweatshirt with a jewelled cat on it sitting next to a sleepy-looking boy who sat hunched over, staring at his shoes. The mother was whispering fiercely, "I hope you're satisfied, you little shit. You've let everyone down. You're just a stupid pothead, like your dad, and that's what I'm going to tell the case-worker. I've covered for you enough. Either your dad takes you and you can party together or they take you, but I've had it."

A big Samoan family occupied half the room, presided over by a large matriarch in her forties, her corona of hair caught in a low-slung ponytail. She was surrounded by a collection of silent teenagers with some little kids running around the floor whooping and giggling. Opposite them sat a teenage girl, alone, weeping and clutching a backpack and a garbage bag that seemed to be full of clothes.

A couple of black kids in gangster gear seemed to be having some kind of a shoving match, and started yelling obscenities at each other. Olive gave them a sharp look. A wimpy-looking security guard went over to them and said, "Say fellows, you wanna keep it down?" and they glared at him until he backed away.

Beside a glass panel, a sign said "Please check in with receptionist".

Olive rapped on the glass with her knuckle, and a moon-faced woman slid open the glass door. "The police sent me here with this young man," Olive said. "He has amnesia and has no idea who he is. They said you could find a place for him."

"We'll see what we can do," she said, staring at Danny with interest. "But it's very difficult to place teenage boys. There are a few group home placements available on a temporary basis. If there are any relatives or anything like that, it's really preferable,"

"I don't know if I have any relatives," said Danny.

"He has amnesia," said Olive impatiently.

"OK. We'll have you talk to a case-worker. Take a seat. What's the name?"

"I don't know," said Danny.

"Has he seen a doctor?" demanded the receptionist. "This sounds like a medical emergency."

"They won't treat him until someone takes legal charge of him," explained Olive.

Danny was starting to feel dumb letting Olive do all the talking. "I need a CAT scan and stuff but there's no one to sign for it. The police said you could find a placement for me. Then there'd be someone to sign for it."

"OK," said the woman, although she seemed confused. "Have a seat."

Olive and Danny sat next to each other on two of the orange plastic chairs, instinctively choosing a distant corner by the exit.

"This place is pretty depressing," said Danny. "You shouldn't have to stick around. I really appreciate everything you've done for me. But they'll figure out what to do with me from now on." If Olive would just leave, he'd be able to sneak out of here before the police figured out who he was.

"I wouldn't feel right leaving until I know what's to become of you," she said, scanning the room with her green eyes. "My, what a lot of unhappy people."

"I guess no one wants to take teenage boys as foster kids. Cute little kids, that's probably what they all want. And girls. People feel sorrier for girls."

Olive took his hand, then quickly released it, because he looked startled. "I feel so much better since we learned that your memory will probably come back in a few days. Your poor parents! And poor you! You're being very brave about the whole thing, I must say. I would be frantic."

"You've been really nice," said Danny. "Most people wouldn't have been so nice. Considering I'm a teenage boy and all."

"I like boys. I had a very nice brother. I was a tomboy and I always played with his friends. There's nothing wrong with boys."

He smiled. "I'm glad I found you then. It's weird, I really don't remember anything, but when I saw that lawn bowling brochure, I got a good feeling. I think maybe I've had some connection somehow with it, 'cause it made me feel good."

Danny hadn't heard of lawn bowling before reading the brochure, but he wanted to say something nice to Olive.

"That's wonderful," she said beaming. "And unusual. Very few young people are interested, to be honest. But it really is such a pleasant game. People of any age or fitness level can enjoy it."

Just then a young teenage girl burst out into the lobby from the door that presumably led from where the social workers were. She was an ample girl with big breasts, wearing a tight, short dress and big platform shoes. Danny had seen hookers standing by the side of the road from a car, but he'd never seen one this close. She looked like an ordinary kid from some mall or whatever, but dressed as a hooker. "No fucking way," she screamed into the inner office. "And when that bitch gets here, you tell her that Sunshine already came and got me. You tell her he takes real good care of me. Not like her."

A thin man in a green sweater came into the lobby after her. "Come on, Anna. Just talk to her. Your mom's really worried about you. Please? She's on her way down here."

Anna flounced through the lobby, and said to no one in particular, "Fucking bitch. Won't leave me alone!" She pounded a trash can with her fist a couple of times, and stormed out the door.

The man in the green sweater sighed as the girl slammed the door.

"Aren't you going after her?" asked Olive. "She's leading a dangerous life. Anyone can see that!"

"We can't keep them here legally," said the man defensively. "If they aren't arrested for criminal behaviour, we can't hold them, and she wasn't busted for hooking. Just picked up off the street."

"I see," said Olive. Turning over a young girl to a man like that! It was criminal. The girl looked about fourteen. There used to be places for girls like that, angry girls, and sometimes stupid ones, where they could be protected from bad men.

Olive could tell that the boy found all this fascinating but disturbing. He kept staring at the other kids in a way that gave her the distinct impression his own life had been fairly sheltered. Now, presumably, he was going to be flung into some group home for boys. He was a slight kid, and she was suddenly fearful that he wouldn't be able to handle himself with a bunch of roughnecks. Olive Chapman knew how tough teenage boys could be on each other. She didn't feel they should be put in groups at all, unless it was to fight a war.

And she didn't like the way this place was run, either. It had the feel of being an underfunded enterprise, with harried workers. Olive could well imagine these people losing paperwork and letting the children slip through the cracks.

If she worked here, she'd bring in her own broom and sweep out this filthy lobby on her lunch break, and scrub the orange chairs and sticky-looking plastic coffee tables with hot soapy water. But these people were apparently too overwhelmed to even try to set a professional tone. Scrubbing things with hot soapy water would have been good for the workers here too. Olive knew that from personal experience. When things seemed hopeless, cleaning something always made you feel better.

After the thin man in the sweater left, Olive turned to Danny. "Let's get out of here," she said. "There's no legal requirement that you stay, and frankly I cannot think that these people have anything very reasonable to offer you."

As soon as she said it, she regretted it. She couldn't just take in a strange boy. Not these days, when there were so many maniacs running around loose.

But when a look of incredible relief came over his face, she decided her impulse had been right. He just needed a quiet place to stay for a few days. She couldn't do anything about all these unhappy families and children around her, but she could at least make a little difference to just one person for a day or two. And something about the boy reminded her of her brother Frank, who had been killed when he was really only a few years older than this boy here.

Like Frank, this boy had retained into adolescence some of the straightforward lack of self-consciousness that younger boys had, and that made them, in some ways, more satisfactory than girls.

Louise hoped she hadn't made a mistake by urging Flora to come with them tonight. She could spot the signs that Flora's brittle, sophisticated, quasi-adult persona had been trotted out for the occasion – the economy of movement, the formality of speech, the dignified expression on her face. Louise suspected Flora was trying to make Daniel look immature by comparison. Why? Because of her residual resentment of Richard? Because she felt threatened by the idea of another kid in the house?

On the way to the restaurant, Louise pointed out some sights from the car. Daniel, in the back seat with Flora, made a polite show of interest. "I've heard Seattle is a great city," he said.

Louise craned around to see Flora staring unsmilingly out of the window through her sunglasses, exuding the world-weary, existential air of someone in an early-sixties foreign film. Why couldn't she make polite conversation with Daniel, for God's sake? For that matter, why couldn't Richard? He seemed to think that the fact he was driving meant he was off the hook.

As they went into the restaurant, Louise lagged back a little, took her daughter's arm and whispered enthusiastically, "It's really nice of you to come. I know you can help make this evening easier."

She was rewarded with a startled, guilty look from Flora and congratulated herself on having appealed successfully to her daughter's better nature. Sure enough, as soon as they sat down, Flora turned gracious. To Daniel's eager, "Wow! This is great. Look at those sailboats!" she replied. "Your dad has a sailboat himself. Did he tell you?" She took off her sunglasses and smiled at him. Louise felt herself relax little. Maybe it would be all right after all.

"Really?" said Daniel, turning to Richard. "I always wanted to learn about boats. I wanted to be a Sea Scout once, but then we moved again."

"Did you move a lot?" said Flora.

"A lot," said Daniel, frowning. "My stepdad was in the military. It was kind of hard changing schools. Now that he's out of the service, he's had trouble keeping jobs. 'Cause he's so mean. The guy has serious anger management problems."

"Really?" said Flora.

"Yeah. You know, these military guys can be pretty tough."

"Actually, I've never moved," said Flora. "My life has been pretty boring. I really want to go far away to college, and maybe live in Europe."

Daniel gave a bitter little laugh. "Carl says college will just make me into a snob, and I should learn a trade. And he says if I really want to go to college I should go in the army and they'll pay for it after I do my hitch. He says the army will make a man of me."

Louise shot her husband a concerned look.

Richard replied, "Well, Daniel, maybe your education is something we can talk about while you're here. Meanwhile, I hope you like seafood as much as I do. But if you don't they've got steaks and stuff."

Louise was irked. Richard had deflected a serious topic – his son's education – to talk about the menu.

Daniel didn't seem to mind. "Seafood is great. I love it.

Maybe I inherited that from you." He gave Richard a big, loopy grin.

"The salmon should be pretty good now," Richard said.

"Let me see how much you guys look alike," said Louise playfully. Father and son turned to gaze at each other with shy curiosity. Finally! She'd got some eye contact going. Seeing them both in profile, Louise admired her husband's nose. It had a strong, aristocratic shape. The two of them turned back to Louise for her inspection and verdict.

"Your eyebrows are kind of the same," she said thoughtfully. Daniel's were darker, but had a similar arch. Both of them looked intelligent. It was funny how intelligence was so clearly evident in the set of the mouth and the look of engagement in the eyes. Daniel's blue eyes, apart from being slightly crossed, which Louise was beginning to find endearing, also had an analytical, intelligent light in them. "And I think the shape of your jaw is the same. But you know what, Richard? He looks more like Gordon than you."

Richard examined his son's face carefully. "Maybe you're right," he said with a trace of doubt that annoyed Louise.

Daniel nodded. "Gordon," he repeated softly.

"Gordon is Richard's brother," Flora explained.

"Your uncle," Louise added.

"That's interesting," said Daniel.

"I guess you don't know anything about our family," Richard said. "My dad died five years ago. My mother lives here in Seattle in the summer and in Arizona in the winter. She's there now. Gordon and his wife Marcia have three kids."

"Wow! A family I never met. Cool."

"When we get home, we can look at some family pictures," said Louise. "Your Uncle Gordon and your dad run the family business your great-grandfather started."

Daniel nodded. "Yeah, a furniture store. Mom did tell me that, but that's about all. I'd sure like to learn more about the family."

"My mother knows probably more than you want to know," said Richard with a smile. "They've traced it all back to the seventeenth century. We're mostly English, with some Scottish and Alsatian French. But I never pay much attention to any of that genealogy stuff. I mean who cares what your ancestors did? It's what you do that counts."

"Right!" said Daniel.

Good. Now Richard was talking to Daniel. Louise settled back in her chair and smiled over at Flora, but Flora seemed to be flirting with the handsome young busboy who was hovering around the table filling water glasses and providing bread. She was giving him a sly little smile and a slightly raised eyebrow. His mouth twitched back at her in a little smile of his own. Then she looked down coyly at her plate as if she were shocked at her own boldness.

Daniel seemed to be noticing Flora too, although he was ostensibly listening to Richard describe how Great-Grandfather Blakely had been on his way to the Yukon Gold Rush from Missouri when he decided to stay in Seattle. Daniel rolled his eyes up at the busboy jokily, and then gave Flora a knowing look of amused triumph that seemed to say, "You can't fool me. I've intercepted your little moves".

To Louise's consternation, Flora was staring back at Daniel resentfully, beginning to blush at having been caught out.

"That's interesting," said Daniel turning back to Richard. "My mom never told me very much. I go by my stepfather's name, Murdock. But on my birth certificate I found my real name."

"When you were little, did you think your stepfather was

101

your real father?" asked Louise, noting with a sidelong glance that Flora had now hidden her rosy face behind the menu. Poor thing! She could be so sophisticated one minute – flirting with the busboy rather elegantly – then have her poise abandon her suddenly a moment later.

"No, I always knew he wasn't my real father." Daniel shook his head in a resigned way. "He made that pretty clear. He's always pointing out the difference between me and Amy. His kid."

"Oh, that's terrible," Louise heard herself say, even though she knew she should try and shut up and let Richard do the talking. "That's so unfair."

Across the table, Flora put down the menu. She seemed to have composed herself. Louise gave her a smile meant to reassure.

Richard now addressed his wife. "I've told Daniel how sorry I am the way things turned out." He cleared his throat self-consciously. To Daniel he said, "I hope your mother told you that none of this was my idea. I would certainly have taken some responsibility for you. I want you to believe that."

Daniel shrugged. "Mom wouldn't talk about you. I quit asking. But I always wondered. Like on ethnic heritage day at middle school. I could only talk about my mom's side."

"What was her ethnic background?" asked Louise.

"Mom? Oh, you know," Daniel shrugged and grinned at Richard. "I never paid much attention to that family tree stuff either."

"Wanda's family was Polish, actually," said Richard.

"Yeah," said Daniel. His face took on a very serious look all of a sudden. "To tell you the truth, I don't feel good talking about her much. She and I don't get along that well."

"I'm sorry," said Richard. "But I'm not surprised. Wanda

was always very—" He paused and Louise knew he was searching tactfully for some euphemism for "completely nuts". He took a deep breath and started again. "She was a highly strung, intense person."

"That's it exactly," said Daniel with the eagerness of someone who hasn't been believed until now. "And my stepfather, Carl, well, that's a pretty long story." He sighed and looked down at his plate, biting his lower lip.

Louise said gently, "It all sounds pretty rough, but you've only got another couple of years until you're eighteen. Then maybe you'll be going away to college." She felt suddenly stupid. How could she be so tactless? The poor kid had just explained that if he wanted to go to college he'd be handed over to some recruiting sergeant and shipped off to boot camp as soon as he graduated from high school.

"Whatever," said Daniel.

There was an awkward silence. Richard turned to Flora and said coldly, "You're awfully quiet, Flora."

Flora was angry. She'd been enjoying a flirty little moment with this cool guy with a great haircut and great eyelashes who smelled like CK One, her favourite fragrance, and this Daniel guy gives her a really sleazy look like she's some total slut. It was a creepy look, a leer, that said, "I see right through you". And just when she'd tried to be nice to him so Mom would be happy!

Thank God her blush seemed to have gone away. At least her face felt cool again. She gave Daniel a half-lidded look and said, "So how long are you staying?"

"That's the thing. I was kinda hoping…" He sighed and ran his fingers through his lanky hair. "The thing is, to be real honest, my mom and stepdad kinda threw me out. I was going to live in a foster home until I finished high school, but the child welfare people said my parents would have to pay for it and my stepdad said he wouldn't. I don't know what to do. Maybe I should just get a job."

"Oh my God!" said Louise softly.

"When I called my mom today, she told me not to come back."

Richard gave Daniel a grave look. In the confident voice that Louise had come to think of gratefully as his take-charge, problem-solving voice, he said, "I'm sure we can work something out, Daniel."

"I'm sorry," Daniel said weakly. "I didn't know where else to go. I had some money saved up from my after-school job and I just went to the airport and bought a ticket and came here."

They all stared at him.

"I was afraid if I called first you wouldn't want me to come," he said, meeting their stares one by one, then gazing down at his hands on the table in front of him.

Flora looked over at her mother. What did Richard mean by "work something out"? Was Daniel going to have to live with them? It was impossible! There was no room for him. The basement was all torn up, and wouldn't be finished into Flora's new suite – bedroom, bathroom and TV room – for weeks. And after that, her old room upstairs was supposed to get remodelled into a study and dressing room connected by a big arch to Mom and Richard's room.

Her mind was racing. Would he go to Madison High School? Would everyone know that this weirdo lived at her house? She'd have to call him her stepbrother. God! She'd finally gotten used to Richard living with them and now another total stranger shows up! But Mom would never let this happen. Daniel would just have to go home.

Mom was looking back at her with a glazed-over expression, like she'd just been hit. Flora's eyes widened dramatically, and, in the visual shorthand she and her mother had developed over the years, she let her mouth fall stagily slack to indicate she was weirded-out herself.

"I didn't know what else to do," said Daniel, his head hanging like a dog's in a surrender display. When he spoke again, there was a catch in his voice. "I guess no one wants me," he said.

Flora watched her mother lean sympathetically towards Daniel's slumped form.

## 11

Olive and Danny ate dinner on her stiff, squared-off living-room sofa in front of the TV news. This had been Olive's idea. She wanted to see if anyone was looking for Danny. "Maybe they'll have your picture and everything," she said.

On the way back from the DSHS office, they had stopped at the supermarket and stocked up on groceries. At Olive's urging, Danny had selected some of his favourite foods, like peanut butter crunch balls cereal, jalapeño-flavoured potato chips, and frozen Totino's pizza rolls. "I also drink a lot of milk," he'd said apologetically.

"It's interesting that you know what foods you like," said Olive. "Should we have steak for dinner? I think you need protein." She peered closely at him like Mom did when she was afraid he might be getting the flu or something. "I'm glad we've got all those doctor's appointments lined up."

Olive lived in a rectangular blue house with white trim and a neat garden. Rows of rosebushes, recently pruned and now leafing out, lined the walk. Danny carried the groceries up to the front door, while Olive unlocked it. They stepped into the living room. Danny took in the giant console TV with a green vase of yellow forsythia on top of it, the plaid sofa and chairs, and shelves with lots of books and knick-knacks. There was a fireplace of painted white brick, and on the mantel, a model ship in a bottle like they had in old cartoons, and a clock that ticked loudly.

After they put away the groceries, Olive fetched the TV trays from the hall closet and asked Danny to assemble them while she got dinner started. The trays were old-fashioned with little clips that attached to a black, tubular folding stand. Danny liked them. The surfaces of them had painted scenes of Paris, with the Eiffel tower and ladies with French poodles at sidewalk cafes and guys with berets and striped shirts.

"How do you like your steak?" she asked after he'd finished snapping the TV trays into place and positioning them in front of the sofa.

"Good question," said Danny, looking thoughtful. "I'm pretty sure I like it medium rare."

She nodded. "After the news, let's see if we can't get some clues to who you are. We'll see if you can play the piano or have any special knowledge of any region. We already know you have pleasant associations with lawn bowling. I'm sure we can narrow down who you are."

"I hope so," said Danny.

"Meanwhile, I'll have to have something to call you."

Wow! He was going to get to choose his own name.

"How about Antonio?" he said thoughtfully.

Olive looked slightly taken aback. "Maybe I could call you Tony," she said.

"OK." He liked the sound of Tony.

"I wonder why you chose that name," she said thoughtfully, shaking salt and pepper on the steaks and sliding them into the oven. "You certainly don't look like the Latin type. Maybe there's some connection with San Antonio, Texas. Or Saint Anthony."

"The guy you pray to for lost things?" said Danny.

"That's right," said Olive, looking a little surprised.

Danny's mom had been brought up Catholic and she once confessed to him that even though she didn't believe in any of that stuff any more, she still did that Saint Anthony thing when her car keys got lost, because it calmed her down while she was ripping apart the sofa cushions. Maybe she was praying to the guy right now to find out where the hell he was.

"Are you online?" asked Danny. "We could do an Internet search for Antonio and see what happens." He had a sudden idea that he could zip around the net and string together a bunch of fake clues that could point totally in the wrong direction.

"No, I'm not, Tony. But I've been dying to. I signed up for a course at the library to try and understand it all."

"I can help you out," said Danny. "I know a lot about computers."

"Really?" Now she was stirring some frozen peas and carrots.

"At least I think I do," said Danny, once again wrinkling his forehead into a puzzled frown. "I'm pretty sure I do."

"We'll find out," she said. "What time is it? Turn on channel five, will you?"

Danny turned on the set, and imagined the screen filling up with his picture, and an announcer saying, "Meanwhile, as they wait for word of Danny, the family clings to hope," followed by interviews with worried-looking neighbours on his street in Arleta, now lined with shrubs and trees full of yellow ribbons in his honour.

But then he remembered he wasn't really lost and amnesiac. He was a fugitive, and he and Olive were more likely to see a picture of him and one of Keith, and the newscaster saying, "These dangerous young men may be in our area. Be alert." He decided to suppress that thought. And if the TV did say all that, he'd stick to his memory loss story, then slowly remember being victimized and abducted by the brutal Keith.

"There's something wrong with the TV," he called to Olive. "I can only get a couple of channels. I think your cable is gone."

"Oh, I don't have cable," said Olive. "But I guess you did, wherever you were."

In a weird way, Danny thought it was kind of cool she didn't have cable. He'd never met anyone who didn't have cable before.

By the time he phoned Wanda's number in California, Richard was desperate to get the situation under control. Daniel and his crazy mother would just have to patch things up, and Daniel would have to go home. It was that simple. Richard had only just learned of his son's existence, and now he was being asked to take him in. It was too much!

On top of all that, Daniel had just fled out the front door in a hysterical manner, which unnerved Richard, and made him even more wary of him. He seemed like a nice enough kid who'd had a hard time, but what if he took after his mother in the mental health department? Richard was prepared to help him in some vague way, but he wanted to do that from a distance, without a lot of up front personal involvement.

After his initial collapse in the restaurant, Daniel had seemed to pull himself together, but when the family got back to the house, he'd completely flipped out. First, when Richard announced he needed to talk to Wanda, the boy had refused to give him his home phone number. "Daniel, I *have* to talk to her," Richard had said firmly. The four of them were standing in the entrance hall, Louise and Flora together like spectators at the side, Richard and Daniel facing each other a few feet apart.

"There's no reason to call Mom!" Daniel had declared. Richard found his voice way too shrill and assertive. "Why do you need to call her, anyway?"

Richard hesitated before replying. He could hardly say, "Because I don't want you either, and I'm going to try and convince that bitch to change her mind and take you back." And he didn't really feel that harsh, he told himself. It was just that he didn't think taking on a teenage boy that he hardly knew would be easy. He sighed and said, "Because I want to make sure she knows what's going on. We can't make any rational decisions about your short-term or long-term future until I have assembled all the facts." He supposed this sounded cold. In a softer tone, he added, "I know you've had a hard time."

"You got that right!" Daniel shouted wildly, and fled out the front door into the darkness. They heard his feet pounding down the sidewalk.

"Aren't you going after him?" Louise had asked in a loud, panicky voice.

"No. I'm going to call his mother." Jesus! Richard felt surrounded by hysterics. All he needed at a time like this was the usually placid Louise going berserk on him.

Flora said, "Don't worry Mom, he has to come back. He left all his stuff here." Thank God Flora sounded reasonable! Richard couldn't have coped with two females going off the rails and one distraught boy running out into the night, all emoting while he tried to make some sense of the situation.

"Maybe he's afraid he'll have to go back home," Louise said, her voice rising. "Maybe he's run away. We have to go after him!"

"No! We can't start in letting him make scenes," Richard heard himself say harshly. "Listen, I have to handle this my own way, OK?"

Louise looked hurt and angry. Well, that was just too bad. She'd have to wait until he sorted out a few things before he reassured her. Fortunately, Directory Assistance had a listing for a Carl and Wanda Murdock in Arleta, California.

Not particularly anxious to have Louise and her daughter staring at him throughout the conversation, Richard went up to the bedroom to make the call, pointedly closing the door. He sat heavily on the bed, sighed, and punched in the number.

A man answered.

"Is Wanda there?" Richard said in a businesslike way.

"No she isn't. Who is this?" Richard didn't like the man's belligerent tone.

"My name is Richard Blakely. Apparently, I'm the father of her son. Who's here with me now, by the way." There was something basically humiliating about all this, Richard felt. His ignorance of paternity seemed to imply that Richard couldn't handle things well, and that he had led a messy, poorly managed life. It seemed so terribly unfair that he had to go through all of this just because he'd once dated a nutcase.

"Oh," said the man, sounding surprised. "Really? Danny? He's with you?"

"Yes. He called Wanda earlier."

"Oh. Right. I just got in."

"You must be Carl. Didn't you notice he was gone?" asked Richard.

"Of course we did," said the man, who neither confirmed nor denied that he was Carl. "Naturally we've been concerned. I take it he's OK."

"I think I'd better talk to his mother," said Richard.

"She's not in," said the man. "She's, um, at a Weight Watcher's meeting. But I'll tell her he's with you. Where are you exactly?"

"I live in Seattle."

"Oh." Carl seemed awfully casual about all this. Richard had heard a lot more enthusiasm and gratitude from people who'd recovered a lost umbrella, never mind a lost child.

Richard tried to inject a note of seriousness into the proceedings, and reclaim some of his dignity by appearing to be taking higher ground. "Frankly, this has been quite a shock. No one ever even told me about this boy."

"Yeah, well that was my wife's idea," said Carl. "She thought it would be easier. What's your number there? Hang on. I'll get a pen."

A Weight Watcher's meeting! His mother had told him years ago that Wanda would turn to fat someday. He suddenly took a horrible pleasure in imagining his former girlfriend transformed into a big, white slug, lying on a stained velveteen sofa, her ample flesh draped in a tent-like garment, reaching with sausage-shaped fingers into a box of chocolates on the coffee table.

Carl came back on the line. "Here I am," he said. "Now what's that number?"

Richard repeated it, and said, "I presume if he comes home you'll take him in. He led me to believe you wouldn't."

"I'll have Wanda call you," he said

Evasive little creep! Richard's voice rose. "Daniel says you and your wife threw him out into the street!"

Just then, Louise opened the door and sat gingerly next to him on their bed with a look of concern. He could hardly break off the conversation and ask her politely to let him deal with this alone, so he shot her an irritated frown which she either didn't see or chose to ignore.

Carl had the nerve to giggle a little. A psychopathic giggle, no doubt. "He said that? Well it's not exactly like we threw him out. We had him signed up for a survival course.

Kind of a character-building thing. It wasn't cheap, either, let me tell you."

"What do you mean 'survival course'?"

"You know. A rehab-type thing."

"I see. And just what kind of rehab was he in?" asked Richard. Next to him, Louise flinched at this question.

"I suppose you have a right to know. He's experimented with marijuana. I have a younger child. I can't expose her to that. And he's had some problems. He's oppositionally defiant."

"What the hell does that mean?"

"It means he won't do what we say," said Carl in slow, exasperated tones, as if he thought he were talking to an idiot.

What a jerk, thought Richard. Typical Californian. As if everyone were supposed to be up on the latest made-up syndrome.

Carl paused, and his voice took on a friendlier tinge and some enthusiasm. "But listen, maybe a little time-out, a break from his home environment, would be a good thing for him."

Carl didn't sound as cretinous as Daniel had described him – maybe he presented well to outsiders – but he was certainly making it clear he didn't want Daniel in his life.

"I think I'd better speak to Wanda," Richard said stiffly. "When will she be back?"

"I'm not sure. Frankly, she's very upset about the boy. But he needs to get away from her apron strings. Like I said, he just needs some time out. We all do. Can he stay with you for a while? I think it's about time he got to know you." Pause. "You know, he's really a terrific kid." Richard detected the salesman's fake enthusiasm. Carl was trying to get him to take Daniel the way the reps who called on him tried to offload some extra recliners or credenzas.

"He told us you just threw him out into the street!" said Richard. The guy hadn't come clean about that.

"Maybe it would be good for him to spend some quality time with his real father," the man continued in a friendly tone.

"What?"

"I mean, legally, and financially — let's be frank here — think about it — you haven't done anything for him for almost sixteen years. There's only two more to go."

"I really should talk to Wanda," said Richard.

"I'll have her call you," said Carl.


Across the hall in her bedroom, Flora was lying on her back on the bed, talking on her own phone line to her best friend, Claire. "I couldn't believe it. He just said he'd been thrown out and wanted to live with us. And Richard doesn't even know him or anything. Plus, I think he's a liar."

"How come?"

"He took the portable to call his mom on the porch, right? But there weren't enough beeps for another area code, you know what I mean? I only heard seven beeps. I was counting because I wondered if he was from around here. And now it turns out she lives in California."

"Weird."

"I couldn't hear what he said, though."

"Is he cute?" asked Claire.

Flora didn't tell Claire that her new stepbrother had a pretty good body, with nice shoulders and pecs, and that even though he was younger he looked really mature for his age. "God!" said Flora, "He is seriously not cute. Really bad hair."

"How bad?"

"Hockey cut. I told my mom he looked dysfunctional, but I didn't tell her I could tell from his clueless haircut.

Anyway, when we all came back home, he got in this, like, fight with Richard, and ran out the front door."

"Wow," said Claire. "Did he come back?"

"Not yet. Richard's calling Daniel's mom right now. I hope to God she takes him back. I do *not* want that geek around here."

"God, you poor thing," said Claire. "And after you went through all that shit with your stepfather, too."

"Yeah. He used to come down on Mom for not having total control over me, you know, and making her make me clean my room. Remember? Now we'll see what his parenting skills are like."

In California, Carl hung up the phone, and gazed out the window to the patio where Wanda was watering her fuchsia baskets by twilight. She looked so peaceful. He didn't want her agitated. How was he going to pitch this one to her? He still had almost two weeks. And if he worked it right, this could all turn out pretty well.

Meanwhile, he'd turn off the ringer on the phone while he was out, and make sure he got there first when she was in, just in case that Blakely guy called back any time soon. Wanda was such a ditz, she'd never notice, he thought fondly.

Olive had apologized that the guest bedroom at her house was full of odds and ends. "I'm afraid that things just seem to find their way here." She looked around the room critically, her eye falling on a what-not shelf with a huge, pink tropical shell, a wooden shoe, and little vases and candlesticks. There was an old sewing machine, too, and some boxes of Christmas ornaments, and old photo albums.

"I kind of like it. There's a lot to look at," Danny said. He

115

would have loved sleeping there as a little kid. There were all kinds of things to explore. He felt an urge to put the pink shell to his ear to hear the ocean.

"This used to be my room," said Olive, "when I was a child."

"Wow! Have you lived here your whole life?"

"No. I was away for a long time."

Danny was sitting up in bed with crisp white sheets, wearing a pair of striped pyjamas. On their way home from the Department of Social and Health Services, Olive had stopped off at J C Penney's and bought him these pyjamas and a toothbrush, and another pair of jeans and a T-shirt and socks and underwear.

Danny hadn't slept in pyjamas for years. That, and the fact that the old-fashioned bed with its squeaky springs was about two feet higher than his normal bed, made him feel about eight years old.

"Getting the computer in here will give me an incentive to get it all straightened up," she said. After dinner, Olive had decided that she and Danny would go out computer shopping the next day. "I've wanted to do it for a while," she had said. "There are so many interesting things on the Internet that I've played with at the library, but I was afraid I would never be able to get it set up. But now that you're here you can help me buy it and everything."

Danny had been eager to help her. He'd been kind of embarrassed because she was buying food and clothes for him. "Of course," she said, now, "that's only if you don't remember who you are, which I'm sure you will. I just thought, that in case your memory *didn't* come back right away, it would be good for you to stay busy. We can arrange for your first lawn bowling lesson in the afternoon if you want."

"Thanks so much for everything," said Danny. "Wow, I'm

so glad I found you." The police, he felt sure, would never find him here.

She smiled. "Why don't you get some sleep now, Tony," she said, "and maybe, when you wake up, you'll know who you are and we can get in touch with your poor parents. They must be at their wits' end!"

Danny nodded and yawned. Suddenly he was feeling very tired. It seemed like weeks ago that he'd been vomiting in the park after hearing about Richard Blakely and his bitch of a wife.

"I'm afraid this is the best we can do for tonight," Richard said apologetically, gesturing to the sofa Louise had insisted on making up with sheets and blankets, even though Daniel had said his sleeping bag would do. "I guess Louise explained to you about the remodelling."

"Yeah. Louise sure is nice," said Daniel. "A lot of step-moms wouldn't have been so welcoming to a kid that just showed up."

Richard, flailing around for something positive and substantive to talk about, seized the topic eagerly. "Yes, she really is wonderful."

He felt suddenly relieved that Daniel hadn't showed up earlier, during his long, sad bachelor existence. Louise would make all this much easier. She actually liked kids, and she was patient. And if Richard himself fell apart under the strain, she would be there to patch him back together. She was a wonderful person, and he was so grateful for her.

When Daniel had returned to their doorstep after about forty-five minutes, Richard was a wreck, reeling from his conversation with Wanda's husband and overwhelmed by the prospect of taking in a strange kid. He had a horrible, doomed feeling that he would have no choice in the matter

– just as he had had no choice about the child being born in the first place.

Louise had welcomed Daniel back into the house as if his storming out were no big deal. She had just smiled and said in her calm voice that she understood what a strain all this had been on him, and patted him lightly on the shoulder. He'd smiled back at her with a look of complete trust.

Now, sitting on the big oak coffee table, Daniel turned away sheepishly and said, "I'm sorry I just took off like that. I really messed up." Sighing, he removed his shoes and set them neatly side by side under the table.

They were ratty-looking – greasy and scuffed – with the soles beginning to peel off. What was the matter with Wanda and that husband of hers? Couldn't they have bought the kid a decent pair of shoes? Now he was pulling off a pair of greyish tube socks that had holes in them, and stuffing them into the shoes. Richard had thought that maybe the ripped jeans were some kind of fashion statement. But these socks and shoes just looked pathetic.

God, the poor kid was wearing rags! *His* kid. And Richard had been helpless, unable to do a thing about it. He was going to take Daniel shopping as soon as possible and get him some decent stuff – and real shoes, not those cheap sneakers that looked like they cost about a buck and a half at K-Mart.

"Hey, none of this is going to be easy," said Richard. "But I know we'll both do our best. And I never want to hear you apologize for showing up at my door." He put a tentative hand on the boy's shoulder. Louise hadn't had any problem patting him, but for Richard it was almost as hard to touch Daniel casually as it was to touch Flora.

He kept his hand on the shoulder anyway, feeling resentment. By rights, he should be completely at ease with this boy. He should have already put in years tossing him into the air and wrestling with him on the floor and hugging him. Instead, he was approaching him as if he were a live bomb. He forced himself to give Daniel's shoulder a reassuring squeeze before withdrawing his hand.

"I didn't know if you would want me. I just didn't know." He stood up, slid out of his jeans and lay them on the back of the sofa, then pulled off his T-shirt. Looking at him standing there in a pair of plaid flannel boxer shorts, Richard was startled to see how grown-up Daniel looked. There was a lot of hair on his well-muscled calves, and even some on his chest. In fact, he was already a lot hairier than Richard.

"I talked to your stepfather, Daniel. I told him you were here and safe."

"What did he say about me?" asked Daniel warily.

"Frankly," said Richard, "I don't give a damn what he has to say about anything. As far as I'm concerned, today is day one."

Daniel climbed between the white sheets with a happy sigh. "It's great to be here." He lay down and folded his arms behind his head, closed his eyes and smiled.

Richard was horrified to see a large tattoo on Daniel's shoulder. It was absolutely hideous – a skull with a knife through it. "What the hell's that?" he said, pointing. "You got yourself tattooed!"

Daniel opened his eyes and looked down at it sadly. "Pretty stupid, huh?" he said. "I wish Mom'd never signed for me. I was only fourteen. Now I realize how dumb it makes me look."

"Wanda let you get a tattoo when you were fourteen?" Wanda's taste had always been dubious, there was no doubt about that. But this thing made Daniel look like scum. What *had* she been thinking?

"I want it lasered off but Carl says it's too expensive."

"How much does it cost?" said Richard, dazed.

"I don't know. If it costs money, that's enough to stop old Carl from doing anything. Unless it's something Amy – his own kid – wants. He makes pretty OK money, too."

"I see," said Richard, setting his jaw in a determined way. This was it! No kid of his was going to walk around with that thing on him. It was going to be off of there as soon as possible. "We'll take care of it," he said grimly.

Daniel stared up at him with a round-eyed expression. "Hey, that's great. Would you really do that for me?"

Richard managed a crooked smile, and put his hands in his pockets. "Sure, Daniel. Good night."

"Good night, Dad."

When Richard came upstairs, Louise was sitting up in bed ostensibly reading an article in an old copy of *Sunset* about holiday-decorating using native plants, but although she looked at all the photographs and read the captions, nothing registered. All she could think about was how Richard and Daniel were getting along. And whether Daniel would be going home again.

The very real possibility that he would come to live with them had set her to imagining a vast array of scenarios – a slightly better-groomed Daniel as a member of a cosy family gathering around the Christmas tree, or, many years in the future, in black tie, toasting with a champagne flute at Flora's wedding. Louise imagined the four of them together on the sailboat or on vacation on some tropical beach. Four was a more satisfactory number than three, she thought.

But, no matter how pleasant the scenes were, Louise knew that in her heart of hearts she wanted Daniel to go back to his own home. It really was better for kids to be with their mothers, and Richard hadn't ever properly bonded with him. Maybe some family therapy would smooth things out for Wanda and Carl and Daniel.

The truth was, Louise was threatened by the idea of a strange, nearly-grown male in the house. Teenage boys got up to all kinds of horrible things – vandalizing, getting drunk, wrecking cars.

Sure, he seemed sweet, but what kind of rehab had they put him in? Maybe he was a pothead like her friend Valerie's son, Preston, who still lived at home in his mid-twenties. Or worse.

From downstairs, she heard them talking to each other, but couldn't make out the words. When Richard came into the bedroom, she put the magazine aside and looked up at him expectantly.

He sighed and gave her a tired smile, then sat down on the bed next to her. "God, this is all so intense."

She reached for his hand and held it quietly for a while. Finally, she asked, "Is he all settled in?"

"Yeah. He says he's really glad to be here."

"Good."

"And he says you're really great." Richard bent over and kissed her forehead. "He's right. Thank you, darling."

Louise smiled. "I'm glad."

"He's had a rough time. He's wearing rags. He seems neglected and pathetically grateful for any attention."

Louise murmured sympathetically, then said, "Richard, I hope you know how I feel about this. I'll do anything I can do to help you and your child."

Richard looked relieved. "Oh, darling," he said, "I was afraid you wouldn't want him, but I feel as if I've got to try and do something for the kid. Maybe even have him stay with us for a while. At least until we get that tattoo off him."

"Tattoo? Really?" Louise wrinkled her nose.

"Some stupid skull thing. Wanda signed so he could get it when he was fourteen or some damn thing! What an idiot she is. Apparently you can laser them off now."

Louise nodded. "That's what Cher did."

"If it's the only thing I ever do for the poor kid, that tattoo has got to go!"

"I think he should see an ophthalmologist, too. Have you noticed his eyes are kind of crossed? I'm sure that can be corrected. And his bite looks OK, but he has a couple of overlapping teeth. I don't think he's had orthodontia."

Richard sighed. "We'll start with some clothes and shoes. I'll take him shopping tomorrow. I can't believe that Wanda. She was kind of a nut, but she came from a solid middle-class family. I can't believe she would ignore her child to the extent she clearly has. He looks like a street thug."

"I'm sure he's really sweet underneath it all," said Louise. "Like you."

"Oh, darling, then you won't mind if he stays for a little while? Wanda's husband seemed really to be pushing that idea. I don't think he wants him back."

"Of course I won't mind. God knows, it's not going to be easy. But you can't just send him away. He's your child. And I'm your wife and I'll back you up all the way." Louise smiled serenely, but felt a horrible wave of panic rising within. What else could she say? And where would he sleep? If only he hadn't showed up in the middle of the remodel. Louise knew that she was lying to her husband when she said that Daniel was welcome to stay here. But sometimes it was kinder to lie. She wondered if he ever lied to her.

## 12

"We're just going out for coffee," said Flora, plaintively. "Just a couple of my friends. He wouldn't like them, anyway. I can tell."

"All I'm saying," said Louise, "is ask him if he wants to come. When he starts school after spring break he'll make his own friends, but until then he doesn't know anyone." They stood outside Flora's bedroom in the upstairs hall and were back to whispering.

Although Daniel was downstairs somewhere, presumably in the kitchen where they had just heard the fridge door slam, they had learned during the last few days that he could emerge silently anywhere, at any time, looking amiable but unsure of where he should be in the house.

"I can't bring him. My friends would *not* understand." Flora closed her eyes to indicate the heaviness of the burden her mother was trying to inflict upon her.

Louise tried not to sound as irritated as she felt. "Think how you would feel if you were in his position."

"You can't *force* me to take him!" Flora's eyes flew open and fixed her mother with a rebellious smoulder.

"No, but I can deny you the car tonight if you don't at least have the decency to ask him along. The car is a privilege—"

"Yeah, yeah," snapped Flora. "Not a right. I can't *believe* you're doing this to me. This is not my regular posse. It's some cool people from Drama that Claire and I are hanging with for the first time. I don't know them that well."

"And you're afraid they're going to judge you on the basis of Daniel, and you don't think he's cool enough, is that it?" said Louise coldly.

"Fine! I'll just tell them I'm grounded or something. I know you want me to be nice to everyone like you are, but my social standing isn't strong enough for me to take him on, *OK*?"

Louise felt herself wavering a little, but then she wondered how she could tell Richard that Flora had refused to invite Daniel along. There was no tactful way she could tell him that her daughter thought his son was a loser.

When she'd brought up the idea earlier, phoning from work, Richard had been enthusiastic – partly so that Daniel could get out and meet some people – partly because he said he looked forward to an evening alone with Louise. He expected Louise to arrange the whole thing.

"I don't think it would kill you to be nice," Louise told her daughter.

Flora sighed. "OK. Let me talk to Claire." She went into her room and pointedly closed the door. Louise sighed in return. Maybe it wasn't fair to expect Flora to take Daniel under her wing when she was still struggling herself with teenage social life.

Simply on a practical level, Daniel's presence was going to cause her daughter a lot of grief. She'd have to share the new TV room they were building in the basement with him and his friends. When he got his driver's licence she'd have to compete with him for the car. Flora's phone line would now become the "children's" phone line.

Flora, Louise knew guiltily, wasn't used to sharing. All the co-operative nursery schools and play groups and team sports that Louise had arranged over the years didn't alter the fact that Flora had never had to compete with another kid for anything on home ground. Louise went into her own bedroom, took off her shoes and lay down on the bed.

The decision to take in Daniel had happened so fast, precipitated by the shocking fact that Wanda hadn't even bothered to call back to discuss her son's future with Richard, or even to talk to her son. Louise couldn't believe the woman could be so heartless. Any normal mother would be heartbroken that things had gone so badly. Louise had expected a tearful phone call from Wanda, begging Daniel's forgiveness for the fact he had felt unwanted, and pledging that the family would work hard on its problems.

Tellingly, Daniel hadn't even seemed surprised at his mother's apparent lack of interest. He had just shrugged and said, "That's typical."

In the end, the shadowy Wanda had left it up to her husband, Carl, to suggest that Daniel spend the rest of the school year, until June, with his father, and then see how everyone felt.

After they decided to take Daniel in, Louise began to come around to the idea. She told herself that this was a chance for all of them to bond together as a family. Another child would help balance things out. She wouldn't feel so much that she was at the apex of a triangle. Besides, she was so shocked at the callousness of Wanda that her heart had gone out to poor Daniel. Her nervousness about boys behaving badly, wrecking cars, running around spraying graffiti and getting high, was still there, but now there was also a surge of sympathy. In fact, she'd put both hands on his shoulders and looked him straight in the eye and said, "You're Richard's son and you are welcome here as long as you like." He had to believe that he was unconditionally welcome *somewhere*.

But now, three days later, Louise was beginning to panic again. She felt like a hostess watching her own party flop. He drifted around the house in an unsettling way. Of course it was bound to be difficult until he got to school and made friends. Because the workmen were there, he didn't even have his own room, which made it all even more awkward.

Daniel had been spending time watching MTV in the study until long after the rest of them had gone to bed. He was always asleep when they went to work in the morning, and he spent the early evening leafing through magazines or going for long walks.

Richard had made a series of desperate attempts to keep him occupied, taking him along on trips to the supermarket and enlisting his help feeding the lawn and clipping hedges. They'd also gone out to a mall and bought loads of clothes for Daniel.

Louise had called and made an appointment with a dermatologist to see about lasering off his hideous tattoo. She also made an appointment with an ophthalmologist, and an orthodontist, and an appointment with a high school counsellor at Madison High School to get his class schedule set, so he could start as soon as spring break was over. The Murdocks were mailing his birth certificate from California, so he would be able to register for school and get a Washington State learner's permit and a driver's licence when he turned sixteen.

From Flora's room, she heard the animated buzz of her daughter's phone conference punctuated by an anguished wail. Maybe she had been out of line to ask her daughter to include Daniel in her plans. Flora was entitled to her own social life, and it wasn't her fault that poor Daniel had nowhere else to go.

On the other hand, Louise thought it wouldn't hurt Flora to tone up her altruism. But should altruism be imposed by a parent? Wouldn't that make the whole thing backfire, and guarantee that Flora would resent Daniel?

Louise began to form phrases in her mind to explain to Richard why Flora had left for a festive evening out, leaving Daniel to sit alone at home with the two adults — adults who, after a stressful week, felt desperately in need of a Friday night alone by themselves.

Maybe she and Richard should take Daniel out to a movie or something. Maybe, she thought crossly, *Richard* should be figuring out how to handle all this. Daniel was, after all, his son.

And Flora was her daughter, she thought with a pang. How could she ask her to sacrifice her own social life for Daniel? Louise hadn't really taken in the gist of Flora's protests. These were new friends. "Cool Drama people." Flora had just auditioned for, and got, a small part in the school play. This was a first for her, and she was terribly excited about it, not least because she had aspired to befriending an artier, more intellectual bunch of kids. Some of her old friends from middle school, the tightly knit group of eight, four sets of best friends, had been drifting away.

As soon as Flora hung up, Louise would apologize, and tell her she could have the car with no strings.

In her room, Flora had finished outlining her mother's unreasonable, insensitive and completely out-of-line demand to her friend, Claire. "I can't *believe* she would do this to me," she said. "It's so humiliating."

The girls debated the question of whether a back-handed

invitation would dissuade him. Flora listened carefully to Claire's suggestions along these lines. "Like, you could say 'Ingrid's nice but she has a lot of problems and she never shuts up about them. Some people can't take it, but maybe she'll be in a better mood and not on such a downer tonight.' Or maybe you could say we're really meeting to talk about a boring team project for Language Arts or something."

"I just don't know," said Flora. "I mean, he hasn't spoken to anyone but my parents for days. He'll probably take a chance on anything, just to get out of the house."

Claire mulled this over. "I see your point. I bet he'll say yes. But what about me?" she went on. "I was counting on you to drive. If you bail now, I get screwed out of a fun time. Could you put it to your mom like that and would she get it?"

Flora's voice took on a tinge of despair. "I don't know. I swear to God I wish I could have my own apartment, now! I can hardly wait to move out of here. I tried to get into the bathroom the other day and Daniel's in there shaving with his shirt off. It was gross. His chest is totally hairy and he left all these little wispy beard chunks all over the sink. I just about threw up."

"Yew," said Claire sympathetically. "That is so disgusting." She switched back to the problem at hand. "Listen, I'm going to call Ingrid and tell her what's going on. That way, if we don't show, they'll know it isn't our fault and that we're still open to hanging with them."

"OK," said Flora, in a defeated voice. "Call me back." She was glad Claire had more energy to devote to the situation than she did. She felt doomed. This guy was somehow going to totally mess up her life without even knowing it. One thing was for sure, this particular evening was definitely ruined. God! Maybe Mom and Richard

128

would try to get her to play Scrabble with them and Daniel or something.

She heard Mom's shy little tap at the door. "What?" she shouted unpleasantly. Richard wasn't home yet, so she could be herself with Mom.

Her mother opened the door and came in looking apologetic. "Listen, I've thought about it, and I've decided that I can only ask you to behave decently, I can't force you, OK? So you can still have the car, and I'll just have to think up some excuse for Richard why you don't want to be caught dead with his kid."

Flora's face turned radiantly happy, and she jumped up and kissed her mother. "I couldn't believe you'd be so mean to me."

Just then the phone rang. Flora picked it up, and heard Claire's voice. "Hi, it's me again. Ingrid really wants him to come. She thinks it will be so cool to find out what happens to someone who meets their father for the first time when they're fifteen and a half. She actually said 'Wow, finally an interesting conversation.' She thought the way Daniel just showed up was so dramatic."

For the first time, it occurred to Flora that Daniel might actually be a social asset.

Danny watched his bowl roll elegantly across the grass, making a perfect curve to kiss the white jack at the other end of the lawn. The thing had done just what he'd wanted it to. There was something very satisfying about that.

"Not bad, Tony, not bad at all," said George, the man from the club who was teaching him. "You're getting it." He turned to Olive. "I think I can do a lot with this young man."

"All *right*," said Danny enthusiastically. "I want to be a lawn bowling *machine*!" At first, Danny had thought these

129

old folks were just rolling things that looked like big ball bearings around the lawn. The whole thing looked kind of pathetic. But when he learned that bowls weren't actually round and didn't roll in straight lines, he realized there was a lot more to it. You had to figure out inside your head just what the heck the bowls would do and try and position them carefully. And, there was all kinds of neat stuff you could do to your opponents, too, like smacking their bowls away from the jack.

Plus, he was sort of enjoying all these old people here at the club. Danny hadn't ever really had much to do with old people before. They talked like people in really old movies. Mom and her friends, and his friends' parents, often sounded like teenagers, even though they were in their forties, but these old people sounded like real grown-ups. They were polite, and they never whined. And he thought it was cool that here at the club, on tournament days, anyway, everyone was dressed in white. It made them look nice and peaceful against the bright green lawn. After what he'd been through lately, with Mom and Carl and the Nazis, and then him and Keith running away from a prison sentence, a little peace and quiet seemed particularly satisfying.

"How long are you staying with Olive?" George asked. "We'd sure like to get you up to speed and on the team."

"We're not sure," said Olive. Danny had asked her not to tell everyone about his head injury. He was afraid it might make him sound like a mental case. She had respected his wishes, and told the other lawn bowlers simply that he was a distant relative. "It's sometimes best not to tell people too much about your past," she had said. "People jump to all the wrong conclusions."

"While I'm here, I'd like to play a lot," said Danny. Some girls in shorts and T-shirts that read Madison High School loped around the perimeter of the green, and Danny watched them as they ran by.

"That's what you say now," said George, following his gaze, "but you'll probably meet some sweet young thing, and drop us like a bad habit. But while I still have your attention, let's see how you do with a different sized bowl."

Danny turned his gaze back to George. He wondered how much longer he *could* stay. If he stayed much longer, would he have to go to school, where there were other kids? He hadn't talked to other kids for four days now, not since he'd last talked to Keith, and it felt pretty weird.

"OK, Daniel," Flora said later, as they went out to the car. "You can sit in the front now, but when we pick up Claire, she gets shotgun."

"OK," said Keith, with a shrug, dutifully getting in beside her. He tried not to let her know how resentful he was. She acted like she had the right to run everything, just because she was all set up at Richard's house, but she wasn't even his kid.

"You aren't really going out for coffee like you told your parents, are you?" said Keith with just a touch of a sneer.

"Sorry, but we are," said Flora crisply.

"You mean like sitting around at Starbucks?"

"No. Around here, Starbucks is a place you go when you want a cup of coffee. But there are other coffee places that are more for just socializing with your friends. Sometimes they have live music and stuff. There aren't any underage clubs in Seattle, nowhere where you can dance or anything. I hate this town and I'm moving to Europe or New York as soon as I can." Flora popped in a Blondie tape. "I hope you don't mind vintage chick music," she said with a little smirk, as she adjusted her seat belt.

"Yeah, I do," he said, grinning at her, ejecting the tape and grabbing it.

"Hey!" she said, clearly pissed off. She reached for the tape in his hand and he pushed her arm away. She turned to confront him now, squirming in the seat belt. It made a diagonal line across her body that showed off her breasts.

"Give it back!" she said, feebly pushing him back in the chest.

"Only if you're very nice to me," said Keith, checking out her tits, which were nice and round, then looking straight into her eyes and smiling. He was delighted to see how uncomfortable she looked now, flushed and confused.

He handed the tape back. After that Keith didn't say anything. He just stared out the window silently until they got to Flora's friend's house.

The friend, Claire, was waiting at the kerb, wearing baggy overalls. Her blondish hair was in two rubber band bunches on the back of her head, and Flora told her how adorable it looked. Keith thought Claire looked babyish and stupid and she was probably hiding a big butt under those huge overalls. Still, he gave her his nice smile and got into the back seat. The girls ignored him, chattering away while he gazed out the window at the street life on Broadway. This looked like it might be the serious drug neighbourhood.

Their destination was an old brick industrial building that had been recycled into a loft-like, two-tiered space with raw wood walls and uneven concrete floors. French bistro tables and chairs in bottle green spilled out on to the cracked sidewalk. The main downstairs area was full of patrons reading, earnestly writing in notebooks or chatting quietly. Keith thought these people looked seriously boring, and the whole place had a snotty feel to it.

Up a steep staircase was the smoking section. Here,

rickety battered tables and tired-looking old oak office chairs were jammed together in a haze of blue smoke. Music, just a tad too loud to make conversation easy, droned from corner speakers. Keith thought the action on the main street they'd driven down to get here looked a lot more promising than this.

Flora felt self-conscious with Daniel trailing behind her, as she and Claire balanced their coffees and made their way through the crowded tables. Ingrid and Nick sat on a large sagging pink mohair couch at the edge of the room. Max sprawled in a chair beside them. Flora was glad to see him. She remembered having had a crush on him in fifth grade. Recently, he had shot up and looked tall and kind of attractive again. She introduced Daniel, who was scrutinized in a narrow-eyed way by Ingrid. They scraped some chairs together, and while making polite, squeally greetings – "Wuzzup?" "Hey!" "So, what are you guys doin'?" – Flora checked out all the fashion details.

Ingrid looked fabulous, having recently bleached her hair an ethereal white blonde, and she had arranged part of it in a nappy tiara-like clump on top of her head, in a kind of parody of a Country and Western singer. She wore an orange and blue plaid polyester housecoat with big orange pockets and big white buttons, the kind of thing eighty-year-old women wore in old people's homes, and a real find at ThriftCo.

Nick, half-white and half-Asian, with beautiful cheekbones and eyes, went for the minimalist look, with blue-ish stubble all over his nicely-shaped head, a plain white T-shirt, and black shorts.

Max, a big, rangy, auburn-haired kid, wore old khakis and a T-shirt with a picture of Felix the Cat on it. A mustard-coloured Mr Rogers cardigan hung on the back of his chair. Flora was charmed. They all looked great. Finally, cool people!

"So, Daniel," said Ingrid, leaning back on the sofa with the smoky, mysterious, half-lidded expression Flora admired, "it must have been pretty weird to just show up at the door and ask for a dad you didn't even remember."

"For sure," said Daniel, leaning towards her. "It was a total risk, but I felt I had to go for it. I had no idea how he'd react or if he was a nice guy or whatever."

"Wow," said Ingrid. Flora could tell she was impressed, and that Max had noticed it too and he appeared to be irritated. He said, with what Flora took to be fake sympathy, "Weird. My parents can drive me crazy, but at least I know where they are in case I need them."

"So are you going to go to Madison?" Nick asked pleasantly.

"I guess so," said Daniel, without enthusiasm.

Flora supplied details. "He's waiting for his birth certificate and his transcripts from his other school. It should take a week or so."

Without asking, Daniel fished a Camel out of Ingrid's pack on the table and fired it up from the dripping candle in the middle of the table. Flora was surprised at the ease with which he performed this manoeuvre. Maybe he wasn't a total geek. "So what's Madison like?" he asked.

"Oh, God," said Claire in a world-weary tone. "There are all these horrible preps who are only interested in where they're going to have their weekend kegger and how many outfits they have from Polo and Ambercrombie and Fitch."

"Ambersnobby and Bitch," said Nick.

"Most of the classes totally suck," Ingrid added helpfully. "They don't care whether we learn anything, just if we follow their bureaucratic rules."

Claire went on. "The preps cheat on all their tests and

they'll get into really good colleges and they're total ass-holes. They run the damn place."

Nick added, "We get so much pressure to do stuff for college applications. Like volunteering and stuff. Everyone is just so insincere."

Daniel looked bored and said, "Whatever." Flora felt that Daniel, who had been promoted as a stimulating, even possibly deviant, character with a dramatic back-story, was not living up to his billing. He was just sitting there sucking on his Camel. To pull him into the centre of things, Flora said in a playful way to the whole table, "Don't you think Daniel should get a haircut?"

"I guess," said Max with a shrug.

"Like how?" asked Daniel, giving Flora a hard look.

Claire piped up, "Something a little less, no offence, redneck, you know? I don't know what it was like where you were from, but around here a haircut like that is totally trailer-trash – and not ironic trailer-trash, which would be OK." She smiled at him.

Daniel leaned very close to her and said, "Where I'm from is the fucking streets, bitch." He rose from the table, batted at his empty chair, lurched clumsily into Max as he made his way to the stairs and said, "You kids enjoy your coffee."

They were silent for a moment and then Nick ran his hand thoughtfully over his blue scalp and said, "I don't think he likes the makeover idea."

Max laughed, and Ingrid turned to him and said, "You guys hurt his feelings!"

"God, Claire, that was maybe a little cold," Flora said. "That trailer-trash thing." She had been shocked by Daniel's abrupt departure. He'd looked really angry.

"Shut up, OK?" said Claire in a half-hearted protest.

"Maybe he did live in a trailer. A real one," Flora went

on. Daniel was so evasive about his past. Now it occurred to her that it was because he was ashamed of it. She imagined the kind of rusted out trailers surrounded by dogs and weeds that she'd occasionally seen from the freeway.

"He wasn't really pissed off," said Claire defensively. "He just wanted to split."

"Yeah, he was pissed off," said Max thoughtfully. "You girls have such a double standard. If I told you that your hair sucked you'd be pissed off too."

"Well you agreed he needed a haircut," said Claire, self-consciously fiddling with her own two ponytails. "Besides, he does need to get a haircut before he starts school. I mean, it does look really bad, admit it."

"Maybe he's at a twenty-four hour SuperCuts right now," said Nick. "He's leafing through the style book as we speak."

"To be honest," said Flora, letting her head fall into her hands, "I'm kind of relieved he ditched. I could use a little break from being his babysitter. Besides, I have no idea what he'll tell my mom about what I do." Her head snapped back up. "Which reminds me, can I bum a smoke?"

Flora admired the gun-metal grey fingernail polish on Ingrid's bitten nails as she pushed the pack towards her. "Wow, Flora, it must be so weird having some strange kid living right in your house. Like a play where a new character just shows up in Act Two."

Flora, a very occasional smoker, struggled to light her cigarette with a practised-looking hand. "So weird," agreed Flora, puffing gingerly. "Plus, I totally do not get him. I mean, he shows up wearing gangster clothes, then he goes out with his dad to Nordstrom's and comes back with yuppie middle-aged gear just like his dad wears – little junior stockbroker, cellphone, sports utility weekend wear, you know, Dockers and stuff. I mean I can't tell whether he's just a total dork, or if he's like some kind of total sociopath."

"He doesn't seem happy," said Ingrid.

"Yeah, that's right," said Flora. "I mean apparently he's led this tragic life. His mom is supposedly completely crazy – like there isn't enough Prozac in the world. And his stepdad is some kind of militia guy or something." Flora felt a slight tweaking from "retired military" to "militia", with its connotation of scary gun freaks in camouflage gear, was justifiable in making the story more interesting.

"Wow," said Ingrid.

"God, my mom will kill me," said Flora, suddenly panicky. "I'm supposed to be out showing him a good time and I lose him."

"He did say he grew up on the fucking streets," said Claire defensively. She was clearly embarrassed at having driven him off.

Ingrid said, "I met this guy here last week who said he'd been living in the woods totally off the land for a whole summer. It was total bullshit. I think he goes to Garfield. Someone I know said his dad was their orthodontist."

They all laughed, then Max stood up and rummaged in the pocket of his Mr Rogers cardigan on the back of his chair. "I'm getting another coffee," he announced.

Flora wondered just how she would tell Mom about Daniel's abrupt departure. She was about to ask the group for suggestions when Max shouted, "Fuck! Someone jacked my wallet, I swear to God. I had it in my sweater pocket, I know I did. And I used it just like an hour ago to buy that." He gestured at his white china cup with its ring of dried espresso.

"Maybe you left it at the counter," said Flora. But the image of Daniel lurching clumsily into Max's chair where the cardigan with its gaping pockets had been hanging, then his rushing away, came back to her very clearly. It gave her a fluttery feeling in her gut – part fear, part excitement.

## 13

Louise and Richard were stretched out on the living room sofa, needlepoint pillows wedged comfortably beneath them, sipping white wine and listening to Chopin. "Gosh it's nice to be alone, just the two of us," said Richard.

Louise felt the jolt of her inner maternal clock and checked her watch. "It's exactly midnight," she said. "The kids will be back any second."

Richard sighed. "Maybe we should scurry up to bed now, before they get back. I don't know if I'm in the mood to listen to a rehash of a teen evening."

Louise knew that Flora's habit of returning home and providing animated descriptions of her social life irritated him. For one thing, it usually took her a while to shed teen dialect for the standard English she usually spoke at home.

Louise, on the other hand, was thrilled that her daughter confided in her, and she followed the cast of characters in Flora's life with interest.

But surely tonight Richard would want to know how the evening went for Daniel. Intermittently, throughout the evening, Louise had thought about how the two kids were getting on, feeling nervous and hopeful in turns.

Richard picked up their empty wine glasses sulkily and went into the kitchen. She trailed after him. "Don't you want to hear about Daniel's evening?"

The phone rang.

"Saved by the bell," said Richard happily. "That's gotta be them. They want some extra time on their curfew. Give them another hour."

The phone rang a second time. "Shouldn't we be consistent about the curfew?" asked Louise nervously.

"Look, Flora will be perfectly safe with a guy to protect her," Richard said, coming up behind Louise, wrapping his arms around her waist and kissing her neck. She smiled, tilted her head to accept his embrace and picked up the portable phone off the counter.

"Hi, Mom, it's me," said Flora brusquely. "I called just in time."

"Hi, darling. Do you want a little extension?" said Louise.

"Well, actually," said Flora, "I was wondering if I could spend the night at Claire's. We're at her house now and we've been listening to some music."

"What about Daniel?" said Louise. Richard released her waist and came around to face her, his eyebrows raised in curiosity.

"Isn't he home yet?"

"No. I presumed he was with you. What's going on?"

"He ditched," said Flora. "We were having coffee and he just ditched us."

"When was this?"

"A couple of hours ago."

"But where did he go?" Louise stopped monitoring Richard's facial expression. It was too distracting. Instead, she looked down at her feet.

"I don't know," said Flora impatiently. "I couldn't just run out into the street after him, could I?"

"Darling, what happened? Was he upset about something? Didn't he say where he was going?"

"Let me talk to her," Richard interrupted sternly.

"Richard wants to talk to you," said Louise in a contrastingly sweet voice.

"God, Mom! Do I have to? *I* don't know what happened to his kid!"

Louise handed the receiver to her husband.

"So what's going on?" he asked crisply. Now it was Louise's turn to hover. Judging by the rapidity with which Richard barraged her with questions, Flora's replies were brief. "Where's Daniel? Did he say where he was going? When was this? Was he alone? Did he say he was coming back to the coffee place? Where is it exactly? Where on Capital Hill? On Broadway? Did you guys discuss curfew? You had the only key, right? Well what kind of a mood was he in? How had things gone up to that point? I see. Just a sec."

He pushed the phone into his chest to muffle it and said sharply, "She wants to know if she can spend the night at Claire's. I think she should come home. She should have called us when he disappeared. I'm really pissed off."

"OK," said Louise weakly, reaching for the phone. If Richard was pissed off, she'd just as soon keep Flora out of range until he calmed down, but maybe he had a point. Louise had a sense that Flora was trying to hide out at Claire's and shirk responsibility in some way.

"I want you to come home right away," she said, bracing herself for a struggle. "You girls will stay up late then sleep till noon and I might need the car."

"When do you need it?" said Flora in a reasonable voice. "I'll come home in time."

"It's not just that. Richard and I are worried about Daniel. We want to talk to you about what happened."

"For God's sake, Mom! I've been debriefed twice already."

Louise didn't know what to say. It was easier to scrap with Flora without Richard there listening. He tended to tell her afterwards what a softie she was and how Flora walked all over her.

After a second of her mother's silence, Flora sighed heavily and said in a leaden voice, "Fine. I'm coming home."

Louise pushed the off button on the phone and set it down. She went over to Richard's side. "Let's not make a big deal of this," she said. "I don't think it's Flora's fault. Apparently he just took off. After all, he did that the other day when we came back from Ray's. Just flounced out of the house."

Richard frowned, and she wished she hadn't said "flounced". She sensed she sounded critical of Daniel – as if he were hysterical, like Wanda. "He came back then," she continued calmly. "He probably just needs his own space. I think girls tend to hash things out more and boys need their own space to calm down." Actually, Louise didn't know a damn thing about boys, but she was extrapolating from *Men Are From Mars, Women Are From Venus*.

"Well, that theory is all well and good," said Richard. "I'd just like to know where my kid is."

Louise didn't like his defensive tone. He hadn't known where his kid was for almost sixteen years, for God's sake! Still, she was determined not to get into a fight about this. His aggression clearly came from his being worried. A while ago, she'd learned that situations that made her panic and wring her hands helplessly made Richard testy instead.

"Oh, he'll be fine," she said soothingly. "He's a big kid, and he's a guy. It's a lot different than having a daughter wandering around in the dark." Louise had spent many an evening terrified that Flora was being raped or abducted. It wasn't really fair that parents of sons didn't have to do that, she thought with resentment. Or that they should have more relaxed rules as a result.

"I know that. I'm not worried about someone jumping him," said Richard in a contemptuous tone. "I'm wondering what he's up to. Wanda's husband said he'd experimented with marijuana. Capital Hill is dope central, isn't it?"

"I suppose so. Why didn't you tell me before about his pot problem? You said that rehab thing was for adjustment problems."

"It didn't seem like that big a deal. Besides, I'd like to give him the chance to make a fresh start. I didn't want him typecast him as a troubled kid."

"I think I have a right to know what kind of kid is in the house with my kid," Louise said, then, realizing she didn't want to go down that path, she backtracked and said soothingly, "I'm sure he's a good kid. He's got a very sweet smile, Richard. He's just been unhappy. I want to do everything I can to help him. Because I love you."

She put her arms around him, and while he stiffened a little, he eventually patted her on the back in a begrudging acknowledgment of her sincerity.

"I'm just worried that Flora and her friends put him down," Richard said. "I've heard her on the phone trashing people in that bitchy way."

"All young girls talk like that. It doesn't mean anything."

"To boys it does," said Richard grimly. "I can still remember what some of those snobby girls at my high school did to whack off our balls." He shuddered. "Lisa Pendergast. She was the worst."

"I resent your accusing my daughter of whacking off balls," Louise retorted sharply. The slur on her daughter's character aside, Louise especially objected to Richard's using a metaphor in which Flora had direct contact with male genitalia.

"I was talking about Lisa Pendergast, actually," he said. "Don't get so defensive."

They heard someone on the front porch, and Richard perked up, apparently thinking Daniel had returned, but his face fell again when they heard the key in the lock. This was Flora returning.

She came into the kitchen with an unsmiling look of dignity, braced to stand her ground in the face of criticism.

"What do you think happened to Daniel?" asked Louise. She deliberately used a neutral tone, as if she were inquiring about any missing item – the portable phone or the car keys.

Picking up the cue, Flora answered in the same manner. "Wow. I really don't know. We were just chatting like I said, and he got up and he was like 'See you guys later'. I guess he was just bored."

Richard nodded thoughtfully. Flora went over to the sink and got herself a glass of water. "So, can I go to bed now?"

"Of course, darling," said Louise.

Flora drained her glass, kissed her mother good night, and gave Richard a wary nod. As she was about to leave the kitchen she turned and said, "Oh. One bad thing happened. You know Max who was in fifth grade and played the clarinet? Someone stole his wallet tonight. No one knows how it happened. It was in the pocket of his sweater, just hanging on a chair." She stared over at Richard.

"What a shame," said Louise. She remembered Max. She'd known him since he and Flora had been in kindergarten together – an amiable red-headed boy.

They heard Flora's feet going up the stairs, and Louise said, "It doesn't sound like there's any big story here," she said. "He just got bored and restless. These kids have a much more free-flowing way of socializing than adults do."

"I know," said Richard. "Rationally, I realize there's nothing to worry about."

"Maybe," suggested Louise, "it's as if you're telescoping a whole childhood's worth of worrying into one evening. This is the first time he's been away from you."

Richard didn't seem to find this as comforting as she had intended, so she went on. "It's everything from the first time you left him with a sitter to the first day of kindergarten to the first time he had the car by himself all rolled into one."

"Yeah," said Richard, turning away. Maybe he felt she was patronizing him. "Listen, Flora gave me a funny look when she talked about her friend's wallet. Do you think she was accusing Daniel?"

"Oh, I'm sure she wasn't," said Louise nervously. Richard seemed to be totally paranoid.

"Listen," she said. "Let's go to bed. We can leave the key under the mat. He'll think to look there. Or he can ring the doorbell and wake us up." She stroked his arm. "Come on, sweetheart."

"You go on," he said. "I'll wait for Daniel."

"For heaven's sake, don't be too hard on him," said Louise. "Just ask him gently what happened. He should feel like you trust him."

"I'll handle it," said Richard irritably.

"When you yell at kids for telling the truth, you make liars out of them," explained Louise. "They have to feel they can be honest without catching hell."

"Louise, just go to bed," he said wearily. "I appreciate your concern, but I'm not in the mood to discuss your child-rearing philosophy right now."

"Fine!" she snapped. God! She'd done everything she could to be helpful where Daniel was concerned. Tonight, for instance, Richard had completely overreacted to

Daniel's bailing out, but she'd taken his worries seriously instead of simply dismissing them. And, she'd tried to smooth things out with some helpful suggestions so that when Daniel did come back there wouldn't be a big scene.

And was Richard appreciative? No! He'd turned on her, dismissed her and said, "Just go to bed". Well from now on he could muddle through on his own.

She left the room and went upstairs, hoping he'd follow her and apologize. Surely he could see that she was hurt, that he'd been stupid and unkind.

He showed no signs of coming after her. Now she was getting angrier. She undressed and flung her clothes on a chair, pulled her nightgown jerkily over her head, then went into the bathroom and brushed her teeth with furious vigour, slamming the medicine cabinet door. Back in the bedroom, there was no sign of him. She slid between the sheets, rigid with resentment.

Downstairs, she heard Richard walking around. He clearly wasn't coming upstairs to say he was sorry. While she lay here alone and hurt, he was worrying about a kid who was a little late. It seemed so unfair. She'd done everything she could to make things easier. Much more than he'd ever been willing to do to accommodate Flora. She'd been the one who'd made all the arrangements to enrol the boy in school and everything. God, she hadn't even demurred about Daniel moving in with them. Lots of selfish wives would have said "No way", or at least, "Let's find out more before we make a commitment".

Louise began to weep silently, hot tears forming puddles around her eyes and rivulets on her face. As a matter of pride, she avoided loud, convulsive gasps and sobs that would make it sound as if she were trying to lure him upstairs to reassure her. Neither did she want Flora, in the room across the hall, to hear.

As she wept, Louise hoped desperately that Richard would come in, find her crying and put his arms around her. She wanted him to kiss her and tell her that he was truly sorry and that he still loved her as much as he ever had, even though Daniel was here now.

## 14

Keith had walked up to Broadway, a main street where it seemed a lot of things were happening. He ended up in a parking lot by an all-night hamburger place. There were a few people buying hamburgers but a lot more of them doing other things which seemed to involve pagers and cell-phones. There were a bunch of freaky-looking kids leaning on cars, sitting on the kerb, smoking cigarettes and talking. He heard a few girls laughing too loudly. A skinny girl and two pale guys sat on the kerb, arms around their knees, nodding off.

Keith went into a phone booth and idly flipped the change return button, but he was not rewarded by the sound of quarters. He seldom was, but Keith felt it was always a good idea to try it, just in case. It was a matter of principle.

Not that he needed spare change now, anyway. He had the feeling that if everything worked out, he wouldn't need to worry about much of anything for a while. He probably didn't even need that snotty red-haired kid's wallet either, but it was just sitting there, fully visible in the guy's gaping sweater pocket. He deserved to have it jacked. Keith took the wallet out of his pocket and transferred the cash to his back pocket. Thirty bucks and change.

He looked at a driver's licence and a library card, then

grinned when he discovered a second driver's licence, this one from Arizona, in the name of Philip VanderGraaf, aged twenty-two. He unfolded and examined a pay cheque from Taco Time. He let the real licence, the library card and pay cheque fall to the bottom of the booth, next to a nest of cigarette butts, French fries, and an empty malt liquor bottle.

Reaching into another compartment of the wallet, his fingers encountered the shiny surface of a credit card. VISA. He looked at both sides. Flora and her friends were all rich brats. There was probably a fantastic limit on this thing. He could also use it as an ID to cash that pay cheque, but he dismissed the idea as too risky. No, the smart thing to do under the circumstances was get rid of the card as soon as possible. Flora and her friends might have guessed he'd taken the wallet, but no one could prove a thing if all he had was actual cash. He'd keep the fake ID, though. It was a pretty useful thing to have, and Max wasn't going to come forward and tell anyone he'd lost it.

Keith fingered the credit card again. It seemed a shame not to profit from this windfall. It was just like flipping the change return in a phone booth. It would be lame and somehow wrong not to take advantage of an opportunity. He dropped Max's wallet, and put the credit card and fake ID in his back pocket.

Ten minutes later, he was talking to a scruffy-looking guy with a pager on his belt. Keith chose him because he looked stupid, just standing there trying to look hard, waiting to get busted.

"The thing is," Keith said in a whiny little voice that he thought matched the brand new expensive clothes Richard had bought him, "my parents are looking for me, and they can trace me when I use it. But it's good, it's real good. And there's a $10,000 limit. I just want a hundred bucks for it."

"Fifty," said his new friend, unsmiling. "Maybe more if you got a PIN number."

"Wow, but you can buy so much shit with it before my parents figure it out and call it in. See, the thing is, they want me to keep using it so they can find out where I've been, so they don't cancel. If you just keep moving—"

"I'm not interested in your problems, OK? These things are worth a hundred bucks, period. People cancel them right away. You got to use them fast. But you don't know where to sell them for a hundred and I do. So I'll pay you fifty." He reached into his pocket and peeled off a fifty and held it low on his hip, away from general view, the bill dangling nonchalantly from his fingers while he surveyed the parking lot with a bad-ass look in his eye.

Keith shrugged, and took it. He turned on his heel and walked away briskly. He bet little Max would phone his parents right away and they'd call some twenty-four hour toll-free number, and the thing would be dead in the water in twenty minutes. Fifty bucks was exactly what it was worth. Besides, he already had the thirty he'd jacked from Max, and his new dad had given him twenty bucks and promised him a nice allowance, starting on Saturday, when Flora got hers. And maybe, like Max, he'd get his own family credit card soon.

Keith sauntered up Broadway feeling pretty good about the near future. He'd be getting his own room for the first time in a long time, as soon as the workmen were through. All the money he needed. Pretty good food. Maybe he could even get Flora to put out, and teach her not to be such a little snob. As far as he could tell, nobody was fucking her now, which was kind of a waste because she had great tits and long legs.

The Blakelys' house was way better than any foster home, because foster home people did it for the money, and gave you bowls of cereal for dinner and made you sleep on cots in the basement with weird kids. People like the Blakelys didn't need to share with people outside their family. As long as he could keep them thinking he was Daniel, he was set.

And when he did move on, there was the prospect of cashing in big time on some of the stuff around the place. He'd already checked out everything – besides the stuff in the desk there were silver candlesticks, laptops, stereo stuff. Both Flora and her mom had jewellery boxes. Everything was just lying around. All he needed was somewhere to offload the shit.

Keith decided to try out the fake ID, and step in some place for a beer. He didn't look much like the guy on the Arizona driver's licence, but then, neither did Max. He checked out one place, but it looked like a gay bar. Further down the street, next door to a convenience store, he found a cosy-looking pub with a sign boasting it had twenty micro-brews on tap. It looked dark and busy, so the chances of his being rejected were less. No more drinking Budweiser out of a paper bag in the parking lot of some convenience store. His life had changed. He was a Blakely now, and he bet Richard drank micro-brewed beer.

Before he stepped in, however, a pretty dark-haired girl approached him and smiled at him shyly. "Excuse me," she said. "Are you twenty-one?"

"Sure," said Keith, checking her out. She was wearing a tight knitted top with little strings tying it on to her smooth shoulders.

"My friends and I are, like, going to this party? And we need someone to buy some beer for us." She gestured over at the convenience store.

Keith surveyed the rest of the group. Four guys and two girls. They looked like they knew what was up, and they had shrewdly sent the best-looking chick over here to ask for his help. "Yeah, I can help you out," he said.

Richard sat alone in the semi-darkened living room sipping a large Scotch. While he waited for Daniel, he tried to figure out how the evening had fallen apart so quickly. Just a short while ago, he and Louise had been relaxing, and having a great time. Now, she was one flight up, angry. And he was sitting here alone in the dark at one in the morning, wondering whether his kid was jabbing needles into his arm, impregnating some trollop who'd give birth to his grandchild, or getting run over by a bus.

His brother, Gordon, had been right. "Life's biggest irony is the way sex creates kids then kids kill sex," he'd once remarked in the course of a bitter monologue about his wife, Marcia, who had somehow morphed from insatiable courtesan to soccer mom in a few short, child-bearing years.

According to Gordon, the first kid had completely de-railed their sex life, always crying out in the night, guzzling at her breasts. Then after that part was over, she'd read some stupid book that said the kid was supposed to sleep in-between its parents until puberty because that's what some Stone Age tribes in New Guinea did. Gordon had ended up on the couch after one memorable evening of being kicked, peed and thrown up on. And now, Daniel, without even being on the premises, had managed to disrupt his evening with Louise.

Not that that little snot Flora had helped. Couldn't she just have introduced her stepbrother to some nice kids and kept him occupied for the evening? Was that too much too ask, considering Richard would be paying for college for her next year? Richard felt he had bent over backwards trying to be kind to Flora for his wife's sake. But all he'd got back was resentment.

152

Richard heard the creak of a foot on the staircase. Oh, hell. Louise was coming down. She'd want to talk. About them. About Daniel. About her feelings. Richard glanced at his glass, and wished he'd brought the bottle over to the coffee table so he could top it up. Now, he'd have to go over to the liquor cabinet in front of her, while she was talking, and it would look like he was using alcohol to deaden emotional pain.

Louise came into the doorway and stood there with the tremulous, bittersweet look on her face that he knew only too well. Yes, she wanted to have a serious talk, all right. Richard felt his heart sink. While he knew that Louise was sincere, and that for the first time in his life he was really loved, he also felt that whether she admitted it to herself or not, these heart-to-hearts were always launched with a single, specific outcome in mind. She would present her case until he agreed that his take on things had been wrong and hurtful.

Well maybe he was kind of irritable sometimes. So what? He got mad and he got over it. Couldn't she just wait? Why did she have to get hurt and then make him feel like a bastard?

"No sign of the kid," he said, trying to sound casual and conversational.

"He'll turn up," she said in a soothing voice. "Come to bed, darling. I can't stand it when we fight. I just need to be cuddled." She glanced down at his glass and frowned. "Are you drinking Scotch?"

He picked up his glass, said, " 'Here's looking at you, kid'," took a sip, set it down, and allowed his head to fall back on the sofa in a world-weary manner. Then he put his arms around her, pulled her down next to him on the sofa and closed his eyes. "No talking. Just cuddles."

She clung to him and buried her face in his chest. "I

guess I was jealous because you were so worried about Daniel. It was stupid."

"Forget about Daniel," he said, leaning over to kiss her. Just then, the front door opened, and Daniel walked into the darkened room. They leapt apart like teenage make-out artists. Louise adjusted her nightgown on her shoulders and arranged the diaphanous folds primly around her knees.

"Wow," said Daniel. "I'm sorry. Want me to sleep somewhere besides that sofa tonight?"

"Of course not!" said Louise briskly. "I'll get your sheets and things." She rose, scuttled around behind the sofa and left through the kitchen, presumably too self-conscious to walk past Daniel in her sheer nightgown.

"Where the hell have you been?" demanded Richard.

"Just, like, out," said Daniel.

Richard narrowed his eyes and scrutinized his son, who looked to be a little unsteady on his feet and fuzzy-eyed.

"What do you mean 'out'?"

With an air of surprise which Richard didn't quite buy, Keith said, "I met some kids. They invited me to a party. Is that a problem for you?"

"Yes, that's a problem for me. And that means it's a problem for you, too." Richard rose and with his fists clenched, walked over to his son. "You smell like beer."

"Yeah, I had a couple." Daniel shrugged. "What's the big deal?"

"You're underage," said Richard. He thought he smelled pot, too, coming no doubt from the boy's lanky hair and the fibres of his clothes. "This is totally unacceptable."

Louise reappeared, looking now, thought Richard, like the matron at a boy's boarding school, in a tightly-sashed plaid bathrobe with the lapels folded forward so she was bundled up to her chin. She carried a down comforter,

154

pillows and a sheet. She gave her stepson a worried look, and her husband a questioning one.

Richard shrugged. "I'm afraid he's had a few beers at a party," he said, trying not to make it sound like a big deal. He'd just pretend he hadn't smelled marijuana. He didn't want to upset Louise. Early on in their relationship, Louise had begged Richard not to talk about his own adolescent drug use around her daughter, unless it was characterized as much-regretted "experimentation".

"Oh, no!" said Louise, clearly horrified. "Flora wasn't with you when you were drinking, was she?"

"Yes," demanded Richard, "did Flora introduce you to those people?" Of course that was it! Flora had corrupted his son and ditched him at the party. He'd always been a little suspicious of Flora's claim that she spent hours sitting around drinking coffee. Louise was so gullible.

The two adults stared at Daniel, waiting for an answer until his face crumpled and he collapsed into an armchair. "I guess I really messed up. My stepdad was always telling me that I had to drink to be a man. He even bought beer for me. I didn't know it would freak you guys out."

"But what about Flora?" persisted Louise. "Was she at this party?"

Daniel waved his hand dismissively. "Naw. I left her with her friends. I didn't think they really wanted me around, to tell you the truth. I went for a little walk and I met some kids. Outside a Seven-Eleven on Broadway. We were just kind of chilling and one of them invited me to a party. I was feeling kind of lonely and depressed, so I went."

Richard glared over at Louise. OK, so Flora hadn't taken Daniel to some beer blast. She'd just rejected him and driven him out into the street to hang out with God knows what kind of scum.

Louise set her bundle of bedding on the coffee table

and sat down on the edge of the sofa. In a sweet little kindergarten-teacher voice that bugged Richard, she said, "Daniel, tomorrow, we're going to have to go over the rules. I know it's been different for you, but here we have limits. We have to know where you are and with whom. And we feel very strongly about drug and alcohol abuse. It's because we care."

Richard thought that this "we care" routine might just possibly work with a female child, but he doubted it would cut any ice with his strapping son. Power, that's all guys understood. He was about to blurt out his own addendum – "And because we're in charge!" – when Daniel astonished him by letting out a little cry of despair. The boy's face fell into his hands for a moment.

"God! I really messed up," Daniel said after a beat, straightening up and apparently struggling to regain his composure. "You guys are great, and I messed up. Before, no one ever cared when I came home or what I did or any of that stuff. It'll take a while to get used to." He smiled shyly. "But I swear to God, I'm really going to get with the programme. That's a promise, Dad."

## 15

Upstairs, Flora huddled on the floor with her ear to the heating duct that led straight into the living room. On her other ear was her phone. She sat up and whispered to Claire, "My God, I can't believe it. You should have heard him. This big phony thing about getting with the programme. It's disgusting."

"I wonder what kind of a party it was?" said Claire. "I mean he doesn't know anyone. It's so weird." The girls left unspoken the thought that they didn't manage to get invited to parties very much.

"I don't know," said Flora. "Listen Claire, there's something really important. I don't want you to tell anyone I think he jacked Max's wallet."

"Why not?"

"Because it's so sleazy. I don't want anyone to think I'm related to such a scummy guy."

"You poor thing," said Claire.

The next day, Louise was pleased that she had planned to have lunch with her friend Valerie. Valerie would be the perfect person to tell about last night.

Valerie had had years of experience with a difficult son. Louise had always felt sorry for her, and terribly relieved that Flora, despite difficult patches, seemed to be turning out just fine.

The women met at a Greek restaurant. Valerie was astonished and fascinated by the appearance of Daniel in their lives, and sympathetic about the events of last night – Daniel bolting, and coming home late after drinking. "I suppose I should let Richard worry about him," Louise said, "but the idea of teenagers drinking and staying out until all hours really scares me."

"Believe me," said Valerie, "short of putting one of those leg-cuff monitoring devices they use for felons under house arrest on them, there's only so much you can do." She sipped her avgolemono soup with a resigned air.

"He starts school next week. I'm worried about him. I hope he'll make friends easily."

"And the *right* friends," said Valerie with a knowing bitterness. "If only Preston had got in with a better crowd back in the seventh grade – that's when his problems started."

Preston, whom Louise remembered as an adorable, perky eight year old, had turned into a complete lout in junior high school, and stayed that way into adulthood. At various times, Valerie had had the boy diagnosed as dyslexic, hyperactive, depressed, learning-disabled, hypoglycaemic and allergic. For a while, she'd pumped him full of weird nutritional supplements she got from a naturopath, and he broke out in a rash. But whatever the diagnosis or the therapy, Preston remained passive, slothful, messy, and marginally delinquent. He showed no interest in an education or a career, hung out with similarly unmotivated youths, and seemed unable to make any long-term plans. He was the kind of boy who, in less enlightened times, would have been sent off to sea as a cabin boy or apprenticed to a blacksmith by fourteen. Those options, however, hadn't been available to Valerie and Bill.

The couple had spent a fortune on shrinks. According to

all the tests, Preston was very gifted underneath it all. Valerie always liked to point out that he actually had more intellectual potential than his older sister, who was now a PhD candidate at Berkeley. At one point, Valerie had lamented, "He's just a slow developer. Some day, he'll get it, and start identifying with the adult culture. Until then, we can't reach him."

The most alarming aspect of all this could never really be discussed. The truth was that despite all Valerie's efforts, Preston had grown into someone who seemed to come from an entirely different social class than his parents. It was evident in his interests, his vocabulary, even his walk and the undisciplined way he let his mouth hang open and his vaguely belligerent, yet sloppy, enunciation. But of course there was no condition, never mind disorder, called inappropriate proletarian affect or negative class mobility.

"What are you going to do about the space?" Valerie asked. "You guys will be packed in there like sardines. Teenagers take up a lot of space."

Louise sighed. "We've pretty much decided that Flora gets the new downstairs bedroom, because she's already planned it and chosen the furniture and everything. But the two of them will have to share the new TV room."

"And Daniel gets Flora's old bedroom?"

"Yes. Frankly, we'd rather share our bathroom with him than with her. She's always taking huge, long baths and leaving Q-Tips and nail polish bottles around." It was kind of liberating that Valerie was always so frank about Preston's problems. It meant Louise could be a little more unguarded about Flora's shortcomings.

"So you won't get that dressing room and little study you planned," said Valerie sympathetically.

Louise shrugged. "Oh well, maybe that was all a little extravagant anyway."

"You should move," said Valerie decisively. The two women, while often immobilized by their own problems, were quick to point out reasonable solutions to each other.

"We've been over all that," said Louise. "The thing is, I've got the house and the garden just how I want them. And they'll both be going off to college in less than two years."

"If you're lucky," said Valerie.

Louise realized how tactless she'd been. Before she had a chance to soften her statement or add some disclaimer, Valerie laid down her spoon and leaned over the table. "Preston is moving back in."

"Oh no!" said Louise. "He just moved out!" Preston, she rapidly calculated, must now be at least twenty-four.

"God, I could just kill him," said Valerie. "Just when Bill and I finally get the place to ourselves after a quarter of a century! Oh well, at least we've had a few months of adult living."

"How was it?" asked Louise.

"God! It was so peaceful. And clean. And you know where everything is, like the scissors and the keys. Not to mention the privacy!"

"Oh, Valerie, I'm so sorry."

"Preston and Bill are going to start up again, I just know it. And I'll be in the middle."

"Don't. Refuse," advised Louise.

"Refuse to get in the middle or refuse to let him move back in?" Without waiting for a reply, Valerie added, her voice rising, "Oh! And get this! He's bringing a dog with him."

"Can't he share a big house with a bunch of other young people?" Louise was bristling with indignation. Valerie was a wonderful person, cheerful and good-humoured. She didn't deserve this.

160

"I don't know. He doesn't seem to be able to get anything together. I don't know what I did wrong."

"Nothing. You didn't do anything wrong," Louise said stoutly, not knowing if this were true or not, but feeling it was what Valerie should be told for her own peace of mind.

"Sometimes I think he just hangs around waiting for Bill to love him." Louise was sad to see her friend look suddenly older and defeated, and reached across the table to pat her hand. Valerie gave her a grateful little smile. "It's the unfinished business between them. He's still after Bill's approval."

"What does Bill say?"

"He says he doesn't approve of Preston and he's not going to fake it. He says telling a kid he's great when he's screwing up isn't going to help."

"I think you can say no to the dog," said Louise decisively.

"It's always the boys who pull this," said Valerie. "Girls move on."

Louise remembered how pathetic it had been last time she'd been to Valerie and Bill's. Preston, slack-jawed and shambling, had burst into the living room where they were having drinks and said in an oafish voice, "Hey, Mom, can I have twenty bucks now if I paint the back fence next week?"

Daniel wouldn't end up like that, would he? She thought of her stepson's nice smile. He did seem determined to please in a way that Preston never had. But of course, Daniel *would* be ingratiating at first, wouldn't he, seeing as he was still kind of on probation in the family?

The women asked for the check and when it came time to pay, Louise was startled to see that she didn't have enough cash. "I was sure I had a twenty in here," she said, fumbling for a credit card.

161

Valerie raised an eyebrow. "I've had to hide my purse for years," she said.

Mrs Carmichael slipped on the glasses she wore on a cord around her neck and skimmed over the transcripts and birth certificate in front of her. From across the desk, Keith tried to read them upside down.

"Oh," she said brightly. "I see your birthday's coming up soon! You're going to be sixteen a week from Saturday."

"Yeah," said Keith. This was interesting news.

She turned her attention to the transcript. "And you've already passed Driver's Ed. Good. Are you going to get your licence right away?"

"I guess so."

"OK, I see we're definitely talking a college prep schedule here, right. It says here you're planning on a four year college or university." She was a middle-aged lady with big teeth and a lot of frizzy hair, wearing a baggy green sweater with a lot of little fuzz balls all over it, and a necklace made out of silver dolphins.

"That's right," said Keith, smiling back at her.

"You're a junior now, so I imagine you've given some thought to what kind of school you're aiming for. Your Pre-SATs look pretty good." She nodded approvingly and drew a bitten fingernail down a column of letters and numbers. "Hmm. Your last semester in California looks pretty bad, though. She removed the glasses and looked across at him questioningly. "You went from a 3.2 to a 1.4. What the heck happened?"

Keith shrugged and transferred his gaze to a poster behind her on the wall. It showed four kids, one black, one Hispanic, one white, one Asian, smiling under a banner that read "In Us We Trust. Diversity = Excellence". The white kid was in a wheelchair.

162

"I don't know," he said. "I had a bad time there for a while."

Mrs Carmichael frowned. "This is something you might want to address in an essay."

Keith wasn't sure what the hell she was talking about. "Whatever."

"I mean, college admissions officers will consider some extreme emotional hardship. Especially if you can use it to illustrate how you overcame a problem."

Keith perked up. This was familiar territory. "Oh. Yeah. Well, I had severe family problems. It was like, an abusive situation." He winced a little as if taking a blow from a battering parent. "It kinda took my mind off of school."

Mrs Carmichael's slightly bulging, pale blue eyes widened. Keith gazed into them. "My stepdad, he, um, started drinking again and he got violent. That's why I moved here to be with my real dad."

"I see," said Mrs Carmichael in a hushed, but slightly pleased tone. "You know, we have an Alateen branch here at school. Is that something you might be interested in? It's a support group for people who've had to live with alcohol issues. It's based on AA principles."

"I don't know," said Keith squirming a little. "Now that I'm away from my stepdad it's OK."

Mrs Carmichael nodded. "Just an idea. You may find that even though you're away from the behaviours, you may need to deal with the issues. Even adult children of alcoholics have a lot of anger to manage."

"For now, I guess I just want to get my schedule figured out. To be honest, I'm not ready to deal with my stepdad right now. Anyway, I'm feeling really good. I think I can get my grades back up now that I'm in a more functional home environment." He gave her a nice smile.

Mrs Carmichael gave him an approving nod. "Well, if

you need to talk about these other issues from the past, Daniel, I'm here for you. I do more than just get kids into college, you know. We're all trained in substance abuse issues and dysfunctional family issues, as well as general issues of adolescent adjustment."

"That's really good to know," said Keith solemnly.

"The teen health centre deals with sexuality issues," she added, clearing her throat and replacing her glasses. She directed her attention once more to the transcript.

"Well, you'll need to take at least another semester of Spanish. Three years is good. Four is better. And I think you probably belong in Integrated Math Three. You can be tested to make sure. And then there are the core requirements, Language Arts, US History and Family Life Choices. Oh! You were in band. What's your instrument?"

"Oh, I'd really rather not be in the band any more," said Keith, scowling.

Mrs Carmichael looked worried. "But with your GPA, you'll need to show admissions officers you're well rounded. Our band programme here is really excellent. They've been state champions, and this year they're going to a festival in Tashkent, Seattle's sister city in Uzbekistan. If the political situation stabilizes, that is."

"Yeah, but see, I never even wanted to be in band. My stepdad made me. He was a military guy. He liked all those marches and stuff. I really developed a lot of hostile feelings. I'd get majorly stressed if I was in band again."

"How would you feel about orchestra?" she said, tilting her head to one side enquiringly and tapping her ballpoint pen on her handcrafted earthenware coffee mug. "You know, I got a French horn player into Oberlin on a full scholarship last year."

"Look, I'm sorry, I just can't deal with it, OK?" said Keith, turning slightly aggressive. "I want to make, like, a fresh start." He leaned across her desk and said intently, "I feel like I have a chance at being a brand new person, and expressing my very own individuality."

Mrs Carmichael nodded slowly and gave him a very serious, respectful look. "I understand completely, Daniel," she said. "It's just that we have to think about electives to balance your academic achievement. Do you like sports? Athletics count too, well rounded wise." She ran an eye over his torso, as if sizing up his athletic ability.

"Can I be in art?" he said. "I really like art, but my stepdad wouldn't let me do it. He said it was too, well, you know…" He looked embarrassed.

"Too what?"

"'Faggy' was the word he used," said Keith.

"That's terrible!" she said, bristling, then looking momentarily embarrassed at having made a value judgment about Daniel's stepdad, she gushed, "We have a fabulous art programme. There's a state-of-the-art kiln, too." She started scratching away on a notepad. "I'm going to get this all set for you."

After a second, she set down her pen, put her chin in her hand and gave him a meaningful gaze. "Daniel, I have a really good feeling about your experience here at Madison. You seem ready to succeed. I want you to check back with me in a few weeks and let me know how you're doing." She rose, beamed at him and extended her hand. "If you ever have a problem, just let me know. I'm here to facilitate. You know, you're at an important stage in your life. It's hard to give up childhood and assume adult responsibilities, but you have to start planning now. For the long term. What you do today determines your future."

"Thanks Mrs Carmichael," said Keith, rising, and giving her a shy smile. "You've really been supportive. I feel comfortable coming to you with my problems and stuff."

This place totally sucked, Keith reflected. He was pretty sure the Blakelys would expect him to show up here at Madison High School every day, do his homework and get good grades, and there was no way he could fake third year Spanish. After school started, it might be time to move on.

It was getting to be a drag dealing with the midnight curfew, and coming up with excuses about the new friends he'd met at that party on Capital Hill. He always had them park around the corner when they picked him up, but the Blakelys were saying they wanted to meet them. Maybe have them over for a barbecue or something. Yeah, right!

He should do like Mrs Carmichael said and make plans. Get himself a big bank roll and maybe go to Vegas. Keith had always wanted to go there.

The funny thing was, though, in some ways, Keith didn't want to leave. As soon as the remodel was over, he'd have his own room where Flora slept now. It would be really pleasant there. They were letting him pick out his own furniture.

Olive was making gravy, and had just handed Danny the potato masher and pointed at steaming potatoes in a ceramic bowl. "It's so nice to have a strong person around the house," she said, as he put all his muscle into mashing.

After a pause, she said, "Tony, I've been thinking about this, and I've called my lawyer to see what we should do about you."

He looked up at her, startled. "Your lawyer?"

"Yes. When you first came here, I assumed you'd know who you were very quickly. But you still don't remember. You may be here some time. You'll need to register for school and things like that."

"I suppose I do." He had kind of hoped that he could just hang out and work on his lawn bowling for a while longer without actually having to do anything.

"He said I should ask to be licensed as a foster home, and then they'll assign you to me officially. They'll even give me some money to buy you clothes and food and all that."

"They will? But what if they come and just take me away and put me somewhere else?"

"Oh, I don't think they'd do that," she said. He resumed mashing. "They said it was hard to get people to take boys, didn't they?"

"Wow," said Danny. "When does school start?"

"I checked on that. Madison is the closest high school. They resume classes a week from Monday. It's so difficult, we don't even know how old you are."

"How old do I look?"

She squinted at him. "About fourteen or so, I guess. Maybe fifteen."

Danny was almost sixteen, but he had always looked young for his age. He turned away so she wouldn't see that he was disappointed she thought he was younger than he was. If he really didn't remember, how could he be disappointed?

"Maybe you can be tested to see how far along you are in math and so forth," said Olive.

"I'm kind of nervous about starting a new school, to tell you the truth."

"Of course, but any school would seem like a new school to you, wouldn't it?"

"That's true."

"I think you'll really enjoy having friends your own age. If you aren't already, you are going to get very restless just hanging out with the lawn bowlers."

She was certainly right about that. Whenever Danny saw people his own age, he felt like galloping over to meet them.

"But I want you to be very careful about the new friends you make, very particular," said Olive. "You're at a dangerous age, you know. Most people make it through these years, a little bloodied and battered, but some people don't. And it's so often because of their friends. Believe me, when I was a teacher I saw *plenty*."

"You were a teacher?" Danny found this astonishing.

"Yes, I was. And later I was a principal."

"So, did you like, expel kids and stuff?"

"A few eighth graders. Things were different then. We had a different attitude towards children."

"Like how?"

"Oh, we believed in punishing them quickly and getting it all over."

"Like detention and time out?"

"Oh, cleaning the erasers after school. And actually, we sometimes hit them with rulers. On the hand."

"Did it hurt them?"

"Oh, probably not very much. We tried to scare them. I now believe that some of them were humiliated more than hurt. I think that was the whole point."

"Are you kidding! If you did that today you'd probably go to jail." Danny found the idea of Olive smacking some eighth grader fascinating. "But you told me you were a book keeper."

"That was later. Anyway," said Olive, frowning, "the main thing is to pick your friends carefully, even if you have to wait a while to make better friends. The bad kids will always take you in right away."

Danny promised solemnly not to get in with the wrong crowd.

"Gosh, Olive, you're really taking on a lot here," said Danny. "I really, really appreciate it. I hope I deserve it. What if we find out I'm a bad kid?"

"Well, you're not now," she said. "I can't imagine you were before, either."

Charmaine and Eugene Philbreck sat in the office of their insurance company lawyer, Donald Keene, and watched while he skimmed the complaint, familiarizing himself with the details of the case against them.

Brian Kessler vs Youth Intervention Therapies, Inc., alleged that Dr and Mrs Philbreck, owners and operators of Youth Intervention Therapies, had put their employee, Brian Kessler, in mortal danger by hiring him to escort Keith Lloyd and Danny Murdock to a therapeutic desert retreat, and that the Philbrecks were responsible for head injuries which had resulted in continuous headaches, emotional trauma, anxiety, diminished trust in his fellow man, and permanent brain damage. These disabilities rendered Brian Kessler unemployable for life, and had made the possibility of his ever finding happiness and personal fulfilment extremely unlikely, as another result of his injuries was sexual dysfunction.

Youth Intervention Therapies was therefore being sued for actual damages, including pain and suffering, mental anguish, lifetime financial support, and decades of physical and mental therapy, not to mention an unlimited supply of Viagra. The amount came to ten million dollars. Additional punitive damages, because of the Philbreck's egregious behavior in failing to provide proper training for Mr Kessler and to adequately screen violent young felons, amounted to an additional million.

Keene took off his reading glasses and sat back in his chair. "Well, now," he said.

"I'm sure he'll settle for considerably less," said Charmaine with confidence.

"It better be less," said Keene. "*Very* considerably less."

169

"Frankly," said Dr Philbreck, "we really would like this settled. Our business depends on community goodwill. This kind of publicity is counterproductive to our ongoing—"

Keene cut him off. "Our business, the insurance business, depends on us not rolling over for everyone who comes after us with a highly inflated claim. And if this guy prevails, you know the other guy that got clobbered will be showing up with his hand out too."

"Oh, Brad hasn't said anything about suing." Dr Philbreck seemed not to have considered this possibility.

"Is he still your employee?"

"For now," said Dr Philbreck nervously. "He seems happy enough."

"Tell me more about Brian Kessler," asked Keene. "What was his background?"

"He was a Naval MP," said Charmaine with a slight snort. "He went around busting up bar-room brawls in Manila. But those two little punks were too much for him."

"Presumably Mr Kessler received training in arresting people and so forth in the Military Police," said Keene, jotting down a note. "What was his job title with Youth Intervention Therapies?"

"Client escort and counsellor," said Charmaine. "Dr Philbreck trained him in the counselling part. Working with the kids and motivating them and dealing with their issues and so forth."

Keene turned to her husband. "Are you a medical doctor or a psychologist?"

Dr Philbreck looked slightly defensive. "I have a doctoral degree from Long Beach State College in Recreation Management."

"Recreation Management? I'm afraid I'm unfamiliar with that discipline. What was your thesis topic?"

"Um, it was about managing small groups in natural settings."

"I typed it," said Charmaine chattily. "It was called 'Establishing Successful Strategies and Performance Matrices in the Organization of Recreational Volleyball Leagues on Southern California Beaches'."

Her husband shot her a look.

Keene nodded. "I see." He sighed and fell silent.

The Philbrecks continued to look at him with hopefulness. He resumed his questioning.

"We'll also have to take a look at the client screening process. How bad was this Keith kid? The one that did the actual hitting?"

Dr Philbreck cleared his throat. "Well, he had juvenile arrests for assault, but most of his arrests were for burglary. Non-violent stuff while the house was empty." He waved his hand airily. "Some vandalism. We diagnosed him as having poor anger management skills and low self-esteem."

"OK, so what happened to the kids? Have they been tried yet? For either the car theft or assault?"

The Philbrecks exchanged glances. "Well, no. Actually, no."

"Have they been charged?"

"We didn't file a criminal complaint," explained Charmaine. "In our business, you don't want people to get the impression you can't handle things."

"But you presumably filed an insurance claim," said Keene, startled.

"Yes, but we left it kind of vague about how the car was stolen," Charmaine explained.

"Do we handle your auto insurance?" demanded Keene.

"No," said Dr Philbreck, looking frightened. "It's—"

"I don't want to hear about anything that could be construed as a fraudulent claim!"

The Philbrecks flinched and Keene sighed and shook his head just a millimetre. "OK. We'll deal with that aspect later." He leaned back in his chair and placed the tips of his fingers together thoughtfully. "The main thing is, I've seen the medical report and we can't completely discount the guy's claim that he was hurt. Somebody has got to take, or at least share, the blame for those injuries. And I can't think of anyone better than the kid who wielded the crowbar and his accomplice. Getting them arrested and charged is probably the first step."

"Except, we have to find them first," said Dr Philbreck pointedly.

"With eleven million dollars at stake," said Keene, "I'm pretty sure that can be arranged."

"So, how's it going with the kid?" As they did most mornings, Gordon and Richard sat in Gordon's glassed-in office drinking coffee. With the soundproof doors shut, Richard hoped that he and his brother appeared to the employees as if they were developing lofty strategies for Blakely Home Furnishings. In fact, they were often enjoying the same kind of desultory conversation they'd had in the mornings when they were kids, lying in twin beds with wagon-wheel headboards, staring up at their Roy Rogers wallpaper and waiting for Mom to come in and tell them it was time to get up.

"Things have calmed down since the beer thing," Richard said. "He's been very quiet and co-operative. Goes out at night with some friends he made when he went out with Flora, but he always gets home by curfew." He sighed. "He starts school next week, thank God. He's been driving us nuts just hanging around the place. We've told him to ask his friends over if he wants, but he says they all have jobs. They don't seem to be ready to go out and do things until ten at night or so. I mean he's a good kid and all, but it's sort of a strain."

Richard was looking forward to his upcoming weekend away with Louise. Some time ago they had bid on the getaway weekend at a charity auction, and despite Louise's reluctance to leave so soon after Daniel's arrival, Richard had insisted they go because he needed the break.

Gordon looked slightly apologetic. "So when are we going to meet our new nephew? Marcia asked me about it again this morning."

"Oh. Well, to tell you the truth, I wanted him to settle in a little first. But I guess we should have you guys over soon."

Gordon nodded. Richard guessed that his response had been too vague to satisfy Marcia, and she'd snap at Gordon because he hadn't nailed down Richard and wangled a specific invitation to dinner to check out the new kid.

"Or maybe we could wait and have Marcia meet Daniel at the company barbecue," Richard suggested.

"Oh yeah," said Gordon. "The barbecue. That reminds me. Doreen keeps nagging me for a budget for that thing."

Richard shrugged. "What do you think? Same as last year?"

"I guess. We wouldn't want the employees to think we're on the ropes or anything." Gordon laughed nervously.

"Well, are we?" Gordon handled most of the financial aspects of the business.

"Not exactly," said Gordon. "But those mall guys want another meeting. I have a bad feeling they want to shove us over to the Siberian end of the mall by that pathetic fishing tackle place and get a Gap or something in there."

"Shit," said Richard. "I hate those bastards. I wish we'd never gotten involved with them in the first place."

"I'm thinking we should have gone for a lower overhead

location in a nearby strip mall with decent parking," said Gordon. "Hell, you know who makes out OK in those high overhead malls? Candle shops. Shoe stores. Bed and Baths and Sunglass Huts. Impulse items, not the big ticket stuff. That's what those teenagers and bored women are buying."

Richard sighed. Why hadn't Gordon thought of this before they signed the lease? Sometimes, he wished that at least one of them had bothered to major in business. "How bad is it?" he asked, not really wanting to know.

"We're bleeding over there," said Gordon. "Want to take a look at the figures?

"I guess I'd better," said Richard plaintively.

"Maybe it's the product mix," mused Gordon, rummaging around in a drawer for some computer printouts. "Anyway, Marcia's still making noises about our getting a bigger draw. I finally told her to forget it until we settle this problem with the Eastside store once and for all."

"Good," said Richard. This was a relief. Gordie had finally stood up to her. Richard thought about the cost of his basement remodel. Even with his own ample salary from the business and Louise working, he'd felt lately that they were getting in a little deep, financially. God, his own parents had lived so modestly. He and his brother had shared a room all through high school, and no one thought that they were deprived. He'd even paid for half of his own bike with paper-route money.

"Yeah," said Gordon, "I got Marcia all resigned about the draw thing, I think. But now she wants to know what the deal is with Daniel."

"I'll talk to Louise tonight. Maybe you can come over this weekend."

"I mean are you writing a new will? Marcia says we deserve to know how much of the store our kids can expect."

174

Richard felt sudden anger. That greedy bitch! "Of course I'm going to redo my will," snapped Richard, who hadn't given it a thought until now. "And I think Daniel should start getting more involved in the business. I'll bring him down here for a tour tomorrow." By the time Marcia and Gordie's kids were old enough to be involved, Daniel, if he was interested, could already have a thorough working-knowledge of the place. That ought to keep Marcia's little brats in their place.

## 16

"But my son isn't missing," said Wanda, staring down at the card the woman on her doorstep had handed her. It said her name was Cheryl Snow and that she was an insurance investigator.

"He isn't? Where is he?" asked Cheryl Snow. She was a pleasant-looking woman with curly auburn hair.

"Well, he's in a sort of character-building programme out in the desert."

"Run by Youth Intervention Therapies?"

"Yes." Wanda was confused and frightened. "There must be some mistake. I don't understand. Why did you say he was missing?" She put a knuckle to her mouth.

The investigator took on a concerned look. "But I assumed you knew. May I come in? We should talk."

Wanda led her into the living room and gestured vaguely at the sofa. "Why are you asking me where he is? Is he all right?"

"He disappeared. I understood you'd been informed. He and another boy assaulted the men who were taking them to the site and stole the car. We want to find them. I assumed you'd be anxious to find them too."

Wanda screamed and sank on to the sofa. "My God! I told Carl this was a bad idea. Jesus! My baby."

"It's likely you'll hear from him," said Cheryl Snow.

"The vehicle was recovered in Oregon."

"Assaulted those men! Danny wouldn't hurt a fly. Who is this other kid?"

"His name is Keith Lloyd. He's apparently the one who actually struck the men repeatedly. With a heavy metal object."

"Oh, my God!" Wanda began sobbing.

Cheryl Snow sat beside her and patted her hand. "I'm so sorry. I assumed you knew. Didn't Youth Intervention Therapies tell you?"

"They told my husband everything was fine," wailed Wanda. She began to shake.

Just then she heard Carl at the door. He gave his characteristic "Honey, I'm home" whistle, and Wanda leaped to the door and flung herself at him. "Danny is gone!" she said. "You said everything would be all right. What are we going to do?"

Carl embraced his wife and looked over her shoulder at the woman sitting on the sofa. Who the hell was she?

"Listen, sweetheart, it's all right. He's not lost. I didn't tell you because I wanted to break it to you gently, but Danny never actually made it to Wilderness Survival School."

"Where is he? Do you know where he is?" shrieked Wanda. "Why didn't you tell me he was missing?"

"Well," said Carl, "the fact is, he's with his dad up in Seattle. I was going to tell you very soon. I've discussed this with Dr Philbreck, and he agrees with me that a little time out with his dad is probably a good thing for Danny right now. The Blakelys sound like very responsible folks.

"In fact, he's spending spring break there, and I've talked with the Blakelys about his finishing the school year up in Seattle. It really is a good idea. He's really quite happy there." He moved his wife from his shoulder. "Who are you?" he asked Cheryl Snow.

177

Before she had a chance to reply, Wanda hauled off and slapped him hard across the face. "You bastard!" she said.

Danny could tell Olive was asleep. She snored. But he wasn't sleepy. He kept thinking about his real dad. He couldn't imagine that he was as much of a jerk as Keith had said. After all, while Danny loved his mother, he had figured out some time ago that he was actually a lot smarter than she was. And Amy, the product of Mom and that idiot Carl, wasn't that bright either – just sneaky and shrewd. Danny was definitely a cut above other members of his nuclear family, so his dad had to be smart or genetically *he* wouldn't be as smart as he was. Well, maybe *smart* wasn't the exact word. His dad had to be more focused and together, and not flapping around emotionally all the time like Mom.

But the guy Keith had described sounded like a wimpy loser. Danny couldn't believe that he wasn't related to *someone* decent. He sighed. Maybe he was a mutation. When they'd learned about mutations in Biology, Danny had taken heart about himself.

Now Olive, even though she was an old lady and all that, seemed to have some of that focused, sensible, kind of classy quality that Danny felt had eluded all of his own relatives except himself.

She didn't have any relatives, as far as he could tell. She told him she'd had a brother who was killed in World War Two and that was all. Still, there were those photo albums.

Danny slipped out of bed and padded over to them in his bare feet. Sitting on the floor cross-legged, he opened the first one, its cover a faded wine-coloured leather. Inside, photographs were mounted on black construction paper. The album began with a picture of a couple and a baby. There were more pictures of this determined-looking,

178

large-eyed baby. Underneath a shot of a toddler with a large bow in her hair, blowing out candles on a birthday cake, a caption in white ink read "Olive is two!".

Soon, Olive was joined by a younger brother, Frank. Danny realized that many of the pictures had been taken right here, at this house. Olive, at about seven, sat on the front porch in a tiny plaid dress, a protective arm around her little brother.

Fascinated, but feeling slightly guilty for snooping, Danny leafed through the albums as Olive and her brother grew into teenagers. Olive wore skirts and sweaters and saddle shoes. She looked serious and smart, with a cute, turned-up nose and wavy dark hair parted on one side. Frank wore patterned sweaters and smiled a big open smile, and later was shown in a studio portrait in a sailor's uniform.

Turning a page, he was surprised to see a black and white school picture of a classroom full of kids. Next to the three rows of children stood a nun in a black habit with some white around her face. Danny stared at the picture. He didn't see Olive or her brother in the classroom. Then he examined the nun. The little round, serious face looking out from veil and wimple belonged to Olive, an Olive who looked about twenty.

Olive had been a nun! Danny was fascinated. Mom, who had been to Catholic school, said some of them were nice but some of them were mean. Danny assumed that Olive had been one of the nice ones. But there was something creepy about the whole thing – dressing up in that weird outfit and never having anything to do with men.

There were a few more school shots, of Olive in her nun outfit. In one of them, she was playing baseball with a bunch of kids. Then, suddenly, a middle-aged Olive – looking pretty much like she did now but with dark hair in a kind of sixties bubble – reappeared with her two old parents. They seemed to have gone on a trip to the Grand Canyon or some place like that with a lot of rocks. Eventually, there was just Olive and her mother, now looking very frail, sitting by a Christmas tree in the living room. Danny recognized the fireplace screen and the poker and tongs, and the ship in the bottle on the mantelpiece.

Danny was confused. Olive had been kind of cute when she was young. He assumed no cute girls would want to be nuns. He wanted to ask her why she decided to be a nun and, later, why she quit and came back home.

Danny was also curious about the God aspect of the thing. He'd never been to church or Sunday School. When he was younger and asked his mom about God, she had said it was OK to be spiritual but that religion was kind of a bad thing, and that God is in all of us, kind of mushed around throughout the universe. She said she had been taught to pray as a child. But now she did affirmations, and thought that if you believed enough that something good would happen, you could make it happen, and if you didn't, it was somehow your fault for not being in touch with your inner core. When he asked her what happened to dead people, she said she thought that they became one with the universe and their spirit continued in trees and stuff.

It would be interesting to talk to someone who believed in an actual God and heaven. Or at least did once, anyway. But he couldn't just bring it up, though, without admitting he'd gone through her photo album. He'd have to ask her some questions about her life and then it would come out that she'd been a nun and they could go on from there.

At dinner, when Richard had asked Keith if he wanted to make some extra money working at the store on weekends,

180

Keith had appeared enthusiastic. "That would be great," he said. "Maybe I could start saving for college." Privately, he thought the idea was stupid. The Blakelys were rich. Why should he have to have a J-O-B?

"Well, I'm glad you're thinking about that, but there's more to it," Richard said. "The fact is, you may as well find out how interested you are in the family business. After all, when I'm gone, you'll own part of it."

Keith dropped his fork with a clatter. "Wow!" he said. "I never thought of that!" He was taken aback. If he really had been Danny Murdock, he could own a huge business and be rich some day.

He looked over at Flora with a wicked grin. He just had a great idea. What if he knocked her up, and she had the kid? Then he would be related, kind of. Maybe they'd let him be part of the family then. Flora looked back at him with a slightly puzzled look. He dropped the grin.

"I'll give you the tour tomorrow," said Richard. "It's about time you met your Uncle Gordon."

Keith had imagined his job at Blakely Home Furnishings would have something to do with the office – maybe wearing a tie and talking to people on the phone or something. Or even being on the floor selling. Keith thought he'd make a good salesman. He had always prided himself on his ability to influence others. Anyway, as the owner's son he shouldn't have to do anything demeaning. People would have to respect him. That was part of being a Blakely.

So he was disappointed when Uncle Gordon led him back to the delivery department, a large area with a loading dock, where a bunch of young guys were moving furniture around. Keith and Gordon watched an employee preparing a set of dining chairs for the truck, wrapping the legs with foam and tape.

"What you don't want is a bad delivery. There's a lot to go wrong. Legs are a vulnerable area. Corners are vulnerable. Improper packing of shelving can be a disaster. We once wiped out a whole china closet because of some loose glass shelving that should have been put into separate boxes, taped."

"Interesting," said Keith. "Will I be driving the trucks and stuff?" That might be fun.

"We'll start you out here, loading. That's how I started. There's a whole art to delivery. First you learn how to make sure the piece arrives in good shape. Then we'll teach you how to work with the customers in their home, place the furniture, get everything assembled properly, and all the little touches that are real important – like putting down padding so you don't track stuff on to their carpets, and making sure you remove all packaging material."

"I see," said Keith doubtfully.

"The thing to remember is that the sale doesn't end on the floor here when the customer says 'yes'. It ends in the customer's home. That's why delivery is so important. We're very particular about our guys. They have to look good, wear a uniform, be personable and pleasant. People don't want to think some thief or axe murderer is casing the joint."

"I get it," said Keith. "They're letting strangers into their home."

"Exactly."

Keith smiled. This could be great. People would tell them where keys were hidden and stuff. The possibilities were endless.

Just then, Richard came into the area. "Hey, can we borrow Daniel?" he asked his brother.

"What for?"

"Catalogue picture for the youth furnishings shot."

"What do I have to do?" asked Keith.

182

"Nothing," said Richard. "Just sit at a desk. We've got a toddler shot in the same room, but we want to show the same furniture will work all through high school."

"OK, Dad." Keith grinned. "Glad I just got a haircut."

"Thank God you were here," said Richard. "This catalogue is way behind schedule. It runs in next week-end's paper! We were going to use Peter from book keeping – he looks real young – but he called in sick." Keith trotted behind Richard out on to the showroom floor. A photographer took him by the shoulders and manoeuvred him into position, sitting in a chair behind a desk. There was a stack of books, a spiral-bound notebook and a mug of pens and pencils on the desk.

"Don't smile or anything," said the photographer, rearranging some lights. "You're supposed to be doing homework. Just pretend to be a normal kid, like you belong here."

"I am a normal kid," said Keith. "And I do belong here." Despite the photographer's admonition, he couldn't help smiling a little as he sat at the desk, pen in hand, head bent as if in concentration over phantom homework.

"But he has to talk to me," sobbed Wanda into the phone. "I'm his mother! *I have to hear the sound of his voice!*"

Richard sounded cold and hard and disapproving. "Sorry, he's chosen not to."

Wanda sure as hell wasn't going to explain to Richard why she hadn't called sooner, and how her husband had lied to her – it made her sound like an idiot. Well, maybe she *had* been an idiot. And she certainly wasn't going to get into it with him about the escape from Youth Intervention Therapies, another one of Carl's bright ideas, or that Danny had been involved with that criminal, Keith Lloyd, when two men were assaulted.

"I want my child back!" she insisted.

"We already worked that out," said Richard.

"Well, I've changed my mind."

"Oh, for God's sake, Wanda, he's registered at school here and everything."

"Why won't he talk to me?"

"He says he doesn't want to," said Richard.

"Well can I at least send him an e-mail?" asked Wanda desperately. "Are you on-line? What's your e-mail address?"

"The good news," said the doctor, "is that you're just fine. There's nothing on this chart that reveals any lesions or other abnormalities." Danny and Olive were sitting in the neurologist's office looking over some blotchy pictures of his brain from the CAT scan.

"And the bad news is that I still can't remember anything," said Danny, trying to look sorry about this.

The doctor turned to Olive. "I think at this point, you might consider some kind of psychological evaluation. Maybe therapy or hypnosis."

Olive clicked her tongue impatiently. "Frankly, I think there are very few people who benefit from talking about themselves at great length. There's absolutely nothing wrong with him, mentally, except for his memory loss. But I feel terrible about his parents. If hypnosis would reveal who he is, I suppose we have to try it. What do you think, Tony?"

"Hypnosis? It kind of creeps me out," said Danny. Would he be able to resist? Would he just blab out everything and end up in prison? Maybe he could fake it somehow. He wished Olive would stop worrying about his parents. If she knew what heartless people they were, she wouldn't be so worried. "Can we think about it first?"

"Of course," she said.

184

Outside in the parking lot, Danny thought that maybe he should pretend to remember a couple of things. Then she would think his memory was coming back, and she wouldn't pressure him into seeing some horrible shrink.

He stopped and put his hand lightly on his forehead. "I have a vague recollection, a little flash. There's a woman. I think she's my mother! Yes, I think she is! She's yelling at me and I can't hear what she's saying."

"Oh, Tony that's wonderful!" said Olive.

"She doesn't seem to like me very much."

"Believe me, if she did shout at you I can guarantee that she's crying her eyes out and feeling very, very guilty right now that she's hurt you and lost you," said Olive. Danny wondered if it were true that his mother was crying. When he was about eight he had once come into the kitchen and found his mother sobbing, after some fight with Carl or something, and he remembered how disturbing that had been. Was she sobbing like that now? Danny thought that perhaps he should at least let her know he was alive.

Keith sat at the computer in Richard's study and read off the screen. He was going to have to think about this one carefully. This Wanda bitch sounded so upset he was afraid she might just show up on the Blakelys' doorstep to get her kid back, and then it'd be all over. Keith wasn't ready for it to be over just yet.

Keith was also concerned to see his own, real name in the message and to learn that a detective had come around to Danny Murdock's house. This was weird. He hadn't really hit those two guys that hard. What was the big deal, anyway?

He re-read the message.

*Danny! I'm so sorry, honey, just call me and I can*

*explain everything. Things will be different, I promise. Oh, darling, I'm sorry I ever let Carl even think about sending you to that horrible place. And in such bad company. The detective told me what that Keith Lloyd did, but I know you had no part in it. You're a good kid and you'd never do anything like that. Please call me, sweetheart, and let me know you are all right and when you are coming home. I love you so much!*

Keith sucked his teeth. A reply was in order. He didn't know much about computers but he couldn't mess this up. He needed to get in touch with this woman and tell her something that would keep her away from here.

Across the room, Richard was watching him.

"If you don't mind, Dad," Keith said, "I don't feel ready to share this right now."

"That's all right," said Richard, looking relieved, just as Keith knew he would. "Are you sure you don't want to answer her? She was pretty desperate to talk to you."

"Hah!" said Keith bitterly. "First she ignores me, then she pretends to you that she really cares." He turned to face the wall, and allowed his shoulders to shake a little as if he were weeping. "God, it's been so hard!"

Richard came up behind him and put a hand on his shoulder. Keith immediately positioned himself so Richard couldn't read the screen and appeared to recover his composure. "Listen Dad, I think I'll send her a message back, OK. But we have, uh, like, a different program on our computer, so I'm not sure I know how to send it."

"I'll help you," said Richard. He leaned over and clicked on "Reply". "Just type your answer in here, and click on this when you're through. I'll leave you alone."

"Thanks, Dad."

It took him a while, as his keyboard skills were limited,

186

but when Keith finished and read the results, he felt as if it might work.

*Dear Mom,*
*Please back off. I do not want to talk to you for a while.*
*I love you very much, but I think it is important for my*
*own self-esteem that I have some time to think about*
*the kind of person I am and the kind I want to be. For*
*now, let us just e-mail. I need my space. I am happy*
*here, but of course I want to come home some day. I*
*need to relate to my dad for a short while.*
*So please don't call. Just e-mail. It's important to me.*
*Love, your son, Danny*
*PS What else did the detective say about that Keith*
*guy? He was pretty hardcore.*

In the kitchen, Flora came in and saw her mother unloading the dishwasher. "Hey, Mom?"

"What?"

"I've been thinking. It's going to be weird having Daniel at school."

"I hope you'll do what you can to make sure he gets along," said Louise. "I'm worried about him."

"I'll do what I can," said Flora bravely. "I can't imagine what it would be like to go to a new school. But it will be hard for me too." There was no way Mom could possibly understand how seriously uncool Keith was.

# 17

Danny had seen a whole bunch of movies about kid-
nappers and terrorists where the FBI or somebody would
whisper, "Keep them on the phone, we're trying to trace
the call, but you have to keep them talking", so he
assumed that if he got on and off really fast, he'd be all
right. But just to be on the safe side, he used the phone up
in the park.

He'd already decided that if Amy or Carl answered he'd
just hang up, but he was lucky. It was Mom all right. She
sounded completely normal, not like she was terrified
about him or anything.

"Mom?" Danny whispered into the phone. "Is that you?"

"Danny! Honey! How are you? I'm so glad you called.
You aren't still mad at me, are you?" She sounded pretty
excited.

"Well, kind of. Jeez, Mom, you sent me to a concentration camp!"

He heard a sharp intake of breath.

"Oh, darling. I've told you how sorry I was!"

"What?"

"It's so good to hear your actual voice. Sweetheart, are
you OK?"

"Listen, Mom, I can't talk. I just want to say I'm OK,
and don't worry if you don't hear from me for a while."

Danny had rehearsed this statement, and he let it out all in a rush.

"I know you're OK, darling. I'm over the shock of that detective coming around. Seattle is a really nice place. I miss it. I miss you, sweetheart."

Detective! And how the hell did she know where he was? Danny was so startled he didn't say anything. Then it occurred to him that maybe they had some kind of Caller ID thing on the phone to track him down. Maybe she was letting him know the web was tightening!

"But Danny, I wish you'd called before now. Why didn't you?" She had the usual intense, slightly hysterical edge to her voice. "I love you, Danny."

"Me too, Mom." He slammed down the receiver.

Could they trace the call? Was the phone bugged? Was she trying to tell him that they knew where he was? Was she trying to warn him? One thing was for sure. He'd better not risk calling again.


Carl walked into the room to see his wife holding the phone and staring at it and sobbing. "What is it?" he asked.

"It's Danny. He called. He said he loved me. Then he hung up."

"Well at least he called you," said Carl. "You said you wanted him to call. Now he did. Why are you crying?"

"I want him back. Don't you get it?"

"Isn't that kind of selfish? I mean, we agreed that this was the best thing for him. He needed a change. We all did. This is good for him. He needed a fresh start."

"As soon as the school year is over, I want him back," said Wanda fiercely. "I have rights, too. We'll get a lawyer and fight this!"

"Don't be silly," Carl replied. "You can't make a fifteen year old do anything he doesn't want to do."

"That's not what you said when you shipped him off to that obedience training," she snapped. "I'm calling him back. Where's that number?"

The phone rang in the Blakely's kitchen. "Daniel, it's for you." Flora held up the phone.

"Who is it?" asked Keith.

"I don't know. Sounds like an adult. Do you want me to screen your calls?"

Keith grabbed the phone. "Hello?"

"Is Danny there?"

"Who wants to know?"

"His mother," said Wanda, her voice trembling. "He just called me."

"Oh yeah? Well, he just left. I'll tell him you called." Keith watched Flora as she opened the cupboard and pulled out a box of crackers and a jar of peanut butter.

"Who are you?" asked Wanda.

"Just a guest," said Keith. "I gotta go." He hung up.

"Who the hell was that?" asked Flora, looking puzzled.

"Listen, if she calls again, tell her I'm not here," said Daniel.

"Who is it?"

"Some crazy stalker. Goes for younger guys. Just forget about it, will you?"

"How did she get this number?" persisted Flora. "Where did you meet her?"

"At a party, OK. With older people. She was really drunk and she hit on me and someone gave her my number as a joke. Just forget about it."

"Yew," said Flora, wrinkling her nose. "You better not give out my line to any child molester weirdos you run into."

"Hey," snapped Keith. "It's not your line, it's our line. The kid line. It's about time you learned how to share."

190

Flora let out a loud and indignant "What?"

"Oh, calm down." He smiled at her and gave her shoulder a little push. "Your hair looks good today."

She seemed taken aback. "It does?"

Keith smiled. "I heard you planning your little kegger here this weekend while the parental units are out of town. Thanks a lot for asking *me*."

"For God's sake! It's not a kegger. It's a margarita party. I didn't think you'd be interested. It's just a few of my closest friends. It's not like I'm going to invite the whole school over and get the house trashed or anything. It's a civilized little gathering. A theme party." She was spreading peanut butter on the crackers now. "Just cocktails and salsa music."

"Cocktails," snorted Keith. "Give me a break." He grabbed one of the crackers and stuffed it in his mouth. Something she had just said had given him a great idea. And it kind of fitted in with the fact that Danny Murdock seemed to have broken down and called his mother. He might have to clear out of here fast.

Flora was excited about her party. She'd taken a collection from all her friends and arranged to get Katie's older sister to buy the tequila, which was hidden in the back of her closet behind a box full of old dolls and stuffed animals. Claire and another friend were going to bring extra blenders, so they could have three going at once. They would buy the guacamole and salsa and chips on the day of the event. And, Flora had made a fabulous mix tape of Latin music.

She and Claire had also picked out their outfits. Flora was wearing a short, black dress with heels and pearls, that showed the tops of her breasts very prettily over the square neckline but with no actual cleavage, very early sixties

Audrey Hepburn, and Claire was doing a kind of Carmen Miranda thing with a tropical print skirt and a tight little black top with big hoop earrings.

Everything was set for a very sophisticated, retro kind of party – nothing like what those idiotic preps did every Friday night going through a keg of beer and throwing up in the park and getting totally wasted and eventually busted by the cops.

One problem with a party like this was boys. Most of the people who were cool enough to appreciate the charm of the event were girls. Still, there were a few guys deemed good enough to be invited who might be able to get into the spirit of things.

And then there was Daniel. He had surprised her when he asked if he was invited. He was supposedly house-sitting while Mom and Richard were away, and she was scheduled to spend the night at Claire's. Flora had been pretty sure, however, that he wouldn't bother them. He'd made it pretty clear that he thought her friends were boring snobs.

He'd be out doing whatever it was he did on weekends. Presumably riding around in cars or hanging out on the street with his loser friends, scruffy-looking stoner-type kids he'd kept in touch with ever since that night when he'd ended up at some party on Capital Hill. Or maybe he would end up at the park, trying to suck up to the preps. He'd asked for the precise location of the weekly kegger a few days ago, and Flora had been pleased to give it to him.

But what if he did show up? Would that be embarrassing, or maybe kind of cool? Ingrid was coming. She'd asked if Daniel would be there. Maybe they'd get together. Flora had a sudden image of Ingrid and Daniel making out in the kitchen or something, and found the idea upsetting. She hoped he'd stay away.

In the car on their way to the inn, Louise felt glad Flora would be safely spending the night at Claire's while they were gone. The idea of two adolescents of the opposite sex together in the house seemed wrong.

Of course, they were stepsiblings, but seeing as they hadn't been raised together, the whole thing seemed terribly awkward. Louise hadn't mentioned this to Richard. It seemed too creepy to mention. The fact was, though, that Daniel seemed so physically mature for fifteen. He had a baritone voice. And he was so *hairy*.

Louise had also worried that Daniel might have some of his mysterious friends over, and Flora would be exposed to strange boys she hadn't met. You did hear horror stories about kids getting in trouble while their parents were out of town.

Richard put his hand on her knee. "Boy, am I ready for this," he said. "The idea of a kid-free weekend is so inviting. In fact, let's make a pact. We won't think about kids for forty-eight hours."

"I just hope Daniel will be all right on his own."

"Of course he will. It's great that we have someone to keep an eye on the place. And Flora is gone, so she won't be bugging him."

"What do you mean?"

"Well, she hasn't exactly been welcoming, has she? Let's face it, Flora's not the easiest person to live with."

"All adolescents are a bit of a strain," said Louise. How dare he criticize Flora? God, he knew so little about children. "Naturally there are going to be adjustment problems."

"Poor Daniel's had to do most of the adjusting. Wanda and that jerk, Carl, did a rotten job. As far as I can tell, he's never felt wanted. That's why it seems especially cruel and unpleasant when Flora puts him down the way she does. Let's face it, she's spoiled and selfish."

"All kids are selfish. And I really resent you calling Flora spoiled," said Louise, trying not shout. "At least we know who her friends are, and she doesn't go out drinking at parties." Richard didn't reply, and Louise, unable to stop herself, continued. "I'm glad you're so confident he can look after the house. I just hope he stays out of trouble without supervision."

"Listen, I had nothing to do with the way he was brought up."

"Oh! But I raised Flora, so if there's anything wrong with *her* it's my fault. God!"

"Look, I suggested we not talk about kids. But you insisted. Let's face it, you're obsessed with kids."

"That's ridiculous. I'm just trying to be a good mother. And stepmother."

"How about being my wife for forty-eight hours?" said Richard. He said it in a jokey way, but Louise was furious with him. He was a complete bastard. Why hadn't she seen that before she married him? He didn't know anything about kids, but he acted like he did. He resented anyone else getting some attention from her. God, it was like having a third kid in the house! And to think, she'd looked forward to champagne in front of the fire and some great sex. Right now, the only physical contact she wanted with her husband was to slap him hard across the face.

They finally arrived at the inn, after a long, silent drive in the dark. It was a Japanoid, minimalist structure of bleached logs in a small, rather grim oceanside town.

As they checked in, they tried to look pleasant and happily married. The smarmy desk clerk, a young man with short hair and tiny little gold-rimmed glasses, wearing

194

what appeared to be a pair of roughly-woven lounging pyjamas, greeted them with a Mona Lisa smile, clasped hands, and a slightly tilted head. "How may I help you?" he said. "Are you staying with us this evening?"

While electronically checking the limit on Richard's American Express card, he continued with a quasi-religious hush. "Here at the inn, we foster an atmosphere of complete relaxation," he said. "If there's anything we can do to make your stay with us more serene, please let myself or any staff member know."

Louise looked around the dim lobby, chock-full of dramatically lit Northwest Indian art, which gave the whole place a sinister air. There were also some Italian leather sofas and chairs and glass and chrome coffee tables dotted with earthenware bowls of pot-pourri. The whole place gave her the creeps. And she was checking in with a man she now regretted having married.

Fending off offers from the young man to show them how the hot tub in their room worked, to turn down the sheets, and bring them herbal tea, Richard grabbed the key and led her down a fern-lined path to the door to their room.

Inside, he let their small bag fall to the floor with a thud. The décor was pale, bland and spare. "This looks like a great place for a Zen retreat." He investigated the futon-like bed and a black lacquer cabinet that turned out to include a TV, which, besides some flimsy bed stands, seemed to be the only furnishings. "If this trend continues," he said in a tone of forced humour, "Gordie and I will have to get into some other business."

"It's not too welcoming, is it?" said Louise.

Richard went over to the cabinet and picked up a sheet of rice paper which lay there next to a bud vase with a single white spiky flower.

"Welcome," he read aloud. "Please understand that the inn works to nurture a calm and tranquil ambience. The rooms at the inn are non-smoking. In order to preserve the pristine environment of an oceanside community, the rooms are not permitted to have fireplaces. If you must use the television, please keep the volume low so as not to disturb the other rooms. Talking loudly on the balcony may also disturb the other rooms."

He flung the paper back down. "The rooms seem to have lives of their own," he said. "They don't smoke and they're easily disturbed."

Louise giggled, and he smiled at her and came over. They kissed.

"I'm sorry, darling," said Louise. "I'd heard such great things about this place."

"Well, at least the champagne will be good. Do you think that elfin creature at the desk can rustle up an ice bucket? And then we can try out the hot tub, if the room doesn't mind."

Louise thought no more about the children, nor about any other aspect of the outside world until the phone rang at one o'clock.

"Mrs Blakely?"

"Yes?" she whispered, trying not to disturb Richard who was snoring lightly beside her. Presumably this was the over-solicitous staff, calling to see if they'd found their pillow mints or something.

"Mrs Blakely, this is Sergeant Peterson of the Seattle Police."

## 18

Flora was more irritated than concerned when the first uninvited kids showed up. About fifteen guests were sipping their margaritas sedately in the living room, and the sound of the doorbell meant that more people were coming, which was great.

Feeling festive, Flora opened the door with a flourish, holding aloft the Holly Golightly cigarette holder with which she had accessorized her little black dress, and said, "Darlings!"

Three hulking boys in scruffy, gangsterish clothes stared at her slack-jawed. She had never seen them before, and she was pretty sure they didn't go to Madison. One of them said, "Daniel told us to wait for him."

Oh God! Just what she needed. These losers hanging around! This was not the kind of tone she'd had in mind.

"Well he's not here," she said crisply, feeling suddenly that her chic outfit, out of context, made her look a little weird.

"He's on his way," said the largest of the boys, moving past her into the hall. The other two followed. "Where's his room at?" said the burly spokesman.

"Um, he sleeps in here," said Flora, indicating the study, "but I think you guys better come back later. I have some guests over and—"

"That's OK." The first boy continued walking deeper into the house with Flora following him nervously, and the other two following her. They had now arrived in the kitchen. "Oh, party time, huh?" he said. Claire, doing blender-duty, looked up nervously.

Flora considered briefly offering these three margaritas before herding them into the study, but one of them just grabbed the tequila off the counter and helped himself to a big slurp out of the bottle. Claire, a germ freak, scrunched up her face with distaste.

From the open outside door, she heard the sound of feet coming up the porch steps. Flora, slightly nervous, ran to see who it was. Her heart sank. There, resplendent in the prep uniform of perfect white baseball cap with the bill folded into a funnel shape like horse blinkers, plaid Oxford cloth shirt, crisp jeans and Timberlake boots, stood Jeff Lane, the biggest prep boozer at Madison. "Hey Flora!" he said. "I hear there's a party happenin' here." Behind him, eyes glazed and swaying a little, was a huge kid named Justin who was in Flora's history class.

"Not really," said Flora. "I'm just having a few friends over. We're going to watch a video or something later." The sound of the blender, Tito Puente, and the laughter of at least a dozen adolescents undermined this assertion.

Jeff laughed, turned over his shoulder and boomed out loud enough for the neighbours to hear, "Hey guys, this is the place!"

Car doors slammed, and soon a half-dozen preps of both sexes, bearing six-packs and malt liquor bottles, trooped past a helpless Flora. One of them, a cheerleader named Jenny Karnofksi, who was in her French class but never actually spoke to her, gave Flora a snide little smile and said, "Cute dress." They all seemed to have been partying for quite a while already.

Flora was terrified. Would there be more? Would they just chill here for a while, get bored, then move on? Jenny now seemed to be pounding on the keys of a cellphone. Why did Jenny want to use the phone? To call more people and invite them over?

"My parents are coming back at any moment," Flora said, trying not to sound panicky. "They're really strict. They might call your parents if they think there's been any drinking going on. I'm serious."

"Shut up, I'm on the phone," Jenny said off-handedly.

Flora was actually relieved when Daniel appeared on the porch. "God," she said, "my party's gotten semi-taken over by preps."

"Are you serious?" said Daniel. She felt a little better. He actually looked concerned.

"And some of your friends are here too," she added. "I'm really afraid things could get out of hand. Maybe your friends could get them to leave." Flora's friends, mostly girls, would not be able to do this.

"I don't know," said Daniel dubiously. "We weren't going to stick around. You made a big deal of saying you wanted me to go out."

"Well you could chill with your friends in the study," said Flora. "Then if things get out of hand, maybe you can help me." She bit her lip nervously.

"You were seriously stupid not to get some guys here for security," said Daniel. "If you'd asked me, I would have handled it. But I guess you thought I wasn't cool enough for your friends."

Flora sighed, exasperated. How could he be talking about rejection when these interlopers were capable of anything? "I didn't think you'd want to help me," she said.

"Well, we can't throw them out now," he said. "I mean they haven't done anything yet, right? But if a fight breaks out or something, me and my friends can maybe take care of that."

"Some of these same kids totally trashed Chuck Wong's house, last year. He had to call the cops on his own party." This tragic act had become known as "Doing a Wong" around Madison High School. Flora would never live it down if that happened. "Maybe they'll just get bored and leave," she said hopefully.

The Latin jazz stopped abruptly. Loud rap music blasted through the house. "God, that music is so loud. The neighbours will hear," said Flora.

"I'll tell them to turn it down," said Daniel, striding off purposefully. Flora was feeling better about things. Daniel looked completely fearless.

More car doors slammed. A dozen kids came up the walk. One of them, Eddie Lamont, whose college application had been enhanced by his being elected student-body president, and receiving a Junior Leadership award from a local Kiwanis Club, was rolling an aluminium keg towards the house.

Back in the living room, things seemed all right. Mostly people were just standing around with beer bottles in their hands. Daniel seemed to have managed to get the stereo turned down and was conferring with his scruffy friends. One of them was still sucking on the tequila bottle, the other was quietly rolling a joint, and the third was nodding his head jerkily to the music.

Flora tried to calm herself down. It was a shame about the theme being shot down, but maybe this would be all right. Maybe the preps would even think it had been a cool party. She tried to hold that thought. Flora went into the kitchen and found a lot of saucers. If she put them everywhere, maybe there wouldn't be any cigarette burns or anything.

Margarita production seemed to have stopped. The traitorous Claire, leaning on the counter in a drunken way, was flirting with the repulsive Jeff Lane. As if he'd ever speak to her in real life!

Flora sighed and gave Claire a disgusted look, then went back to the living room where she scurried around deploying the saucers. "Use these ashtrays, you guys, OK?" she pleaded. The volume of the music had crept up a little, and she went into the study to crank it back down. There, Justin, the huge guy who'd arrived with Jeff, seemed to have passed out on the sofa, carefully clutching a twenty-ounce malt liquor bottle. Yes, the preps had already been to at least one gathering before this.

She remembered the story of Chuck Wong's party. Chuck had been majorly stupid and actually told everyone at school to come and party at his house while his parents were at a dentists' convention in San Francisco. It had ended with his dad's computer submerged in the bathtub and his mom's jewellery stolen. Chuck had claimed to be too drunk to know who the perpetrators were, but everyone assumed he was just sticking to the teen code of silence. His dad had gotten him a summer job at a fish cannery in Alaska to pay the family back, because the insurance wouldn't cover the activities of invited guests.

Flora looked around the room. Would that happen here? It just couldn't. But if it did, she could say she hadn't actually invited everyone like Chuck had. The insurance would have to pay.

But if they took Mom's jewellery, like they took Mrs Wong's, she'd never get it back. There was stuff in there from Flora's great-grandmother, and the engagement and wedding ring Mom had had when she was married to Flora's dad.

Flora sneaked upstairs. Through the open bathroom

door, she was disgusted to see Jenny Karnofski, mascara running, vomiting convulsively into the bathtub. God! Couldn't she at least use the toilet?

Two guys, beers in hand, lolled outside the door, viewing the scene dispassionately. One of them turned to Flora. "She's kinda fucked up," he explained.

Cleaning Jenny Karnofski's vomit off the shower curtain was not how Flora had envisioned the evening ending. For just a second she considered getting out a camera and catching the cheerleader not looking her best, but then she remembered her original errand.

A few minutes later, Flora was in her parents' room and had buried her mother's jewellery box, and the special case that held the pearls Richard had given her, under the dirty laundry in the hamper in her closet. Then she slipped unnoticed into her own room and did the same thing with her own jewellery box and laundry basket. As an afterthought, she tucked her journal in under the dirty laundry too, topped the basket off with some socks and jeans from the floor, then pushed the basket into her closet.

She had just concluded the operation when three girls burst into her bedroom. "I knew there had to be another phone somewhere," one of them squealed in triumph. "Alana will be so pissed we didn't call. She's already paged me like five times." The girls laughed merrily.

From the bedroom window, Flora heard young males yelling in the back yard, although she couldn't make out the words. This was an alarming development. The party was moving out of the house. She would try and find Daniel and get him to herd those guys back inside. The voices became louder and now she could understand what they were shouting.

"Fuck you!" yelled the first one,

"No. Fuck *you*!" was the indignant reply.

Flora raced down the stairs, manoeuvring around two people coming up – a boy and girl, arms around each other's waists, gazing into each other's eyes. Great! They'd probably end up *doing it* in Mom and Richard's bed, seeing as the other bedroom was occupied by the telephoning girls. But the action in the back yard was more important. She'd try and contain that, then rout the couple. She really needed Daniel's help.

In the living room, though, she encountered something even more disturbing than shouting boys. A guy was standing on the coffee table with a saucer in his hand, saying, "Wow, they've got Frisbees everywhere." He cranked up to hurl it, while several girls screamed.

"No!" yelled Flora. But he let it fly across the room, where it collided with the wall, then shattered. He gazed drunkenly at the spot where it had crashed. Two other boys now joined him on the table, each armed with a saucer. The first boy's saucer landed in some sofa cushions and he looked disappointed. The second boy's missile, however, sailed straight through the window overlooking the porch, producing a spectacular shower of breaking glass.

"Stop it you guys!" screamed Flora, above the screams of other girls. Some of her friends, similarly attired in nineteen-fifties cocktail gear, surrounded the table and began to berate the three. Flora turned to one of the original guests, her friend Nicola, and said, "We've got to collect all those saucers." Nicola nodded, her face pale and frightened.

Where the hell was Daniel? Flora ran outside where two boys were grappling on the ground, while others watched them struggle, beer bottles dangling from their hands. She realized that the music from the house was really loud out here. The neighbours would be seriously pissed off.

She ran back towards the study and the stereo controls, and in the hall encountered Daniel ushering the amorous couple out of the house. "You guys are gross," he said to them. "Trying to fuck in my parents' bed! Just get the hell out of here."

He stood a few inches from the guy, his body kind of bristling.

"OK, OK. Jesus!" mumbled the boy. "Let's go," he said to his companion.

"My purse is around here somewhere," she whined.

Flora grabbed Daniel's arm. "There's a fight in the back yard, and they're throwing saucers around the living room." Daniel loped off towards the back door.

She tried to get into the study to turn down the music but there was something wedged against the door. Suddenly, however, the music stopped entirely.

Relieved, Flora went to see how things were going in the back yard. Daniel seemed to have waded into the fight, and he was kicking one of the boys. "Get up and get out now," he said in a cold, sober, controlled voice that seem to cut through the collective drunkenness.

To Flora's amazement, the boys rolled apart. One of them lay on his back on the grass panting. The other scrambled slowly to his feet. "I mean it," said Daniel. "I will do something that will make you very sorry if you don't go the fuck home right now. It's over, man."

"OK, OK," said one of the witnesses to the fight. "We have another party to go to, anyway."

Flora hoped that the absence of music would have slowed down the tempo in the living room. Unfortunately, when she went to check it out she discovered that guests there seemed to have formed themselves into two teams positioned behind rolled-over sofas opposite each other, and were hurling saucers and beer bottles at each other over a no-man's-land of debris. The overturned salsa bowl created a large splotch on the carpet that looked like blood.

Then she heard the police sirens.

It was about three-thirty in the morning when Richard and Louise arrived back home. Shattered glass covered the porch. The front door was open, and in the living room Flora and Claire were on their hands and knees, scrubbing a salsa blotch on the rug. Flora looked up at her mother and burst into tears, her bottom lip trembling, her face blotchy, suddenly a child again. Louise ran to her and embraced her and began sobbing too. Richard turned away. Why the hell was she comforting the little brat! And where the hell was Daniel who was supposed to be house-sitting? "God I'm so sorry!" wailed Flora. Sorry! What good did *that* do?

Did that make up for the panicky exit from the inn, the harrowing drive back in the middle of the night wondering what horrors awaited them at home, and then the sight of their violated home?

Richard followed the sound of clanking bottles on to the back porch, where he confronted Daniel who was dragging a huge trash bag up the back steps towards the recycling bin. "What the hell happened?" barked Richard.

Daniel shook his head sadly. "Flora had a party and it got out of hand," he said.

"But you were supposed to be house-sitting, and she was supposed to spend the night at Claire's."

"Well what could I have done? Called the cops on her? The neighbours finally did that, but I couldn't have stopped her. It's her house too."

Richard wasn't quite sure what Daniel should have done, but he felt strongly that he should have done *something*.

Disgusted, he turned away and went back into the house to survey the damage. The girls seem to have done a pretty good job cleaning up, although the rug would probably have to be professionally cleaned. As far as Richard was concerned, that little expense could come straight out of Flora's allowance. As could replacing the window glass. Although maybe their home-owner's insurance would cover it. He looked into the garbage can under the sink and observed a pile of broken crockery.

Avoiding the living room – where Flora and Claire were still babbling at Louise, and the wailed phrase, "But they weren't even my friends!" was heard several times – Richard headed towards the study. He bet the little thugs had cleaned out his liquor cabinet. The idea of teenagers swigging his fifteen-year-old single malt whisky made him sick.

He pushed against the study door but it wouldn't budge. Sighing, he yelled for Daniel to give him a hand. The two of them strained against it for a while, and finally managed to get it moving. "I can't imagine what's stuck there," said Richard. He heard the sound of furniture feet scraping the polished floor, and wondered what their efforts were doing to the finish.

Finally, they got it open enough for the two of them to slide inside. The object against the door had been the sofa, but that hadn't been heavy enough to make it so hard to open the door. That mystery was solved by the fact that a huge kid – he looked to be about 250 pounds – was passed out on the length of the sofa. His mouth hung open. One arm dangled to the floor, and the other was wrapped securely around a bottle of lemon-flavoured vodka.

For a horrible moment, Richard thought he might be dead of alcohol poisoning, and envisioned the boy's family blaming and suing him for their kid's tragic, youthful death.

He was distracted from this thought by some papers rustling on the top of his desk. He looked over at the window, which was wide open, the breeze lifting the hems of the curtains.

Glancing sharply around the room, he realized that it all looked very different and strangely empty. The computer monitor was gone, and the other components too. So was his stereo, television and VCR. He ran to his desk. They got his laptop as well. Yanking open a drawer, he saw that a collection of gold coins his grandfather had left him had also vanished.

"Louise!" he shouted, working his way around the end of the sofa. "We've been robbed! They've taken everything."

Louise screamed and began running upstairs. "My jewellery!" she wailed.

Flora ran after her. "It's OK, Mom."

OK? What the hell did she mean? Richard was furious. It was *not* OK. He went back into the study. The fat kid was still inert on the sofa. "Get up!" Richard shouted, pummelling his shoulder. "What the hell are you doing in my house?"

The kid's eyes opened – small red eyes – and he mumbled, "What the fuck?" It was all Richard could do not to punch him right in the middle of his soft, weak, stupid face.

"What the hell happened?" he demanded, grabbing the kid by his shirt and shaking vigorously. "Who took all my stuff? And why are you here? Serving as a human doorstop while your little buddies left by the window?"

"I didn't do anything," said the kid blearily.

Louise and Flora's feet could be heard clattering downstairs. "Thank God," Louise said through the partially open door. "Flora saved our jewellery." They slid into the room around the sofa and looked around.

"The computer!" gasped Louise.

"And a lot more stuff besides." Richard turned to Flora and gave her a look of fury. "I hope you're satisfied! I don't suppose you know who left with our things, do you?"

"No, no," said Flora, visibly flinching. "God, of course not." She stared at the kid on the sofa. "Has he been here all along?"

"Do you know him?"

"He's in my American History class, and he's on the wrestling team. Justin something."

Justin, sitting up now and weaving a little from side to side, looked initially a little unsure about this fact but after a beat, he nodded in agreement.

"Things were pretty chaotic," said Daniel. "Anybody could have got out of here with all kinds of stuff because of all the distractions – people yelling and running around and stuff."

Flora closed her eyes in concentration. "I do know that I tried to get in here to turn down the stereo but the door wouldn't open. Then the music stopped. Daniel was in the back yard breaking up a fight. I was relieved that the music was turned off, but that must be when they disconnected the stereo."

"Someone ripped off your stereo?" said Justin with a confused frown.

"Yes, and presumably you were a witness," snapped Richard. "I'm calling the cops and I hope they take you downtown and rough you up in the elevator to get the truth out of you!"

"Hey, I was sleeping the whole time," protested Justin.

"Anyway," said Flora, "the cops were already here. They said they didn't care what had happened in the house – as long as everybody went home."

"What time is it?" asked Justin.

"About four o'clock," said Louise.

"Wow," said Justin, "it's *way* past my curfew. My parents will kill me. I gotta go. Sorry about whatever."

"Not so fast," said Richard. "I want him questioned."

"We know who he is," pointed out Louise, with an exasperated sigh. "Let him go home." Her eyes misted up. "Frankly, I just want him out of here. The feeling of invasion – it's so creepy." She started to tremble.

The last thing Richard wanted now was for her to get hysterical. He turned to Justin and shoved him roughly on one shoulder. "Get the hell out of here. Now!" he yelled, taking some satisfaction from the fact that he had at least been able to confront one intruder personally.

## 19

Danny struggled down Olive's rosebush-lined walk to the kerb with the plastic newspaper bin. From down the street, he heard the loud wheezing sound of the recycling truck's heavy brakes, and he started to run. On the top step, he tripped, and while he managed to regain his balance, the bin fell down the steps, disgorging most of its contents.

He scrambled around, picking up the pieces. The Sunday paper with all its advertising inserts had been on top. As he picked up one of them, he stopped and stared. It was a big, multi-page ad for Blakely Home Furnishings. He rolled it up and put it in his back pocket, and continued the gathering operation, then ran back to the porch for the mixed paper and bottles and cans, getting them to the kerb with a rattle of glass just in time. Then, he went to his room, sat on his bed, and unrolled the advertising insert.

It looked like a nice store. There were pictures of sofas and tables and lamps and things. Nothing cheesy. Danny had sort of imagined the place was a warehouse kind of operation with tacky stuff. Some of the pictures showed furnished rooms with people in them. There was one with a smiling couple sitting on a sofa drinking coffee. An Irish setter was lying on the rug next to them. Another one showed an older guy in a plaid shirt and khakis, reading in a big leather chair, with his feet up on an ottoman in front of a big bookcase. "Gear Up for Spring with Savings On Garden Furniture" was the caption underneath a summery scene of parents and some little kids sitting under a big canvas umbrella.

The pictures of happy people in beautifully appointed settings made Danny resentful. He wondered how the customers would feel if they knew that Richard Blakely, who was trying to project this harmonious, family-oriented image for his store, wouldn't even see his own son. Or that Mrs Blakely had called his mother a skanky, trailer trash ho. He bet she didn't talk like that in front of the customers.

The next page showed a toddler playing with a Tonka truck in his bedroom under the headline "Youth Furnishings That Grow with Your Child". Below it was a picture of a teenager sitting at his desk doing homework in the same room with the same furniture but with sports equipment lying around instead of toys.

When Danny looked at this picture, he had a physical reaction of surprise that set him tingling. The teenager at the desk doing his homework was Keith.

Or was he imagining it? No, he wasn't. He'd had his hair cut, and he was wearing a preppy outfit, but it was Keith all right. What the hell was *Keith* doing in his real dad's advertising?

It took Danny a while, but he finally came up with a plan, and he liked it a lot. He went back to the phone booth in the park, the one where Keith had first told him the bad news about his real dad, and where he'd called Mom that time. This time, he called Blakely Home Furnishings.

"This may seem kinda weird," he said pleasantly to the woman who answered, and identified herself as Doreen. "I'm calling about your advertising thing that was in the paper last week."

"You mean the Spring Flyer?"

"I guess. I was kind of interested in the picture on the back page, the youth bedroom set."

"Oh. Do you have a question about it?" Danny heard paper flapping. "I know we have one on the floor if you'd like to come in and take a look."

"Actually, I have a question about the kid in the picture, the guy doing his homework."

"What about him?" the woman sounded surprised.

"Well, I'm pretty sure he's the guy I sat next to at the movies, and when he left, I found his jacket. I didn't turn it in to the lost and found, 'cause I thought I'd catch up with him and give it to him, but he left really fast, so I still have it."

"Oh. Well, that's the owner's son," said Doreen, sounding disappointed he wasn't interested in buying furniture. "Hang on and I'll page him."

Keith had just finished muscling a heavy dresser into the back of the truck. When the other guys had asked him if he wanted help, he'd said no. He didn't want them to think that just because he was the owner's son he was some weak, wimpy, rich kid. He sensed they were just beginning to respect him.

"Daniel, it's for you!" yelled his supervisor.

Keith was surprised. Who had his number here? Maybe it was Louise. What would she want?

When he picked up the phone in the small office off the loading area, he heard Doreen say, "Hang on, I'll connect you."

"Hello?"

"Keith?"

Holy shit! It sounded like Danny Murdock.

"Danny?" Keith said.

"That's right." His voice didn't sound friendly. "I thought you were going to Canada."

"Hey! It's great to hear from you," Keith said enthusiastically. "I wondered what happened to you. I'm really glad you called. I wanted to be able to tell you some shit I found out."

"The lady at the store says you're the owner's son! What the hell is going on?" Now Danny Murdock sounded seriously pissed off.

"Oh, she's new. She probably just thinks I'm his kid on account of she's seen me come to work with your dad in his car. The fact is, I'm your dad's yard boy." Keith had once been in a foster home where he had been told he was to serve as a yard boy and, in fact, had been addressed as "yard boy" for two days until he hit his foster mother in the face with a rake and was placed elsewhere.

"Yard boy?"

"Yeah. I'm keeping up the yard and I wash the car and stuff. The thing is, I thought it made sense to stick around and find out how things were going. Kind of an undercover type of thing to keep track of our problem and all. So after I talked to them and called you, I went back to their house and said I was a homeless kid and I would work for food, and they basically let me be like a slave. I mean they feed me and I live in this little shack thing in the back yard, a garden shed, and I work here for real money sometimes."

"Wow. That is so weird," said Danny. He was silent for a moment then said, "Tell me what kind of people they are. Now that you know them better. I'd sorta like to know more about what—"

Keith cut him off, lowering his voice to a conspiratorial whisper. "We shouldn't talk on this phone." People were always picking up the wrong line around here.

"Where? When?" said Danny.

"I don't know. Is there a phone where I can reach you?"

After a pause, Danny said, "No."

Keith thought fast. "How about meeting at that place we slept in the park? When's a good time?" The little jerk was probably still living in the bushes.

"Um, I'm not sure when I can get away."

Maybe he wasn't living in the bushes after all. "Well, call me on the number I'm going to give you," said Keith. "Call me exactly at ten tomorrow morning." Flora slept in until at least eleven every morning, and Keith would make sure he grabbed the kid phone on the first ring.

It worked out nicely that Olive went to the dentist the next day around nine-thirty. It meant Danny didn't have to make some excuse about going for a walk and then go to the phone booth in the park.

He'd had some time to think about all this since yesterday when he'd called Keith at the furniture store. The whole thing was too weird. Living in a shed in the back yard? Was that legal? What kind of people were the Blakelys, anyway? There was something Keith wasn't telling him.

Danny had copied down the Blakelys' street address from the phone book. It was folded up in his back pocket right now. He had half a mind to just go over there, knock on the door and find out what the hell was going on. The number Keith had given him was different from the Blakelys' number in the phone book.

But he supposed he'd better call Keith first and hear what he had to say. There was no getting around the fact they were in big trouble. After all, Keith had hit those men. They had stolen two cars. Danny remembered the crowbar with the blood on it lying on the back seat of the Bronco.

Keith answered on the first ring and got straight to the point. "Well, the bad news is that the FBI guys keep calling the Blakelys, asking if they've heard from you. Apparently there are warrants out for you and for me, too."

"Then why are you still hanging out there?" Danny didn't think this made sense at all. "Aren't you afraid you'll get busted?"

Keith made a contemptuous snorting sound. "This is the last place they'd think of looking for me. Plus, being here, learning how the investigation is going is the smoothest thing I can do right now. I keep my eyes and ears open, and I find out where we stand. I'm doing it for both of us. And no one would think I'd stick around at my accomplice's parent's home." He gave a laugh of triumph.

"So what's the deal with my dad?" persisted Danny. "I want to meet him. You know, just come over like I'm your friend, and quietly check him out. Chill with you in your hut."

"No. Bad idea," said Keith decisively. "We can't risk it. At least not now. Hey listen, I need a way to get in touch with you. Like a phone number or an address or something. So I can keep you posted."

Danny did not want Keith to know where he lived. What if Keith came over? The idea of Keith, with his death's head tattoo, sitting in Olive's living room was just too weird. He certainly didn't want to give him Olive's number.

"That's kind of hard," he said.

Upstairs, Flora woke with the groggy impression that the phone had rung. But far away. And just once. God, what if it was for her and Daniel had got the call first? He was certainly capable of not passing on an important message. She looked next to her bed. The portable wasn't there. She knew she'd left it there last night. She'd had a long call with Claire from bed last night, seeing as both of them were grounded.

215

God! Had he come in to her room while she was sleeping? That really creeped her out. She grabbed her robe and pattered downstairs in her bare feet.

Keith was lying on the sofa in the living room, his feet on one arm, talking into *her* phone. And he was saying, "But you gotta understand, if we get caught we could go to the slammer. I'm not kidding. And the Blakelys will probably co-operate with the cops. I'm not in that tight with them."

For an instant Flora wanted to scream. Daniel was admitting he'd ripped them off! And talking about it to one of his sleazy little buds. She leaned over the sofa, ready to confront him, but he looked up at her in a way she'd never seen before, a kind of cross-eyed, startled but mean look, and she was suddenly scared and felt all prickly. Instead of confronting him with what she'd heard, she said, "Who said you could use my phone?"

Daniel smiled at her and made as if to pull at the ends of her robe sash. She leapt back. "Gotta go," he said cheerily. He clicked the talk button and handed her the phone with a little smirk. She grabbed it, ran upstairs and locked herself in her bedroom. Then she hit the star button and 69, so she could find out who had called. She carefully wrote down the number.

Flora stayed in her room with the door locked until she heard Keith slam the front door on his way out of the house. Then, she called her mother at work.

Keith knew what Julie would say if he asked her for more, and he was right. "Oh, for Christ's sake! You think I can get what people pay in a store for this? Jesus! If people want to pay what it costs in a store, they'll go to the store. Stupid kids!"

Keith and his friend, Josh, had taken a panel truck full

of the items from the Blakelys' house up north on the freeway, turned into Julie's driveway and then driven into the garage next to her sixties split-level house on a wooded lot in a quiet neighbourhood.

Julie was in her early forties, with long blonde hair, a lot of sooty eye make-up, and tight jeans. She had a lot of rings and long frosted pink nails and she frowned all the time, but Keith thought that was kind of cool. She had that mean look because she didn't want to seem too enthusiastic about any of the merchandise she was offered. He had met her once before, accompanying a new acquaintance on an expedition to sell a box of car stereo equipment, and some airbags, the priciest removable items from inside a car.

Once the vehicle was inside, Julie pushed a button and the garage door lowered. She turned on a bright light and gestured at the boys to open the truck.

Keith looked around the garage. There were stacks of computers and more electronic equipment, intermingled with ordinary suburban garden tools – a lawnmower and rakes with little bits of grass still clinging to them. He also noticed a box of Beanie Babies on a nearby workbench, and some china figurines.

Julie opened the little bag and looked carefully at the gold coins, and carefully bit one. She peered back into the van. "Everyone already has a TV," she said.

"Not one that good," said Keith. "That's top of the line."

"OK." She sighed. "Eight hundred for everything."

"Fuck you," said Keith cheerfully. "The coins are worth at least that."

"Fine, go sell them at some coin shop then. Eight hundred. Take it or leave it. And if you leave it, take all this shit with you. And don't say 'fuck' in my house again."

"This isn't the house, it's the garage," said Keith, trying to sound sassy, because he was embarrassed by the fact that she knew they'd take the money. She was already peeling some bills off a roll.

His two-thirds share was an OK start to his Las Vegas fund but the whole thing made him kind of sad, in a way. It was like she didn't have respect for the high quality of merchandise from his house, from his family. He had hoped for a thousand. People were always exploiting kids.

"So if you don't want TVs, what do you want?" he asked her as he pocketed the cash.

She shrugged. "Jewellery. Silver. Laptops. Collectibles. But no Beanie Babies. I got more than enough of those."

"How about guns?" said Keith jauntily. It irritated him that this woman didn't take him seriously.

"Yeah, OK."

"I may be in touch," said Keith importantly.

Flora didn't like the way this had developed. Mom was just standing there with a worried look, leaning on the counter with her arms folded across her chest, while Richard punched in the number on the kitchen phone. Why couldn't she have taken care of this at work? Or why hadn't Flora herself made the call? Now, Richard was involved and he sure as hell didn't want to believe that Daniel had ripped them off. The only good thing was that Mom and Richard hadn't kicked her out of the kitchen while they made the call.

"Hello," began Richard pleasantly. "My name is Richard Blakely and I'm trying to find out about an incident at our house this weekend. Do you have a teenager by any chance?"

He paused. "I see. Well, did this young man go to a party this weekend, do you happen to know?"

Another pause. "Well, could he have gone without your knowing? Maybe took the car after you were asleep?"

218

Another pause. "Or maybe he could have walked or taken the bus. Where do you live?"

"I see."

Flora bit her lip nervously while Richard was silent again, then he said in a flustered way, "I know. I apologize. I realize this is awkward. It's just that we think he may have been at the party and because some things are missing here, we'd like to know if he saw something." Richard was talking so gently and respectfully. Why didn't he just lay it out with these people?

"Those friends of Danny's got here around ten," whispered Flora impatiently. "Where was he at ten?"

Mom gave her a withering look for interrupting, but Richard was doing such a crappy job of checking this out! Flora knew why, too. If he told this person about the phone call and star 69, he'd have to admit his own kid was involved and he was too embarrassed to do that. "And the stereo stopped at about one. That's when it was stolen," she hissed.

Richard glared at her but he did say, in his same pleasant tone, "If he was here, he arrived around ten."

After a long string of "Uh-huh"s, and "Yes"s, he said, "Oh, I see," with a sense of finality. "Well, I'm sorry for bothering you. Yes. Richard Blakely. Maybe you could have a talk with Tony and see why he — that is, if he knows anything about this. I'll leave you our number."

Flora clicked her tongue contemptuously. She'd been right. He'd started to tell whoever was on the line that Tony had made a call to Daniel, but he'd backed off because that would be admitting his own son was some-how implicated.

"Oh," he was saying now, "well I got this number from another kid who was here, and thought that maybe it had something to do with the missing items." This was so lame.

219

"Yes. Well, I'm very sorry to bother you. Goodbye." He hung up and glared at Flora.

"That phone number belongs to a little old lady over on the corner of Argyle and Burke," he said in measured tones, only thinly veiling his irritation. "She's got a fourteen-year-old relative visiting but she says he certainly didn't leave the house on Saturday. At ten o'clock, he was watching a nature documentary with her on TV. It was about leafcutter ants, apparently. Then he was on the Internet until midnight when he brushed his teeth and went to bed, and then she remembered they'd forgotten to put out the garbage so she went into his room about half an hour later and asked him to put out the trash, which he did in his robe and slippers and then he went back to bed. She says she doesn't always sleep that much at her age and she stayed up reading for a couple of hours more and she would certainly have known if he left the house. She says there's obviously some mistake. This kid's from out of town and doesn't even know anyone in Seattle."

"But that kid must have called Daniel," said Flora. "And they were talking about the rip-off, I swear to God!"

"It's kind of embarrassing grilling a complete stranger like that," said Richard. "She acted like I was nuts. Are you sure you got the number right?"

"Yes!" said Flora.

Louise said, "Are you sure they were talking about the theft? It seems so unlikely."

"As far as I can tell, Daniel did what he could to protect our property," said Richard.

Louise turned to her husband. "But you will ask him about the phone call, won't you? It's kind of strange."

"Of course I will," said Richard irritably.

Flora hadn't been told the names of those friends of Daniel's at the party. She'd heard them talk to each other and vaguely remembered one of them being called Josh

220

and that another one was named Ben. But the name Tony didn't ring a bell. Neither of them looked fourteen either. And they sure didn't seem like the kind of kids who'd be sitting around watching a nature documentary with an old lady on a Saturday night.

They heard Daniel come in the front door, whistling. A second later he joined them in the kitchen, yanked open the fridge door and peered inside. "What's up, guys?" he said cheerfully.

"Daniel, do you know someone named Tony who is visiting a little old lady who lives over on the corner of Argyle and Burke?" asked Richard.

"No," said Daniel. "Who's he?"

"He called you here this morning," said Flora, tilting up her chin aggressively. "I star 69'd him and got his number."

"What?" Daniel gave her a puzzled look.

"Flora says you were talking to him about getting arrested for stealing our things," said Richard.

Now he glared at her. "You're crazy," he said. "I guess you're trying to get me busted because of *your* party."

"Did you get a phone call here this morning?" demanded Richard.

"Yes. But I didn't know the guy's name was Tony," said Daniel.

Flora's hands were in fists. "But I heard you say, 'If we get caught we'll go to jail and the Blakelys will co-operate with the cops.'"

"Oh, God." Daniel laughed. "That was just a joke."

"What kind of a joke?"

"Just a guy thing. You really don't want to know."

"Yes I do," said Flora. Let's see him get out of this one, she thought. God, he was a total psycho and he was living in their house. And her parents were just standing there like it was no big deal!

221

"OK, if you must know," said Daniel in even tones, "this kid called up and said he was a friend of my friend Josh, and he wanted Josh's pager number and I gave it to him and then he said he'd heard all about the party and Josh told him how you were all uptight and snobby, even though you were wearing this low-cut dress flashing your tits around, and this guy, who I guess is named Tony – I don't know – said it sounded like you needed to be taught a lesson for being a tease, and I bet you can guess what he said somebody should do to you, but I basically told him that if he did anything like that he'd have to deal with me and he'd be busted. OK. Are you satisfied?"

Flora burst into tears and ran out of the room and up the stairs, her mother following after her calling her name.

"Did you have to tell her that!" asked Richard after they'd gone. "God, Daniel! You just cannot speak to her like that. And in front of Louise, too! It's totally inappropriate!"

"She asked. I'm sorry, but if she's going to spy on people she's going to have to hear the truth sometimes."

Keith made a mental note to consult the big map posted in the delivery department at work and find out where Burke and Argyle were. So Danny Murdock was living there with a little old lady. That was pretty interesting.

"Look, try not to get Louise and Flora all riled up, OK?" said Richard. "They can be very emotional."

"I'm sorry, Dad," said Keith. "I'm trying. I really am."

"I know," said Richard.

"OK, so maybe you can choose to believe he didn't rip us off but, Mom, I still think we don't know the whole story. I still think Daniel *could* have been the one to tell those kids. I told you he wanted very specific instructions to the place in the park where they party. He could easily have gone there and told them." Flora stood watching Louise scrubbing the sofa in the study – where the 250 pound kid had passed out – with a brush and a can of foaming upholstery shampoo. Louise wanted all traces of intrusion gone.

"*You* gave the party. *You* are responsible," said Louise angrily.

"Will you ever trust me again? Oh, God, I feel so awful. Richard hates me. I just know he does. But I never meant for all those kids to find out. Someone snitched. Do you hate me too, Mom?"

"No, I could never hate you, but I hate what you did. I am very disappointed in you." Louise sighed heavily. "I never would have believed you would do such a thing. And as for all those kids from Madison High School standing around in parks drinking in the bushes, that's got to be busted up. Why didn't you ever tell me about that?"

"I don't know. It's a kid thing. I didn't want you to worry." Flora shrugged. "I try to protect you from some of the facts of life, OK?" Louise didn't respond to this, and Flora continued, "Anyway, you know that Daniel's creepy friends were here. Like that repulsive Josh. They were drinking too. I wouldn't be a bit surprised if they took that stuff. They looked pretty marginal. And the idea of that guy talking about me like that – it just makes me sick." She wrapped her forearms around her stomach and bent forward as though she were actually about to throw up.

"We've been all through this," said Louise. "I can't *believe* you're trying to dump blame on Daniel. From what I can tell, he tried to protect our home to some extent. You know he broke up that fight and kicked out some people."

"Yeah, I know." Flora sighed. "Are you going to tell Richard I think Daniel might be involved in at least telling people about my party?"

223

"No I'm not," said Louise, yanking up one of the sofa cushions. "He's already given me enough grief about the situation. If I tell him you're trying to blame his kid for one more thing, it will only make him more angry. Frankly, this has been a terrible strain on our relationship. You know that, don't you?"

Flora sighed again and said, "If I could go back in time and not invite those people over, I would. This has been the worst experience of my life. I'm probably a laughing stock at school, too."

"That should be the least of your concerns!" snapped Louise. She grabbed the other sofa cushion and flung it aside. Beneath it lay a man's wallet. She picked it up and opened it. There was a driver's licence for a Justin Kramer and a picture of that awful boy whose germs she was now scrubbing off the sofa.

She also checked the section where bills were kept. There was a twenty-dollar bill, and a small piece of paper with the Blakelys' address and a map, showing their cross streets. Underneath, it said "party" in capital letters.

What Louise found so startling about it, however, was that the piece of paper was from a Blakely Home Furnishings notepad with its familiar logo, a picture of the store, and the motto "Furnishing Northwest homes since 1902". Richard brought these notepads home from work, along with matching ballpoint pens, and they always kept one next to each phone in the house.

Keith stared down at the note that Richard was flapping in front of his face. "You tell me, Daniel. How could he have got this from anyone outside of our family?" he demanded. Keith was sitting on the sofa, while Richard paced around the living room. Keith wished Louise was here. That would have made it easier to work. He could hear Louise and

Flora fussing with dinner in the kitchen. Ever since she got busted, Flora had been following her mother around like some pathetic little dog that had been kicked.

"So, why do you think it was me and not Flora," Keith replied belligerently, sticking out his jaw. "I guess you just assumed *I'm* the bad one. Even though it was her idea to have a party. I guess you're more trusting of her than your own son."

"I don't want to give you my theories," said Richard sternly. "I want *you* to tell me the truth. Did you invite those kids?"

Keith figured they'd check the handwriting or something. Besides, they could probably get that fat Justin kid to tell them. There was only one way to go with this one now, and maybe it wouldn't work.

Keith let out a huge sobbing sound, then collapsed face down on the sofa and produced some heaves.

Richard stood there looking nonplussed.

One more big, loud sob, Keith figured, and Louise would come pounding in. She did, followed by Flora, both of them looking horrified.

Keith sniffed and sat up. "Yeah, I did ask some kids," he whimpered, when they were all gathered around him. "It was her party, but I wanted some friends. I thought it would get me some friends. I've been so scared about making friends." Louise rushed to his side, and he looked up at Flora. "You'd be scared too if you'd moved all the time." He flung himself on to a needlepoint pillow, and allowed his body to heave some more, while Louise lowered herself next to him on the sofa and stroked his back.

After a suitable interval, Keith righted himself again and dug at his eye sockets with his fist to produce some redness. He kept his head down as if he were ashamed he'd burst into tears again.

Richard pushed his wife aside and sat next to Daniel.

Louise and Flora backed away, towards the entrance to the room. Richard put his arm around Danny. "Listen," he said. "I know it's been hard for you. We've all been through a tough time."

"I've been trying," said Keith. "I swear to God. I don't want to mess up." Shit! Everything was falling apart. Keith figured he might have to split soon. He was busted.

"This is so pathetic," Flora said. "He admitted it! *Now* do you believe me?" Louise shushed her. Flora gave Daniel a look of utter contempt and stomped out of the room.

Richard patted his back, and said in a soft voice Keith hadn't heard before, "Daniel, I was going to make this a surprise, but I'll tell you about it now. On your birthday, after you go down and take the driver's test, I'm going to give you your present. It's a '67 Mustang that I'm buying from Peter in book keeping. It's in pretty good shape and it's got a V6. It's a safe car, and it's easy to work on."

"Wow!" said Keith, beaming happily at Richard.

"You'll have to pay for the insurance out of the money you make at the store. But it's a great car." Richard sounded eager. "I had one just like it when I was just a little bit older than you."

Keith gave Richard a big, grappling hug. "That's fantastic," he said. "Thank you, Dad." Keith couldn't split right away. He'd have to wait until Saturday. He wasn't leaving without that car. *And* a totally legal picture ID in the name of Daniel Murdock, who wasn't wanted for assault, and would only be sixteen which would keep him out of the adult criminal justice system for two whole years. Things were looking up.

Flora felt just the slightest bit disloyal to Claire sitting here in the coffee place on Capital Hill with Ingrid. It wasn't like she had to tell Claire everything she did, but when

Ingrid called to invite her, Flora realized it would be fun for just the two of them to hang out, so she hadn't told Claire, who she knew would have wanted to tag along.

"So, how's it going with the evil stepsibling?" Ingrid wanted to know.

Flora rolled her eyes. "He's completely conned my mom and stepdad," said Flora. "Even when it got proved he screwed up my party, they acted like he was some poor, troubled teen, and somehow I was the bad kid."

"He's so manipulative," said Ingrid, sipping her latte. "God, can't your parents see that?"

"I've tried to tell them, but they won't listen. Richard has my mom totally brainwashed."

"It sounds terrible," said Ingrid. "You poor thing."

"Do you think it will create problems for me at school?" asked Flora earnestly. "People knowing that I'm somehow connected to him?"

Ingrid shrugged. "If people are going to judge you by something you can't control, then they're shallow."

Flora nodded but didn't feel totally convinced. "Since the cops busted my party, I feel like people will think I'm a complete loser."

"No way," said Ingrid loyally. "Everyone knows that's not your fault. Everyone knows your stepbrother screwed you over. It'll just make people sympathetic. Anyway, it's good it happened at Spring Break because it's going to be old news when we get back to school."

"Really?" Flora felt a little hopeful.

Ingrid waved and yelled across the room. "Hey! Max!"

Flora was pleased to see Max, but still felt embarrassed in case he suspected that her stepbrother had stolen his wallet. She suddenly felt shy. Max gave them a big smile and came over to their table and sat down. "Hello, ladies," he said amiably. "Flora, it's great to see you."

Flora smiled and felt a lot better.

"Sorry I missed your party," he added in a teasing way that reassured her further. "I understand it was pretty exciting."

"It was *not* her fault the cops came," said Ingrid adamantly.

"Everyone knows that," said Max. "I can't believe that someone in your own family would rat you out like he did. It's evil."

"I wish my parents would send him to military school or something," said Flora. "Instead they think he's this pathetic victim of bad parenting and they want to help him."

"Even after what happened at your party?" said Max.

"He has them totally conned. If I discovered he was planning to shoot up Madison High School with automatic weapons they'd probably say he had adjustment problems and I shouldn't be so judgmental," said Flora. "There's not even any point letting them know what he's up to. Not that I know anything, anyway. He never has his friends over or anything."

"You've got to nail him on something," said Ingrid. "And open their eyes."

Flora smiled. "Interesting you should say that, Ingrid. Actually, when I was doing laundry I noticed he had a pair of jeans draped over the dryer. With his wallet in the pocket."

"Did you check it out?" said Max. "Look for signs of seriously criminal activity?"

"As a matter of fact, I did. And I found his fake ID."

"Did you tell your parents?" asked Ingrid.

"I'm kind of waiting," said Flora. "For the next time he tries to screw me over." Actually, Flora had decided not to do anything because she thought going through his wallet would look bad and maybe he'd start messing with her stuff, like her journal or something.

"To be really sneaky," said Max, "you could just leave it somewhere where they'll find it. Is it the kind with his real picture?"

"No. Just some guy from Arizona."

Max looked interested. "Is the guy's name Philip VanderGraaf?"

Flora's eyes widened. "That's right."

"That's my fake ID," said Max triumphantly. "I always thought he stole my wallet. That bastard!"

"God, I feel so bad," said Flora. "I'm sorry, Max. I brought him here and everything." She began to tremble.

Max put his hand on hers. "Don't worry, Flora. It's not your fault. I'm really sorry you have to put up with that guy."

"Me too," said Flora, looking down at their hands together on the table.

"I think I'm going to have a little man-to-man talk with him about my wallet," Max said thoughtfully. "Maybe I could say I'm coming to see you and then I can bring it up with him."

"Come on over anytime," said Flora casually. She made a mental note to clean her room in case Max kept his word.

There were four houses on the corner of Burke and Argyle, but it turned out to be pretty easy to find Danny Murdock. He was out in the front yard of a little blue house, cutting the grass with an old-fashioned rotary lawnmower. There was a weird canvas thing attached to the back of it to catch grass clippings.

"Hey, I guess you got yourself a yard boy gig too," said Keith.

"Keith! How did you know I was here?" Danny asked, leaning on the mower. He looked flushed and sweaty.

Keith stepped over closer to the younger boy. "So who lives here? You find someone to take care of you?"

229

"Kind of." Danny looked over his shoulder at the house. "Listen – about my dad – I need to know a few things about him. Maybe even meet him. But undercover, like."

Keith gestured over to the little blue house. "So you're living there now?"

"Kind of," said Danny.

"Anything good in there?"

"Huh?" Danny scrunched up his face. "You mean, like, to eat?"

"Yeah," said Keith. "To eat. I could use a snack."

"Not really. There's nothing."

"Let's take a look." Keith headed towards the front porch.

"You better not go in there," said Danny. "In fact, it's probably better if you don't hang around here at all."

Keith walked into the house, slamming the screen door. "I understand a little old lady lives here," he said.

"What?" Danny was clearly astonished that Keith knew this.

Danny caught up with him in the living room. Keith was standing in the middle of the room taking things in. "God, that TV is so damn old," he said. "Is she home?"

"No, but she'll come back any moment now," said Danny nervously.

Keith laughed as he went into the kitchen and opened the fridge. He reached inside and pulled out a quart of milk which he guzzled from the carton, then replaced, still open. "Cool," he said. "Pie." A lemon-meringue pie with two pieces removed sat on the top shelf.

"Hey!" said Danny. "You gotta get out of here. I like it here and I don't want to mess this up. Besides, if she comes back and sees you, then she's, like, witness to the fact that we're together."

"Things might be heating up," said Keith ominously as

he rummaged in a nearby drawer, coming up with a fork. He grabbed the pie tin and gouged away at one side of the triangular-shaped opening, helping himself to a few huge bites. "One of those guys is on life support." Keith slammed the fridge shut and stared at the lawn bowling tournament-schedule attached to the door with magnets. Next to it was a snapshot of Danny and a short old lady with a round face. They were standing on a green lawn dressed all in white.

"Is that the old lady? What's the deal with the white outfit?"

"We're in a lawn bowling league. That was taken at a tournament in Tacoma. Listen, Keith, you really gotta go."

"What the fuck is lawn bowling?" said Keith. Before Danny could reply he said, "Seriously stupid move having your picture taken when you're a fugitive." He shook his head sadly.

"I figured it was OK because it was a Polaroid," said Danny, acting kind of insulted that Keith thought he did something stupid. "No negatives. Listen Keith, you'd better go. Seriously." Keith could tell he was trying not to sound serious, and he strolled slowly into the hall, taking his time so that the little jerk would get even more scared. He peered into Danny's room. "Is this where you sleep?"

"Yeah. Come on, Keith. You gotta go, OK?" Keith noted with satisfaction that Danny was looking pale now instead of flushed. There was a computer in here. It looked brand new. It even had the box, sitting over in the corner of the room. That would make it more valuable, he guessed.

"I've been thinking," said Keith, turning to Danny and staring at him straight on. "I'm almost eighteen. They'd try me as an adult for sure. I'm thinking it makes more sense for us to say *you* hit those guys. You'd be tried as a juvenile.

You'd be out when you were twenty-one. Plus you'd do easy time in a juvie jail. I'd make it up to you later. It only seems fair, seeing as we were both in it together, that the person who can do juvenile time should be the one to go. Don't you think that's fair, Danny?"

"What are you talking about! *You* hit those guys."

"Well, in a way, yeah. But we're partners in this. Listen, Danny, it might never come up if I go ahead and take off. But for that I'll need some money. This time, I don't want to be scamming fat chicks in malls for credit cards."

He set down the pie tin, and moseyed back into the living room and eyed the what-not shelf full of china figurines. Ladies in big puffy skirts and men in wigs. "Collectibles. There's big money in that stuff. I know someone who wants collectibles."

"You can't take anything from here," said Danny with a fake laugh, as if Keith were joking. "That would be stupid."

"It's easy. You just unlock the door for me some time."

"What!"

"Oh come on! What's an old lady going to do? Does she have a job or anything? When's the place empty?"

"Never," said Danny. "Someone's here all the time. And anyway, she's a pretty tough old lady. And she's got a gun. There's a great big old revolver in the drawer next to her bed. Which she knows how to use. I wouldn't even think about messing with her. Now would you please get the hell out of here?"

"OK. But maybe I should take the gun now. That way she won't blow me away if I come back later. Do you have, like a backpack or something I can carry it in?" Keith went into the other bedroom. There was a set of matching furniture in dark wood. The bed was neatly made with a white, tufted bedspread. With Danny trailing after him, Keith went over to the bedside table and yanked open the drawer. Inside was a box of Kleenex, a bottle of aspirin, fingernail clippers and a necklace of amber and gold beads.

"So where's the gun?" demanded Keith, holding up the necklace and examining it. There was a gold cross at the end. He wondered if it was valuable, then dropped it back into the drawer. No point taking it now. Danny would get busted, and then who would let him in later?

He yanked back the bedspread and turned over the pillow, revealing a folded blue cotton nightgown. Maybe she kept the gun under the mattress.

From the window came the noise of a car pulling up. The engine stopped and they heard the ratchety sound of a handbrake being pulled.

"She's back! You gotta go. Right now!" said Danny, clearly terrified as he smoothed down the pillow and replaced the bedspread. "Do you want us both to get caught?"

Keith smiled, sidled over to the sash window, raised it and slipped out behind the sheer white curtain. "Later," he whispered.

Flora took a couple of Cokes out of the fridge. She thought about getting out glasses, and ice too, but maybe that would look too much like she thought it was a big deal he'd come by.

"You want ice and a glass?" she said.

Max was sitting at the kitchen table tipping back in his chair. "Sure," he said. "Gracious living. Why not."

She rattled the ice cube tray and said, "I'm sorry he's not here. I don't know where he is."

"That's OK," said Max. "We needed to talk about how to approach him anyway."

She handed him his glass and sat down beside him. "I'm really glad you aren't going to tell him I went through his wallet."

Max looked at her with a worried expression. "Just tell me one thing, Flora. Is it because you don't want to look bad, or is it because the guy actually scares you?"

"Maybe both," she said.

"You shouldn't have to be scared in your own house," he said. "That's really bad."

Danny, his heart pounding, locked the window after Keith. He knew that the car pulling up had been the people next door – their driveway was right next to this window. Thank God Keith believed that it was Olive! He just hoped no one had seen Keith leave by the window, but it was probably OK. There was a thin, scraggly privet hedge on the property line that you could only really see through if you tried.

He gave the bedspread an extra smoothing, made sure the drawer was closed completely, then went to his room and hastily removed the pie, which looked as if a rat had gnawed it. In the kitchen he trimmed the ragged edges Keith had left so that it looked like someone had eaten a normal piece of pie. There was no garbage disposal, but he buried the rough edges he had removed underneath some coffee grounds and a frozen-pea package in the garbage can.

How had Keith found him? How did he know an old lady lived here? Had he been stalking him somehow? And what would he do if Keith came back? Maybe he should move on and get out of there.

But he couldn't now. He had to stay here in case Keith came back. Danny remembered that crowbar with the blood on it. Could Keith hurt an old lady? Feeling sick, Danny felt sure that he would.

Maybe that story about Olive having a gun would slow him down. After all, even an old lady could blow you away if she had a gun. Shaking, Danny sat down at the kitchen table and put his head in his hands. Damn Keith! He had just walked in here like he owned the place. Danny hated him. He had already ruined his life, and now he was making it even worse. If only Keith were dead. That would solve everything. If he were dead, Daniel could say he got his memory back and blame everything on him. Keith couldn't try and get him to take the blame if he were dead. Danny wished Olive did have a gun. Then, if Keith came back, Danny could shoot him and say he was defending their house from a burglar.

Maybe a car would run over Keith right now. Maybe he was crossing the street at this very moment and a car was just about to run over him. That would be perfect. As far as Danny was concerned, it was the only reasonable solution to his problems. Filled with anger, Danny willed it to happen.

He heard the screen door open, and called out nervously, "Olive? Is that you?"

She appeared in the kitchen with a bag of groceries. "Of course, Tony," she said, sounding surprised. "Are you all right?"

"Yeah. I just came inside for a snack. I'll finish the lawn now." He managed a smile, and she set the grocery sack down on the counter and took out a package of meat. "I hope you like lamb," she said. "They had a special on some nice-looking chops." She opened the fridge, and said, "Oh good, I see you had some of that pie."

"It was great," said Danny, rising to go back outside.

"Oh, Tony, I got a strange phone call the other day," she went on, putting away more groceries. "Somebody wanted to know if I had a teenager here who was at a party last Saturday. Something about a burglary."

"What?"

"It was all clearly some kind of mistake. The boy they

were looking for was at their house the night we watched that show about the ants. I didn't quite understand why they called here."

"Weird," said Danny.

"He said his name was Blakely," said Olive, rearranging some cans of soup in the cupboard. "He seemed perfectly pleasant, but he sounded confused. I felt kind of sorry for him."

When Keith returned to the Blakelys', he discovered Flora sitting in the kitchen with the kid named Max.

"Remember Max?" said Flora, acting all friendly, presumably so the guy wouldn't know she was a snobby little bitch.

"Yeah, hi," said Keith, heading towards the fridge.

"How's everything going?" said Max.

"It's OK," said Keith, peering into the fridge. That lemon pie had been pretty good. There was never anything like that in this fridge. Just healthy shit.

"You know what I've always wondered?" Max went on, stepping towards him.

Irritated, Keith turned to face him. The guy was crowding him. "What?" he asked. "What is it that you've always wondered?"

"I've wondered if you stole my wallet," said Max.

"Hell, no," said Keith. He looked over at Flora. "Is that what you think? Is that what you told him?" he snapped. "You've been trying to get me in trouble since day one."

"No," said Max in a calm, phony adult tone, that Keith found infuriating. "She didn't tell me that. But I've been wondering about it myself. You kind of fell on to my sweater that day, and it was gone. I couldn't imagine how anyone else could have stolen it."

"You can't walk into my kitchen and start accusing me of

stuff and giving me your stupid theories," said Keith. "Get the fuck out of here." He had enough problems without these two fools bugging him.

"I didn't expect you to confess," said Max. "I just wanted to see your face when you denied it."

Keith turned and gave Flora a sleazy leer. "Or maybe you're really here to see if you can get Flora here to put out, and used that wallet thing to get into our house. Good luck with that!"

Flora let out a shocked little cry and Max pushed Keith's shoulder.

"Get outta my face!" said Keith pushing back. He didn't think the guy would start something right here in the house. Just then Louise walked into the kitchen carrying a bag of groceries. She looked alarmed.

Keith smiled at her. "We're just fooling around," he said.

"Yeah," said Flora. "You know how guys are, Mom."

Louise looked relieved. Good. Flora hadn't ratted. Keith had already figured she never told her mom anything that might make her upset or worried.

"Mom do you remember Max?" Flora asked.

"My gosh, it is you," said Louise. "I remember you from kindergarten and fifth grade. You're all grown up. Do you still play the clarinet?"

Keith turned back to the fridge while they all made polite conversation and Max sucked up to Flora's mom. In some ways he'd be glad to get out of this place. Finally, Max and Flora left and said they were going to take a walk in the rose garden near the park. Knowing Flora and her stupid friends, they probably were. That's just the kind of lame thing they would do.

"I can't believe it! You pay these guys home-owner-insurance premiums for years and years and years, and

237

then, when it comes time to collect, they just tell you to go to hell."

Richard and his brother were in Gordon's office, away from the stares of the employees.

"Gosh, you're not covered for any of it?" asked Gordon. "Even the stuff that got stolen?"

"He said they're not responsible for the activities of the guests of family members. Then the son-of-a-bitch hints that if I press this claim, they'll cancel me." Richard took on a prissy, parody voice. "'Frankly, an inability to monitor the activities of teenagers looks bad on your record,' he said. Can you believe that?" The cops had implied the same thing, indicating that his burglary case was a low priority because his children's friends had perpetrated it. The police officer had had the same superior attitude as Richard's insurance agent – a kind of world-weary, too-bad-your-kids-are-out-of-control contempt.

"What are you going to do, Ricky?"

"Flora says she can get a job at some juice bar near school, and pay us back." This, however, was more symbolic than anything else. It would take years, he figured. "And I've already arranged for some quotes for new home-owner insurance."

"I bet you feel like killing those kids."

"No kidding! Of course, if Flora hadn't started the whole thing, Daniel wouldn't have been tempted to invite some other kids. I can't imagine he knew how destructive they could be. Believe me, I'm beginning to wonder about Madison. I'm not sure it's the right place for Daniel. He's kind of sensitive underneath it all. He may need more individual attention."

Gordon didn't say anything, but rolled his eyes over in his brother's direction with what looked like a combination of pity and superiority. Richard, sensing that his brother thought his son was weak, added, "Of course, none of this would be necessary if I had raised the boy in the first place."

"Yeah, sounds like Wanda was a screw-up," said Gordon, sounding relieved that there was, as usual, an unreasonable woman to blame, deflecting any potential conflict between the brothers.

Richard, suddenly weary, leaned his chair back against the wall and closed his eyes. "God, it's all so exhausting, this kid stuff! And I didn't even know he existed just a couple of weeks ago."

"I know," said Gordon. "Everything's got very complicated."

"What a tangled web we weave when first we practise to conceive," said Richard, smiling at his own joke. "But you know, in a funny way, I'm starting to get it. I think I've been too hard on Louise, the way she makes such a big deal about Flora. Daniel was so excited about his car. I'm really looking forward to working on it with him."

The phone rang, and Gordon picked it up. "It's for you," he said, handing the phone over to Richard.

"Hello Mr Blakely. This is Donald Keene of Golden State Insurance."

"Well that was fast," said Richard. "I just started collecting quotes an hour ago. But I don't remember calling you." He was confused. Had one of the companies he'd called changed its name in a merger or something?

"A quote?" said Mr Keene.

"On my home-owner insurance," said Richard.

"There must be some mistake," said Mr Keene. "I'm calling on another matter entirely. I am not an insurance agent. I am an attorney, representing The Golden State Insurance Company. This concerns a criminal matter involving your son Daniel Blakely, also known as Daniel Murdock."

"A criminal matter?"

"Assault and car theft. Of course, if he is willing to be deposed in an upcoming civil matter, we may be able to avoid filing criminal charges against him."

## 20

Louise and Richard were in bed, whispering urgently in the dark.

"I'm thinking as Wanda and Carl got him into this mess, they should get him out," said Richard. "I'm also furious that he didn't tell us himself, right away."

Louise had had exactly the same thought. Shipping him back to California tomorrow would give her a tremendous feeling of relief. The whole idea that Daniel had had knowledge of the violent assault the insurance lawyer had described, and had kept it all inside horrified her.

And she felt very strongly that Flora had gone off the rails because of Daniel – not that he had meant to do anything harmful of course. But the shifting family equilibrium had probably rattled Flora to the point where she recklessly invited those kids over for margaritas. And then, because of his terrible insecurities, Daniel had invited those other awful kids. Life without Richard's issue-ridden son would certainly be less fraught.

But they had to do what was right.

"Think how it seemed to him," said Louise nervously. "He was scared. He probably thought you wouldn't take him in if he was in some kind of trouble. Shipping him back to them would send the message that no one really wants to help him work things through."

"Damn that Wanda," Richard said. "If I'd had some kind of influence from the beginning of his life…"

Louise was uncharacteristically silent.

"On the other hand," he said with an ironic little laugh, "maybe I should be glad I got off scot-free for as long as I did."

"Oh, Richard," she said sadly. She was disappointed by this irresponsible impulse, but she was also sympathetic. He had been put in a horrible position.

Now Richard was silent, and Louise went on, "I guess we should just do what that Keene guy, the insurance company attorney said. If Daniel simply tells the truth – that he was in the car the whole time and didn't see the assault behind the gas station, and that he was literally kidnapped by this Keith character—"

Richard snorted. "Sounds like kind of a Patty Hearst defence to me. But Keene made it pretty clear that if we don't place the burden of guilt strictly on this Keith Lloyd's shoulders, the insurance company will come after us."

This made Louise uneasy. They couldn't tell Richard's son to do anything sneaky or underhanded. That was another wrong message to send to a kid. "Well don't put it to him that way. Just tell him to tell the truth."

"The truth as he told it to us, anyway. Why couldn't he have gotten away from that guy?"

"Put yourself in his position. He was scared he'd be arrested or something. This Keith apparently convinced him he'd be considered an accessory. Maybe even go to an adult prison! And he couldn't trust Wanda or Carl not to ship him back to that awful desert camp thing. Keith had managed to put the fear of God in him about that, too. I hope that place wasn't as bad as Keith told Daniel it was, but it's clear Daniel believed him."

"That Keith sounds like a real piece of work," said

Richard. "A cold, manipulative bastard."

Louise had a sudden inspiration. "Maybe we should call Keith's parents. Maybe they could give us some insight as to what really went on."

"Forget it," said Richard. "Keene says we should have nothing to do with them. Their kid is scheduled to shoulder all the blame in this mess. Anyway, the little creep is apparently still at large."

"God," said Louise, her *Pollyanna* instincts bubbling to the surface. "We think *we've* got problems. How'd you like to be Keith's parents?"

Keith lay in bed, analysing his situation. It was only around eleven and he wasn't anywhere near sleepy, but he had to look really sorry, and sticking close to home for a while was the way to play it.

He was furious with the jerk who was suing Intervention Youth Therapies. If it weren't for him, the whole thing would have been forgotten, and he could have just moseyed out of here in his own good time, and no one would be looking for him. Maybe he should have finished the job behind that gas station.

It was pretty clear he was about to get seriously busted unless he got out of here soon. Those insurance company lawyers wanted Danny Murdock's deposition, either in person or on videotape, blaming Keith for everything, and the Blakelys were all for it so that they wouldn't get nailed. He wanted to be long gone by then.

Keith was also worried about Wanda. She could show up at any time. He had done a good job of stalling so far, but maybe Wanda would insist on talking to him or seeing him on Danny's birthday. She'd better not blow the whole thing before he got his car and licence.

That would be so unfair. Because there was no good

reason he shouldn't continue to be Daniel at least until he got that Mustang. He deserved solid, respectable parents with nice things, parents who didn't fuck up. He deserved that at least as much as Danny Murdock did. Danny Murdock didn't even know the Blakelys. Keith had been the one to find them and take the initiative to show up and take his place in the family.

Danny Murdock himself was also potentially big trouble. The lawyers were counting on him to blame Keith for everything. If only he'd gone over the cliff with that Bronco like it looked like he might have.

On the plus side, Keith knew exactly where Danny was. That gave him some control of the situation.

Hell, there wasn't much point lying here in the dark waiting to get busted. He should be doing something productive. Like getting his act together to build up his Las Vegas bank roll, and making sure little Danny Murdock didn't even dare think about coming around here and snitching on him to those lawyers or anyone else.

Keith figured he could work on both problems at once. He slid out of bed and slipped into his clothes, then opened the study window and slid out into the shrubbery that ran alongside the house.

Up close and personal, that was the way to handle it. It would be a lot easier to scare Danny in person. He'd seen how nervous Danny was when the old lady came back. He'd be even more nervous if she was right there in the house while Keith was there.

Tonight wasn't the night to get stuff out of the house, though. He'd have to work that one out. Which shouldn't be too hard. He wanted the computer in the box, all that collectible stuff, and the gun. And there was probably some jewellery and maybe silver. He'd never been inside any house where a woman lived where there wasn't at least some jewellery. Tonight, he'd set it all up and get Danny involved so that he'd take the blame if anything screwed up. He'd go back and pick it all up when the old lady was out and he had his car.

And while he was at it, he'd say that one of those guys he hit was dead. If Danny Murdock was going to blab about any of that, a murder charge ought to slow him down – at least long enough for Keith to get his Mustang and his licence and get out of town in style. Damn, he just needed a few more days.

Burke and Argyle was about a mile away. Keith wished he had a ride, but he set out purposefully. Soon, he'd have his own car, and about time, too. Every moment was bringing him closer to his goal. It felt good to have a goal and some plan for the future.

A few blocks away, Keith saw a kid's BMX bike just propped up against the side of a house. It was a good sign. He felt that he was being rewarded for his diligence. Thirty seconds later he was pedalling furiously down the street. Keith felt great. The evening air was cool and pleasant against his face. Life was full of challenges and opportunities, and he felt capable of achieving just about anything he set his mind to. He did a nice little jump off of a kerb and let out a triumphal whoop as the bike thudded back to earth.

Danny had lain awake in a state of panic for what seemed like an hour. If only there was some way to warn Olive about Keith without getting in trouble himself. He just couldn't imagine what that could be. He had toyed with the idea of calling the number Keith had given him and hanging up if anyone else answered. And if Keith answered he'd come up with some horrible threat to keep him away from here.

He'd rejected that idea on the grounds that Keith had stayed away for a few days, so maybe he'd forgotten about the whole thing. Calling him would just remind him of his half-hearted plan to rip them off.

Danny had also considered telling Olive everything, but he wasn't sure how she'd react. Old people were unpredictable. Why rush into something that could end up with his being in prison?

Keith wasn't being straight with him, that was for sure. First of all he'd said they'd both go to an adult prison. Then he barged in here and said Danny should take the blame because he'd go to a juvenile prison. Plus, he'd said he was some kind of slave living in a hut in the back yard. But Danny realized that Keith had looked pretty sharp when he'd showed up the other day. He was wearing really nice clothes – an Eddie Bauer shirt and Timberlake shoes. How could he afford stuff like that?

Danny began to realize that he didn't really know what was going on. All he really knew was what that psycho Keith had told him. The thing to do was to go over to the Blakelys' and scope it out. Then find out just exactly what kind of trouble he was in back in California. There had to be a way to do that.

God he hated Keith! Maybe he had been run over by a car the other day, just as Danny had willed. It would be fair and just if he had been. Danny remembered his mother telling him when he was little that if he didn't look both ways before crossing the street, a car would squash him like a bug. That's what Keith deserved. The idea of him just waltzing into the house and helping himself to their pie! And talking about ripping off Olive! As if Danny would just stand by and let Keith do that to someone in his own house! Danny couldn't let anyone hurt Olive any more than he would have let some kid hit his sister, Amy, in the playground, when they were both in elementary school.

And *what* was that phone call from his dad, Richard Blakely about? Where did he get the number? Danny had to get clued in to what was really happening, that's what it came down to. He'd start figuring out how to go about it tomorrow. He rolled over on to his side and curled himself into the foetal position. Suddenly, he felt better about everything.

He was asleep when Keith arrived, slid a screwdriver into the gap in the old sash window of his bedroom, and jimmied the flimsy latch. By the time Danny realized what was happening, Keith was sitting on the window-sill with his feet inside the bedroom, then leaning backward and sliding in.

"Jesus!" Danny said softly.

Keith put his fingers to his lips. "Shh," he said. He sat down on the bed and whispered, "We gotta talk. It's an emergency."

"Are you fucking crazy?" Danny whispered back. "Go. Now. Olive will wake up."

"So?" said Keith. "We can take care of her."

"I swear to God," said Danny, sitting straight up in bed, "you will get us busted."

"Oh, come on! What can she do? Whip my ass?" said Keith. "Now, listen. Two things. First of all, I want to come over here and clean this place out when you guys are out. I'll split the take with you. We need to leave town fast."

"Someone's always here," said Danny decisively.

"Bullshit! I've seen that schedule on the fridge, for whatever that kind of bowling it is where they wear those white outfits," said Keith. "Get it now. We'll pick a time."

"What if I wake up Olive?"

"Tell her you're getting a snack or something."

"What's the second thing?"

247

"Get the schedule, OK?"

Danny was silent for a moment and stared at Keith. Keith's slightly cross-eyed look made him look like a weasel. Danny bet that other kids had laughed at him when he was little, maybe even picked on him. "OK," he said. He got out of bed and crept to the door, but instead of going into the kitchen, he went into the living room and picked up the poker next to the fireplace, then went back to his room.

"Get out!" he yelled as loud as he could, bursting into the room. "Get out of this house!" He held the poker like a baseball bat.

"What the hell!" said Keith. Much to Danny's amazement, he looked frightened. He was in a half-crouch now, and he was holding a screwdriver in one hand.

"Tony!" yelled Olive.

"Run, Olive!" shouted Danny over his shoulder. "Call the cops from next door! There's a guy in here."

"You stupid fucker!" said Keith.

Danny advanced and swung the poker just like a baseball bat, aiming for Keith's head. Keith tried to fend him off and Danny got the satisfaction of driving the thing into his forearm.

"Ow!" said Keith, dropping the screwdriver and rubbing the spot Danny had hit. This allowed Danny a second try for Keith's head, and he connected. Keith fell sideways against the bed and started screaming.

"Get out!" yelled Danny.

"OK, OK," said Keith, backing up against the window and starting to climb back out.

Keith's head was outside the window and his stomach was on the window-sill. It was a stupid way to get out, but Keith was clearly panicking. Danny dropped the poker and grabbed Keith's extended legs, pushing him out the window as if he were a wheelbarrow. He was panting with

248

the effort but his adrenaline kept pumping. Keith seemed to be trying to wriggle out the window under his own power but it wasn't fast enough for Danny. "Get out of here!" he screamed, grabbing Keith's belt and shoving him through the window.

"Jesus!" yelled Keith, as the window sash fell down on his back. Danny yanked it back up and went back to pushing, until Keith fell head first to the ground.

"Tony!" shrieked Olive.

"It's OK," said Danny. "I threw him out." He felt like laughing. Keith looked so ridiculous going out that window head first and then taking a dive into the garden bed below.

"The police are coming!" Olive shouted. Carrying the poker, Danny ran out the front door and through the living room where Olive stood holding the phone. She spoke into it. "He's gone," she said. "Apparently he was thrown out of a window. Oh no, just a first-storey window. The young man who lives with me says he threw him out. Tony! What are you doing? Tony, the lady at 9-1-1 says not to go outside!"

Danny ignored her and ran around through damp grass in his bare feet to his window. There he saw a bike lying in the grass, but no sign of Keith. He was completely wired now, his heart was pounding and he was tingling all over. He wanted to find Keith and really let him have it with the poker. But as his breathing became more normal, he realized that it was a good thing Keith had run away. Now he had to hope the cops couldn't catch him.

Louise said, "Daniel, I think you should see a neurologist." She was dabbing at the gash on Keith's head with disinfectant while he stared at his reflection in the mirror above the bathroom sink.

"A neurologist? For a cut on the head?" said Richard, who was watching the procedure.

"No, for sleepwalking. It's scary. How often does this happen?"

Keith shrugged. "Not very often. Just when I'm majorly stressed." They seemed to be buying it.

"Why didn't you wake us up?" asked Louise. "I can't believe you just went back to bed."

"I figured I'd caused you enough trouble lately," Keith replied mournfully.

"So let me get this straight," said Richard. "You woke up after you fell."

"That's right. My head was on the bottom step in the front hall."

"And you just went back to bed?"

"Yeah. I was pretty groggy." He smiled at Louise. "I'm sorry about all that blood on the pillow slip."

After jumping a few fences, with the sounds of police sirens, crackling radios, and alarmed neighbours in the background, Keith had managed to make his way back home and get himself tucked back in by about two in the morning. He hadn't made any effort to clean the wound or bandage it.

What a fucking disaster. Danny Murdock had totally flipped. The guy was nuts coming at him like that. Keith hadn't even had a chance to scare the shit out of him by telling him one of those guys was dead, just to make sure he didn't snitch. Not only did Keith ache all over, he felt at the mercy of a volatile hysteric. Danny Murdock had been willing to risk his getting arrested. This was not a good sign. The kid had to be brought under control somehow.

"Are you sure you don't remember who you are? Please Tony, tell me the truth. There's something you're not telling me." Olive stood facing him in the living room, her arms crossed, her tone cold.

Startled, he stepped back from her. "No. I'm sorry. I really don't remember."

"The man from the burglar alarm company said it was very unusual what happened. An intruder coming into a room where someone was sleeping. Are you sure you didn't know him?" She stepped towards him and this time he stood his ground.

"I'm positive!"

"You were very brave, incredibly brave. Reckless! Are you sure you didn't know that person?" It had occurred to Olive that going after someone you knew with a poker was a lot easier than going after a stranger who had penetrated the house.

"Positive!" His eyes went blank as he stared back at her. She'd seen that dead-eyed, closing-down look before and it made her furious.

"If you're lying, Tony..." Olive hadn't felt this angry in years. She'd tried to help him and she felt betrayed. There hadn't been phone calls about burglaries or teenagers crashing into the house before he'd arrived.

"I wish I could remember. I'd tell you everything," he said frantically.

She put her hands on his shoulders and stared into his eyes. "We're going to have to go to the hypnotist."

"OK. Whatever." His affectless tone maddened her. Suddenly, she grabbed him and started shaking him as hard as she could. He looked completely shocked. Horrified, she let go.

"I'm sorry, I'm sorry," he said, tears welling up in his eyes. He was trembling.

She stepped back. "No, no. I'm sorry," she mumbled. "Please forgive me."

What had she done bringing this boy into her life? What had made her think she could help him? She must be crazy.

After Olive lost it and shook him, Danny crept out of the house. Was she going to throw him out? But if she did, she wouldn't be safe. He had to make sure Keith kept away. He had to do it now, because if Olive threw him out, he wouldn't be there to protect her.

If she let him stick around until they went to the hypnotist, he'd choose that moment to come up with a version of the real events that ensured he'd stay out of trouble. He could do it. He'd have to do it.

He was less worried about it now, because after the cops came the other night, and congratulated him on chasing the intruder away, he realized they didn't know or care who the hell he was. He'd completely relied on Keith's version of events, but now it looked like Danny wasn't a wanted fugitive at all.

After all, he'd never been in trouble before. Keith, he felt sure, based on his knowledge of the criminal justice system, had. Danny would say he'd been kidnapped by Keith, and struck by him on the head causing amnesia. It was all true except for the amnesia part.

If they asked him about the mall and the credit cards he'd say he didn't remember a thing. If they got those girls to testify, he'd say Keith threatened to kill him.

He went straight to the phone booth in the park and once more called the number Keith had given him. He was elated when Keith answered. But a little scared, too. What if Keith came back to get him after what he'd done to him with the poker? The first thing Danny did was to make sure he sounded apologetic. "Listen," he said, "I'm really sorry about what happened last night. The thing of it is, when I went out to get the schedule, I saw the light on under her door. She was already calling 9-1-1. I had to make sure you got away."

"Jesus, you didn't have to hit me," Keith retorted. "I thought you'd flipped." Keith sounded like a whiny little kid.

"Hey, I'm really sorry," said Danny, adding in a slightly patronizing tone, "really. Think about it. I had to make it look realistic."

"God, I was bleeding and everything." Keith actually sounded a little pathetic. Danny remembered with pleasure the time he'd finally screwed up the courage to punch Dylan Esposito, the worst bully in the third grade, right in the middle of his face. Dylan's nose started bleeding and his face turned all pink and he started bawling.

Danny continued. "But listen, any chance of ripping off Olive is gone. After what happened she's installing a state-of-the-art burglar alarm system today." This was actually true.

"Bummer," said Keith.

"Plus, she's getting a trained attack-dog," added Danny, hoping this lie wasn't overkill. "So forget about it, OK?"

"Sure," said Keith. "But listen, we've gotta talk. Can we meet somewhere safe and private?"

"What do we have to talk about?"

"I got new information," said Keith. "Let's meet where we camped out that first night. Can you find it?"

"Sure. How about Saturday morning at about ten thirty? I can get away then." There was a lawn bowling tournament at eleven just next to the glade in the park. He could say he was going early to practise. He wondered what Keith would have to say, and whether he could believe any of it. Whatever it was, it might come in handy when he broke down at the hypnotist's and came up with his version of events. It wouldn't hurt to listen to what the guy had to say.

He hung up, slightly reassured that Keith wasn't planning to come back any time soon. He was also nervous about going back to Olive's. He didn't know quite what to expect.

When he got home, she was sitting in the living room, as if she had been waiting for him. "I'm sorry, Tony," she said. "I just had this awful feeling you were lying. I hate lying. And sometimes I have a terrible temper."

Danny wasn't about to admit that he had lied right now. He'd wait until his hypnotist appointment. Then he could get out of the whole thing gracefully. He hadn't had any choice but to lie. He was too scared not to.

But in a funny way he understood that Olive would be mad at him for lying. She had gone to a lot of trouble for him, and if she found out he was jerking her around with his amnesia story, she'd feel like a sucker. "It's OK," he said. Being shaken hadn't really hurt, but it sure had startled him. "I'm just sorry you think I'm lying. If I knew who I was, I'd tell you all about it," he added with a kind of desperate edge to his voice. "I swear to God."

Danny remembered she'd said she'd hit some eighth graders on the hand with rulers when she was a principal. "Is that what happened when you were a principal?" he asked. "Did you sometimes lose it?"

Maybe this was why she wasn't a nun any more. Danny was fascinated. He'd never met anyone who'd hit a kid before. He'd never been hit himself. Carl raised his hand in a vaguely threatening gesture once in a while, that was all. Danny always smirked and said, "Go ahead, and I'll call the child abuse hotline."

"No one minded so much back then. People kind of expected it. The parents didn't seem to mind, anyway." She sighed.

Danny had a sudden inspiration. He would pretend to have another one of those little flashes like he'd done outside the neurologist's office that time. She'd been so pleased with him then. Maybe she'd get excited and be friendly again. And maybe he could bring the conversation around to the fact that she was a nun, and he could find out more about it. He'd hinted around a little, but she always side-stepped the whole thing when he asked her about her past.

"Wow!" he said with a big wide-eyed look. "I just had another little flash. About my mom. Remember I said before I had a little flash of her? That she yelled a lot?"

"Yes, of course." Olive leaned forward with her shiny green-eyed look.

Danny closed his eyes as if he were concentrating. "Something tells me my mom went to Catholic school. Suddenly I remember someone telling me some of the nuns were nice and some were mean, and I think it was my mom."

"I imagine most of them were nice some of the time and mean at others," said Olive. "Like everyone else. Just because they felt God called them to serve Him doesn't mean He made them perfect."

Danny opened his eyes. She was smiling at him, and he smiled back. She hadn't smiled since before she'd started shaking him. And she was talking about God without sounding embarrassed. This was kind of interesting.

"Oh, Tony, I'm so glad you remembered that little fragment. Maybe everything will be all right soon. But what an odd memory to have pop up."

"Well, we were talking about schools and stuff."

"Yes, but I never said I taught in a Catholic school, did I?"

"No. But you never said you didn't. Did you?"

"Well actually, I did. First I taught, then I was a principal."

"Were you a nun?" asked Danny.

She was silent for a second, then she said, "Yes I was, but I never tell people."

"Really? How come?"

"Because they tend to judge you. If they aren't religious, they think you are an oddball or fanatic of some kind. And if they are practising Catholics, they think you let down the church and God. I don't tell people about it because I'm afraid of what their reaction will be."

"Oh," said Danny. "I can see that."

"It's a little like lying," said Olive. "People usually lie because they are afraid. But it's still a lie, just like other kinds of lies. So, when you asked me directly, I told you."

What was she trying to tell him? Of *course* he'd lied because he was scared. But he was going to put all that right very soon. Well, he wasn't going to just sit here and let her stare him down until he cracked. He put his arm on the back of the sofa and said casually, "So, how come you aren't still a nun. Did you retire?"

"It's not quite like that. You can't retire. It's more like getting a divorce than retiring. One day I just knew I shouldn't be where I was. It's happened to a lot of people. You don't always know how things will end up."

"I hope you don't mind my asking."

"No, Tony. I don't."


*Dear Danny,*

*I've begged you to talk to me. I've tried to respect your wishes. I've talked to my new therapist about this and, while she says I should respect your privacy, I can't take it any more.*

*Our entire family is torn apart. Amy is upset. Carl and I are having a trial separation. Last week he moved into your room and this week he moved in with his cousin Ed in Palmdale. I've been very stressed, and I've gained ten pounds with stress. I worry night and day about you, although it now looks as though you are not in any legal trouble over what this horrible Keith has done and there won't be any criminal charges for you — just Keith. I've apologized for letting Carl send you to that place. I want to apologize in person. I've decided I have to come up and see you.*

*All I ask is an hour at the airport. I'm coming up on Saturday, a special day in my heart, on the United Shuttle, arriving at the Seattle Airport at 8:56 a.m. I hope to see you there.*

Damn. She was coming up for Danny's birthday. Keith hit the reply icon, and typed,

*Mom. Don't come. I don't want to see you. Just leave me alone. I need more time to work through my issues. I mean it. It would be the best birthday present you could give me.*

"Dad?"

"Yes, Daniel?"

The two of them were in the car, driving to Blakely Home Furnishings, where Keith would soon go out on his first delivery. No more wrapping stupid furniture legs and table-tops. He was wearing his new uniform, a perky green coverall with "Daniel" embroidered on one pocket, and a patch with the Blakely logo on the other.

"There's something I want to tell you about Mom."

"What is it?" Richard glanced over at him, but he was turned away, looking out the passenger window. There was a pause. Richard turned down the radio.

Keith sighed. "I'm afraid she's really crazy."

Richard could well believe that. "She was always highly

strung," he said solemnly. Richard had developed the habit
of referring to Wanda as if she were a known quantity, a
significant person in his life, when in fact, she was mostly
a blur. But to indicate that seemed to trivialize Daniel,
somehow, and make Richard seem like a promiscuous
sleaze-bag.

Keith went on. "Lately, those e-mails she's sent, well,
they sound to me like she's totally lost her grip."

"What do you mean?"

"Well, once before, when I was little, she had to go to the
hospital. She had all these wacky ideas. She thought people
were trying to get her and stuff. And she thought I wasn't
really me, that I'd been replaced by a robot or something.
She yelled at me 'That's not my son'. It was pretty scary."

"What?" Richard had known Wanda was highly strung
and prone to hysteria, but he'd never dreamed she was a
full-blown nutcase. That must have developed later. "I had
no idea!"

"It kinda comes and goes. It's just that, judging by some
of the e-mails she's been sending, I think she's off her
rocker again."

"Well, surely her husband can get her some help! Isn't
there medication or something?"

"Carl? What a joke! He just ditches out when it gets
bad. I suppose I should be there to take care of her, but I
can't stand it any more. I really don't want to talk to her, or
have anything to do with her. I don't want her stalking me
or anything."

"Stalking you?"

"She says she wants to come up here and grab me. Can
we keep her away? With some kind of court thing or
something? Seriously. I don't want her around."

"I suppose so." Richard was bemused. "Why didn't you
tell me this before?" he asked.

"I just didn't want to tell you. It's hard to admit, even to yourself, that your mom is completely nuts. But I'm afraid she is."

Richard decided he'd have to talk this over with Louise. And possibly a lawyer. There was no way he could let his son go back to live with a complete psychotic. He'd have to go for full custody.

## 21

On Saturday morning, Flora and her mother hung a large paper banner on the front porch, where Daniel would see it when he came home. He had left early on a mysterious errand, before anyone had even had a chance to wish him a happy birthday, with a note saying he'd be back to take his driver's test that afternoon.

Louise was standing on a chair, adjusting the tape, and Flora stood below, squinting to see if it was straight. The banner read "Happy Birthday, Daniel". Flora thought it was a corny idea, but Mom seemed hell-bent on making a big deal out of the occasion. A cake was baking in the oven, and there were wrapped presents – more new clothes and a new backpack for when school started on Monday – sitting on the coffee table in the living room. Richard was out picking up the Mustang, and planned to gift-wrap the keys as soon as he got back.

"I can't believe his mother hasn't even sent a card," said Louise. Her voice dropped to a whisper. "But apparently, she's practically psychotic." Louise hadn't planned to share this with her daughter. Richard had asked her not to, which she had found difficult. In fact, she was pretty sure she would break down further, and provide more details with the slightest encouragement.

"Really?" said Flora. She gave the banner the thumbs-up sign.

Louise descended from her chair. "She's actually been delusional. Hears voices. Says there are conspiracies against her."

"Wow!" said Flora. "You mean like UFOs are after her or something?"

Louise leaned towards her daughter. "At one point, she apparently claimed that Daniel wasn't her real son and someone had replaced him with a robot."

Flora's face took on a fascinated, thrilled expression. "My God! Has she been hospitalized or anything?"

"No, but it sounds as if she should be. Apparently Carl is in complete denial. Richard's very upset about it."

"Does this mean he'll never send Daniel back to her?"

Louise sighed. "I don't know. I guess we'll have to play it by ear."

Keith hadn't been able to figure out any way of getting a physical description of Wanda, but in the end it worked out OK at the airport. For one thing, while most of the disembarking passengers seemed either bored or happy to arrive, Wanda was searching the area in a panicky way. She was a big, soft-looking woman in a long, flapping denim dress, wearing sandals, and carrying a big straw purse over her shoulder.

When Keith approached her and said, "Are you Danny Murdock's mom?" she clutched his forearm. "Yes! Is he here?"

"I'm a friend. He asked me to tell you to get back on that plane and go home. You're not wanted. He needs his space. 'Tell the fuckin' bitch to leave me alone', that's what he said to tell you." Keith delivered all this in a menacing deadpan tone.

"Who *are* you?" she demanded. "Danny would never say that to me."

"Not only would he, he did. You and Carl treated him like dirt. He told me all about it. I suggest you get on that plane and go home."

Wanda burst into tears, and Keith, running late and worried that they were attracting attention, slipped away through the crowd. Damn! Why couldn't this woman just back off until he got his car!

After he had left, Wanda pulled herself together and went and sat down in a moulded plastic chair. This was not acceptable. She was simply not going to be turned away like this. She had Richard's address. She would rent a car and go straight to his house. They would have to work out some reasonable custody and visitation arrangements. Keeping her from her boy was cruel. And on his birthday, too! He was probably being brainwashed.

She hardly remembered Richard, and had never met his wife. What kind of people were they? They could be monsters. In fact, it seemed likely that they were, not allowing her to speak to her own son.

And that creepy kid who had met her plane! Definitely not the kind of kid Danny should be hanging out with. What was the matter with Richard and his wife?

She went to the ladies room and rinsed the tears off her face. They had made her skin red and blotchy. She didn't want to look demented as she tried to rent a car or when she arrived at the Blakelys'.

The little glade, where they had slept that first night in Seattle, was much less ominous by day. Some pale pink rhododendrons had just come out. Danny sat waiting for Keith on the bench nearby. He was in his white lawn bowling uniform.

While he waited, he thought about Keith living with his

real dad. The more he thought about it, the more pissed off he was. If someone was going to be a yard boy and hang out in Richard Blakely's garden shed, it should have been him, not Keith. He was the guy's real son.

Keith came into the glade and sat down silently next to him on the park bench. Danny was again struck by Keith's changed appearance. His long hair was now cut neat and short, and he was wearing expensive-looking, very un-gangsterish clothes – khakis and a blue Tommy Hilfiger polo shirt.

"I see you've got some new clothes," said Danny sarcastically. "I guess the Blakelys dress their slaves pretty nicely."

Keith shrugged. "I bought these with the money I make at the furniture store."

Suddenly Danny noticed the red scab on the side of Keith's head, and was both thrilled and horrified to see the damage he had done. "Hey listen, I meant it on the phone the other day," he said. "I'm really sorry I hit you with that thing. Like I said, I thought I had to in order to make it look good."

Keith waved his hand dismissively. "Big deal. I've been hurt a lot worse than that. It's nothing compared to what we're facing now. Nothing."

"What do you mean? What's the big deal?" asked Danny.

Keith raised his head and gave Danny a piercing stare with his slightly crossed pale blue eyes. He lowered his voice to a whisper. "The big deal is that one of those guys died. We're wanted for murder!"

"What?"

"I swear to God." Keith looked down at the ground. "It's a pretty weird feeling knowing we took a human life. Life is hella weird."

"*We?*" yelled Danny. "*We* took a human life?"

263

"Well, you drove the getaway car," said Keith. "Your ass is on the line too. Just stay away from the Blakelys. And don't call your family in California, either."

## 22

Danny was trembling uncontrollably by the time he walked back into Olive's house. He was frightened, but he was also angry. Why should he have to be accused of murder? He was just sitting there in the car when Keith hit those men! Suddenly, the whole thing seemed ridiculous. And why should Keith, a killer, be allowed to go free, living at his dad's?

Killers weren't supposed to go free at all. For the first time, it occurred to him that Keith should be in jail. To protect people. People like those men. And like Olive. And maybe him. Danny was furious and imagined himself kicking a fallen Keith sharply in the ribs. In his vision, Keith was down on the ground in the dirt, his knees drawn up, his face frightened.

In the kitchen, Olive was sitting at the table reading the newspaper and drinking coffee. She had changed into her white skirt and polo shirt in preparation for the tournament.

She looked up over her reading glasses. "Hi, Tony," she said. "Have you eaten?"

He stared back at her with a slightly wild expression. He knew he should answer her but he was too agitated to form a sensible reply.

She stood up, her face serious. "You've remembered. You've remembered, haven't you?"

He nodded. "My name is Danny Murdock and it's my birthday today and I'm wanted for murder."

As she drove up the freeway, Wanda managed to calm herself down. There had been a lot of misunderstandings and hurt feelings, but she felt sure that as soon as she and Danny laid eyes on each other, all would be well. She had his birthday present with her, a new computer game that Amy had said he'd been talking about, and she would explain that Carl was on his way out of the picture, and that she had had lots of time to think about him while he'd been gone.

The upshot of her thinking about her son was that she had decided he wasn't such a bad kid at all. All the trouble seemed to start when he got that one inch taller than Carl, and started ignoring him. Well that wouldn't be a problem any more.

She glanced out of the car window as the familiar landscape of firs flickered by. She'd liked it here. This was where her son had been born, and where she had met Carl and married him. She wished Carl had never been transferred down to California. Everything had been so peaceful here when Danny was an adorable little toddler.

"No answer." Olive put down the phone. "Well, if your mother in California isn't around, I think we should take you directly to your father. Especially after what you've told me about this Keith person actually living there." Danny had told Olive that he had run into Keith in the park and that had jogged his memory, and that Keith had brought him up to date.

"You mean just go over to the house?"

"That's right." Olive's jaw was thrust out in a way he had only seen before on the lawn bowling green. She grabbed her purse, and was pawing through it looking for the car keys.

"But what if I get arrested?"

"Don't be silly! If what you say is true, that other boy should be arrested. You are a witness to a crime. Since this boy has confessed to you, you are duty-bound to come forward. Saying nothing makes it much worse but that wasn't your fault, because you couldn't remember. Now that your memory has come back, we must act immediately."

"Well maybe we should just call the cops," said Danny.

"I feel you should be in your parents' care before we call the police. They would want to take care of you at a time like this. Now that I know who your parents are, I'm going to get you back together with them right away. I want to hear what your father has to say about all this."

"But what if he doesn't want me?" He was following her out to the kerb now.

"Then he is not worthy of you, Tony, and we will have to get your mother on board. Or proceed ourselves. Now get in the car."

"OK," said Danny. Olive made it all sound so simple.

"And when we get there," said Olive, a determined gleam in her green eyes, "let me do the talking. The last thing we want to do is tip off this Keith and let him get away. I'd like to ask that young man a few questions."

Wanda Murdock had no trouble finding the house. Although her sense of direction was poor, the Seattle topography had come back to her immediately. She pulled up in front of the house with a lurch. The unfamiliar brakes grabbed. She parked behind an old Mustang that looked just like the one Richard had owned when she had first met him. Awkward in her haste, dragging the straw bag with Danny's birthday present behind her, she clambered out of the rental car. It was a fire-engine red Ford, absurdly vivacious for such a sad errand.

Richard lived in a pleasant-looking house behind a low brick wall. A wrought-iron gate allowed a glimpse of a pretty garden. On the front porch hung a banner that read "Happy Birthday, Daniel". This sight brought tears to her eyes. Would she have done that for him? Had she taken him for granted? Had she been kind enough to Danny before all this happened? Was all this her own fault?

She pushed open the gate, which squeaked ominously, rushed up on to the porch and pounded on the door before noticing there was a doorbell, which she also rang. She was now flushed and nervous. Her heart thumped. She heard footsteps approaching the door.

When Richard opened the door, his first impression was that he knew the person standing there but was unable to put her in context. His second thought was that the woman he was looking at – a flushed, ample, previously pretty blonde – was terribly upset, if not on the edge of hysteria. His third thought was the realization that he was looking at Wanda, a middle-aged Wanda, wider everywhere – across her face and body and cheekbones. The fact that Wanda had seemed to spread sideways, and subsequently appeared bulkier, made her appear more formidable, and her tear-glazed, wild, blue eyes frightened him.

"God," he said in a hushed tone, stepping back.

Wanda took his retreat as an invitation to enter and stepped forward into the hall.

"Where's Danny? I just have to see him." Her tone was shrill.

"He's out," said Richard. Louise came from the living room, and from behind him he heard the thump of Flora's feet on the stairs. The footsteps stopped halfway down, so she was presumably hanging over the banister goggling at the intruder.

"What is it?" asked Louise, staring at Wanda and taking Richard's arm. He felt like shaking her off. It was as if he wanted his arms free so he could beat off Wanda if she came further into the hall.

Wanda turned to Louise. "It's my son's birthday. I have to see him," she said in a calmer, insinuating, woman-to-woman tone. The shrillness had vanished. Now there was the soft but firm confidence that Louise would understand a mother's feelings, and behave accordingly. The wild look in Wanda's eye faded, replaced by a sentimental, dog-like expression. Her head shifted from an aggressive verticality to a supplicant's tilt.

Louise's face crumpled. Richard had seen this expression on his wife's face many times before. It was the crumple of pity, and it invariably annoyed him, even if he was himself the object of her pity. "Oh, you must be Wanda," she said in a gentle voice.

"Wow!" said Flora from the staircase.

Richard felt surrounded. He had to take control of the situation. "Wanda, we had a deal," he said, trying to sound calm. "Daniel has made it very clear he doesn't want to see you. You shouldn't have come here."

She turned her gaze back on him and the wild look returned. "He's my son, my child!" she shouted. "I've missed him so much and I never even knew where he was. It's been horrible. He was taken from me against my will! Stolen!" Her flush grew even redder.

"I can see you're upset," said Louise, which struck Richard as an absurd understatement.

Wanda burst into tears just as Richard noticed that Daniel had walked up the porch steps. He stayed outside, observing the sobbing Wanda through the open door, then strode purposefully inside.

"Mom!" he said. Wanda turned to face him. "What are you doing here, Mom?" He looked intense and frightened. Richard felt horrible. He had promised his son he'd protect him from his lunatic mother, and what was he doing? Nothing. Richard shook Louise off, preparatory to shoving Wanda out the door.

"Mom, what are you doing here?" Daniel asked Wanda again, this time in a tone of defeat and chagrin that broke Richard's heart. "You promised to stay away."

"Who are *you*?" she screamed. "Who *are* you?"

"I'm your son. Danny," he said, in a sad little voice that seemed to indicate he knew she wouldn't believe him, and that he'd been through this horror before.

"No, you're not!" Wanda said. "What's going on?" She turned to Richard. "That's not Danny!"

"Ohmigod," said Flora. She pounded down the rest of the stairs and now stood in the hall next to Richard.

"Yes, Wanda, that's Daniel," said Louise in a kindergarten teacher voice. "I can see you're very upset," she repeated.

"You bet I'm upset!" Wanda shouted. "I don't know who this little son-of-a-bitch is, but he's not my kid! Where's my kid?"

"Mom, please," began Daniel.

"Wanda, you have to go now," said Richard. "I mean it."

"Tell me the truth, Richard," she yelled back at him. "Do you know where my son is?"

The Blakelys were silent. Flora drew in her breath in a frightened little gasp.

"I'm calling the police," said Wanda menacingly.

Richard said, "I'm telling you to leave now, Wanda. Immediately."

"I'll leave, but I'm coming right back here with the cops."

"I'll handle this, Dad," said Daniel. He reached out to put his arm around Wanda.

"Don't you *touch* me!" she shouted. "I knew you were bad news before, at the airport. I hate you! I bet you know where the real Danny is."

He grabbed her by the shoulder and half-pulled her down the stairs. "Where is Danny?" she was yelling.

By the time Keith got Wanda to the bottom of the porch steps, he had managed to pull her head by the hair so that her ear was next to his mouth. "I know where he is all right," he whispered. "Shut up and I'll tell you all about it."

Wanda shut up. Keith dragged her to the gate, with his arm around her. From the porch where Richard, Louise and Flora now stood, staring in fascination, it looked like a protective gesture. Actually it was more like a wrestling hold.

Outside the gate, Keith released his grip and scowled at her. Wanda stood staring back at him with a stunned expression.

"Is that your car?" he demanded, pointing to the red Ford. She nodded and he pushed her towards it. In a low, precise voice, he said, "I know where Danny is all right. After the way you and Carl treated him, he's decided to stay away. I know where he is, but I'm not telling you."

Wanda began to cry again. "Please, please!" she said.

"Forget it. He's happy where he is. And I'm happy here. So don't tell the Blakelys I'm not your kid any more."

"Where is he?" pleaded Wanda. "Please tell me. I don't care about anything else. I won't tell them anything."

"I know where he is. And if you call the cops or snitch on me to the Blakelys, I'll find him and make sure you never find out what happened to him."

"What do you mean?" asked Wanda, leaning away from

his face, which was now about an inch from hers.

"I mean you won't find Danny. No one will. Or his body. Ever," said Keith. "I can get to him any time I want. And he'll be glad to see me. He thinks I'm his friend." Keith yanked open the door and pushed Wanda inside the car. "Now get the fuck out of here!" He slammed the car door shut.

He turned on his heel and bounded back through the gate and up the steps.

In the Ford at the kerb, Wanda, sat, zombie-like. She had to do something. She had to get help. She had to get going. But get going where? And who would help her? She wasn't sure just what she should do. First of all, she supposed, she had better try to pull herself together so that she could drive, to wherever it was she should be going, to find whoever it was who was going to help her.

Keith came back through the gate and joined Flora, Louise and Richard, who were standing on the porch looking at Wanda's car. He was scowling and breathing heavily. Louise put out a hand to comfort him, but he brushed her off.

"Hey, let's forget about her," he said. "It's my birthday."

"I know. Oh, Daniel, I'm so sorry," said Louise.

"Come on," he said irritably. "Let's go inside. Don't stare at her like that. She just wants the attention."

"But she's your mom," began Louise.

"Oh, screw her!" he shouted, then went inside, slamming the door behind him.

Keith was furious. The damn car was sitting right out in front, and that bitch Wanda had to pull up exactly at the wrong time! He went into the living room and eyed the packages on the coffee table. It was the same pile of presents he'd seen there this morning before he left, but now there was a new one on top, a little gold oblong with white ribbon. He was pretty sure that the keys to the Mustang he had seen parked in front of the house were in there.

On the porch, Louise turned to her husband. "This is awful. She's very distraught. She probably shouldn't drive. She should be on some kind of medication. She's delusional. What should we do?" She looked skittishly over her shoulder at the door as if she were worried about Daniel too.

"I don't know. How the hell should I know?" said Richard impatiently.

"God!" said Flora. "Did you see how he pushed her into the car and slammed the door? It looked really rough." She peered through the porch window into the living room and let out a little cry at the sight of Keith tearing away wrapping paper with a determined expression. "Daniel's opening his presents!" she announced. "He didn't even wait for us. And his mom is out there in the street freaking out! This is too weird."

"She's just *sitting* there," said Richard. "Why doesn't she just *leave*?"

Inside, Keith had already stuffed the key into his pocket and was tearing at the biggest present. Perfect. A backpack. If they stayed interested in Wanda and her problems for just a few minutes more, he'd be home free. He gazed out at the porch. All he could see was the back of his three temporary family-members' heads. He moved quickly to the hall and went up the stairs two at a time.

Out on the porch, Louise said, "I should go talk to her. We can't just leave a delusional woman sitting out there in her car." Wanda had now allowed her blonde head to fall into her hands, so they could barely see the top of it. Louise took a step off the porch. Richard pulled her back

273

by the elbow. "Don't go out there!" he said.

"He's right," said Flora nervously. "She's crazy. Who knows what she might do? What if she has a gun in the car?"

"Maybe we should call someone," said Louise. "An ambulance or something. She could be a danger to herself or others."

"That's only in the movies," said Richard bitterly. "Men in white coats who come and take nutcases away." Wanda was clearly still sobbing, with her head down on the steering wheel.

As he spoke, a small, sturdy woman with grey waved hair, accompanied by a fair-haired boy, both immaculately dressed entirely in white, opened the wrought-iron gate and walked up the Blakelys' front walk.

Richard looked down at them. The fact that they were both dressed all in white unnerved him. They must be religious wackos, going door to door. As if he didn't have enough on his hands! He stepped forward aggressively, looking for telltale pamphlets. "What do you want?" he demanded.

The woman gave him a beady eye. "Are you Richard Blakely?" she asked him in a voice that he found reminiscent of his fifth-grade teacher, Miss Schroeder.

"Yes," he found himself saying weakly.

"I have reason to believe this young man is your son, Danny."

"What?"

The woman strode up the porch steps with confidence, and the boy followed, staring at Richard. "My name is Olive Chapman," she announced. "And Danny here has told me an amazing story. I'm sure you'll want to get to the bottom of it."

"But that's not Daniel," said Richard.

Olive looked momentarily taken aback. "He says he is."

"I am too," said the boy. "My father is Richard Jerome Blakely. It's on my birth certificate."

At the kerb, sitting in the red car, Wanda lifted her head from the cradle of her tear-soaked hands, and turned to look despairingly at the Blakely house. What she saw there made her heart soar.

Olive went on, "I believe there is another young man here, named Keith."

"Keith?" said Richard.

Danny said, "He may be using another name. He has a tattoo. A skull with a knife through it."

Richard stared down at the boy and took in his fair, wavy hair, his broad face with its high cheekbones.

Just then, Wanda came running up the path. "Danny!" she screamed. Richard watched the boy turn and shout "Mom!" then clatter down the steps. The two embraced.

Up in the master bedroom, Keith had just finished pouring the contents of Louise's jewellery box into his new backpack, on top of Flora's stuff. Too bad about all the bigger stuff the Blakelys had replaced since the party, like the stereo speakers. But there was room for more in the backpack. And, he'd have his car too, even if he wouldn't have his licence.

And not a moment too soon, what with Wanda making trouble. He thudded back downstairs and went into the study.

On the porch, Olive said to Louise and Richard, "He's a fine boy and an excellent lawn bowling player." They all stood in an awkward circle.

Louise looked down at him and gave him a wan smile, "Let's go inside and sit down. We're all in shock!"

"No *kidding*!" said Flora.

"Where the hell is Daniel? We've got to ask him about this," said Richard.

Olive held up her hand. "Please don't let him escape."

"Escape!" said Richard. "I just want to ask him a few questions." He stood in the hall and screamed, "Daniel! Come here. Right away!"

"Just a sec," said Keith's voice from behind the closed door of the study which served as his bedroom.

Louise led everyone into the living room but no one actually sat down. Louise said, "So you're saying that Daniel is Keith? Do you mean Keith Lloyd? Who hit those men with the crowbar?" She looked horrified.

"I believe that is the case," Olive replied. "Did he, by any chance, kill them?"

"No!" said Richard, horrified to discover he felt insulted at the aspersions she was casting on his Daniel. Who apparently wasn't his after all. But he seemed as if he were. Richard thought of this paler, younger looking boy as the impostor. "Nobody killed anybody. Those men are alive. One of them is suing."

"That's right," said Wanda. "He's suing Youth Intervention Therapies." She had her arm around Danny and was stroking his hair.

"So, Mom, are you saying I'm definitely not wanted for murder?"

"Keith made that up," said Olive contemptuously. "He's clearly an accomplished liar."

"Where *is* Keith?" demanded Danny, shaking off Wanda's arm. Yes, thought Richard. Where *is* Daniel? He was furious with the boy. He felt really let down. He wanted to sock him. He had lied and lied and lied and made a fool out of Richard. God! To think, he'd bought him that Mustang. Well, Richard was going to keep it for himself now, that was for sure!

"I'll go get him," said Richard, striding towards the study door.

276

"We should call the police," said Olive.

"The police?" said Louise, looking horrified.

"He's wanted in California," said Wanda. "For assault. He's a criminal, a complete thug!"

Richard flung open the study door and was startled to see the window wide open, just as it had been the night of the burglary. He glanced quickly around the room. The speakers were still here, but the tuner was gone, and so was his laptop. From the open window he heard the unmistakable, sweet sound of a '67 Mustang's engine starting up. He ran from the room and towards the front door. "He's trying to get away," he shouted. *"In my Mustang!"*.

He ran down the path. The other Daniel, the one who Wanda acknowledged, was running after him – a speedy little streak in white.

"He's gonna get away," yelled Richard in despair.

The kid in white caught up with him at the gate.

"I don't think so." The boy smiled as he bounced down the steps on to the sidewalk. "He can't drive a stick. I bet that's a stick."

The horrible sound of grinding gears, a sound that enraged Richard, was audible proof that this was a true statement. Keith was hunched over the gear-shift, still struggling to find reverse, when Richard reached the car door and wrenched it open. Then, with the aid of his son Danny, he pulled Keith roughly out of the car and on to the sidewalk.

"Oh, man!" wailed Keith loudly. "This sucks!"

## 23

Several months later, at a pre-trial deposition, Keith Lloyd told his story of the unfortunate incident at the abandoned gas station on the road to the Youth Intervention Therapies site. "I hit Mr Kessler again, and I thought of how his trying to touch me like that behind the gas station reminded me of the same bad, inappropriate touching that had happened when I was just a little kid, and all the rage I'd had at my stepfather came kind of surging back, and I just kept hitting him," said Keith. "Because I was big now, and I could stop it. Not like when I was little and helpless."

He broke into apparent sobs and slumped forward, covering his face. The lawyer representing Brian Kessler glanced over and saw that the young court reporter in the room was also weeping, even as her hands flew across her keyboard. Angrily he threw his pen across the table, and said, "OK, OK. Let's stop right now." He gestured to Donald Keene, representing the insurance company that carried Youth Intervention Therapies' liability policy. "Let's step outside for a sec," he said.

In the hall, Keene remained impassive while the man sputtered. "It's all bullshit and you know it," he said.

"Come on, Phil," said Donald Keene, "you saw that court reporter. No jury in the world is going to give your client a dime."

"Yeah, yeah. OK. We'll settle. The kid is good, I admit it."

"Ohmigod!" said Claire. "I can't believe it. It's just so amazing!"

"Mom says she thinks it happened that weekend of the party – when they went to that inn place," said Flora. "It's sort of embarrassing thinking about it, really."

"But aren't you excited?"

"Yes. The idea of a brand new person is really exciting. I can't wait to hold it." Flora's face took on a soft expression. "I remember when I used to babysit little Zachary next door. I love the way babies smell and their nice fuzzy heads."

"How old is your mom anyway?"

"Forty. She always said she was glad she had me when she was young, and how she feels sorry for old parents who have teenagers when they're almost sixty. Now she's going to be one of those mothers."

"Do you think she can handle it?"

"Yeah. She's really happy. She looks so pretty and glowing."

"What about Richard?"

"He's even goofier than Mom. He keeps staring at her with this amazed expression. And Danny is pretty excited, too. He was over last night and we were all thinking up names. I bet this baby is going to be a spoiled brat. And, it's the only person in our family who will actually be related to all of us."

Danny was in his lawn bowling whites, standing at the kitchen sink drinking a glass of milk. Wanda sat at the table with a Diet Pepsi. "You'll need more than that for breakfast," she said.

"Oh, I'm late. But Olive said she'd pack some sandwiches. She always does for the away games."

"Listen sweetie, Carl called last night."

"Oh yeah?" Danny was now rummaging in the fridge, with an ear cocked for Olive's Buick.

"He says he really misses me," said Wanda, "and he's pretty sure he can get transferred back up here."

"That'll be nice for Amy," said Danny.

"If we tried again, me and Carl, how would you feel about that?" said Wanda.

"I don't care," said Danny. "Do whatever you want, Mom. It's your life. I personally think he's a jerk, but I'm gonna leave pretty soon anyway, so you should do what you want. Oh, and don't expect me back after the tournament, because I'm going to the movies with Max and Flora and some other kids. Can I take this package of bologna with me and eat it in the car?"

Eugene and Charmaine Philbreck looked across the table at Keith. Keith gazed down at the large, gem-encrusted rings on Mrs Philbreck's wrinkled hands. These people were rolling in money. They had a real nice scam going here. Parents were willing to pay a lot of money to scare their own kids, and even poor people could ship them out for a couple of weeks if they had a decent health-insurance plan.

"Naturally we appreciate your help," said Dr Philbreck smoothly. "We were delighted when you contacted us and told us you wanted to tell the truth. Your frankness saved us a lot of trouble."

"And a lot of money, too," said Keith. "Before my deposition, I'd talked to you about maybe getting something from you in return for my own trouble. I mean, after all, it was pretty hard having to talk about all that personal stuff."

"That's right," said Dr Philbreck. "Of course we'll have to keep this all very quiet. If it looked even *remotely* like we *paid* you to testify—"

"Oh, I'm talking about something else," said Keith. "I've been thinking. I really want to work here. I bet I could do a really good job as one of your counsellors and escorts. And, because I'm like a graduate of the programme myself, I can tell parents how it turned me around, you know?"

"That matter of assault and stealing our car—" began Dr Philbreck delicately.

"I did a couple of months and my community service," said Keith. "I've learned my lesson, and my attitude has really changed. Anyway, my attorney says my record can be cleaned up when I become a legal adult. You just have to file some paperwork and it's like it never happened."

Dr Philbreck nodded.

"How old are you?" asked Charmaine.

"I'll be eighteen next week," said Keith. "Lately I've been thinking about my future a lot. I can't just hang around any more. I need a career."

Charmaine and Eugene looked at each other for a moment, and then Dr Philbreck reached across the table and shook Keith's hand. "Welcome aboard, son," he said.